INIQUITOUSNESS

(yoo-bik-wi-tuhs)

Extremely Immoral or Wicked

D. H. COOP

ISBN 979-8-9913102-7-7 (paperback)
ISBN 979-8-9913102-8-4 (digital)

Copyright © 2024 by D. H. Coop

All rights reserved. No part of this publication may be reproduced, distributed, or transmitted in any form or by any means, including photocopying, recording, or other electronic or mechanical methods without the prior written permission of the publisher.

Printed in the United States of America

When righteousness is cut off, injustice is increased.
— Sumerian Proverb.

Evil as well as good, both operate to advance the Great Plan.
— Egyptian Proverb

To do injustice is the greatest of all evils.
— Plato

CHAPTERS & CHARACTERS

Chapter 1—1948 Trofim Denisovich Lysenko 1
Andrei - Soviet Union
Georgii – Soviet farmer
Olga – Soviet KGB informer
Yakov – Olga's husband
Boris
Lev
Colonel Zinoviev Soviet Union
Major Whittemore U.S Army
Anna & Greg – Soviet Sleeper agents

Chapter 2—1965 Baby Boomers and Free Speech 13
Andrei
Betty
Randy
Sandy
Ben
Michael
Howard

Chapter 3—1991 Nika's Escape the Iran Revolution 26
Azar
Cyrus
Sarina
Rashid
Nika

Chapter 4—2010 Re-Education Camp 34
Tao Cheng
Zhi Cheng - Tao's sister
Li Jie

Chapter 5—2012 Escape from Mainland China 40
Sun Zhou
Li Zhou
Jiefan
Xiu
Fai

Chapter 6—2020 Lavatory Fire 47
C.E.
Elaine
Nick Thomson
Director Lee Edison FBI
Professor Zhang
Professor Harrison
Lab Assistance Xiu
Lab Assistance Fang
Agent Greg Peterson FBI
Agent Benjamin Barns FBI
Edward Wilson - DEA
Tao analysis FBI
Leader He
Jiehong

Chapter 7—2020 Spies at University 60
Nick
C.E.
Director Edison
Professor Zhang
Professor Harrison
Benjamin Barns
Greg Peterson
Fang

Xiu
Joaquin Miller ATF
Leocadio Blanco
Agent David Lev
Agent Chen Russel

Chapter 8—2020 Pandemic 68
Nick
C.E.
Benjamin Barns – FBI
Greg Peterson – FBI
Edward Wilson – DEA
Joaquin Miller - ATF
Mary Jo Longstreet – Cyber division
Tao – analysis
Diego's Cartel

Chapter 9—2020 Protest or Rebellion 75
Chet Butler
Pete Blanco
Little Miss Hermes

Chapter 10—2020 Cartels 82
Leocadio
Juan

Chapter 11—2022 Election Interference 87
C.E.
Nick

Chapter 12—2022 Chinese police stations 94
Nuan
Liu
Chet
Jenny Zhang
Edward Young

Chapter 13—2022 The Lecture Hall 102
Professor Andrei
Mary Robinson Rush
Joe Turner
C.E. Hall
Director Edison

Chapter 14—2022 Secret Chinese Biolab 112
Leader He
Ying
Building inspector Williams
Chair Person Casimir
Chief Young
C.E. Hall
Mayor

Chapter 15—2023 The Walking Route 118
Officer Davis
Mexican Officer Santiago Perez
Sargent Phillips
Nick
C.E.
Leocadio

Chapter 16—2023 Refugees and Asylum 124
Asylum
Maria
Hector
Blanco Leocadio

Chapter 17—2023 Golan Heights 130
Jiyan
Karwan
Sherko
Soran
Rebaz
Zilan

Leocadio
Haval
Nick Thomson
Agent James Wallace
C.E.
Sherko
Darya
Karwan
Baran
Soran
Azad
Zillan

Chapter 18—2023 West Bank - Palestine 138
Father Giuseppe - Catholic
Father Usire – Coptic
Father Nikolaos – Orthodox
Siham
Hossam
Nidal
Nada

Chapter 19—2023 Drug Smuggling 145
Nick
C.E.
Director
Edward Wilson
Mary Jo
Martin – adult club in San Diego
Santiago – enforcer
Barns
Fang woman & laundry
Martha McKenna FBI analysis
Joan St. Janes FBI analysis

Chapter 20—2023 Sponsors of Terrorism Iran 150
Terrorism Iran
Arzhang
Darab
Dariush
Ervin (Friend of Honor)
Ashti (Peace)
Banc (Small Spring)
Major General Hashem
General Ormazd

Chapter 21—2023 Gaza Strip 156
Rami
Ismail

Chapter 22—2023 Settlements Israel 159
Sarah
Rebecca
Jeremiah
Modi
Shiloh
Naomi
Adam
Jordyn
George / Jergis
Salim /
Paul / Bulos
Samyah
Suzan
Ahmad

Chapter 23—2023 Education Subversion 168
Professor Andrei
Harriet
Dan
Jose
Sandy

Peggy
Peter
Martin
Abraham
Naomi

Chapter 24—2023 International Money..179
Mary Jo
Director
Nick
Casimir Dubanowski
C.E.
Barns
Peterson

Chapter 25—2023 Funding Terrorism...185
Rachel - Israel
Micah - Israel
Charbel - Lebanon
Qateel – Lebanon
Samir – Lebanon
Hadi – Iran
Erfan – Iran
Cyrus – Iran
Rebaz – Iraq
Haval – Iraq
Crown Prince - Saudi
Abdullah
Ibrahim
Ahmad
Saad
C.E.
Nick
Director
Mary Jo
Casimir

Chapter 26—2023 October 6th 195
C.E.
Mary Jo
Director
Nick
Juan
Javier
Zai
Old Chinese Couple
Bahman
Rashid
Tao
Nika (wife)

Chapter 27—2023 Massacre 207
Samer
Malik
Mostafa
Hasan
Hussein
Ava
Levi
Fadi
Abdel
Naomi
Shiloh
Lilah
Eva

Chapter 28—2023 Aftermath 214
Chet
Eric
Nick
Elaine
C.E.

Sara
Director
Burt
Joan
Mary Jo
Tao

Chapter 29—April 17th Meeting 224
Director
Tao
Nick
Mary Jo
Agent Peterson
C.E.
Elaine

CHAPTER ONE

The Barefoot Biologist
Trofim Denisovich Lysenko

> The line between good and evil is permeable and almost anyone can be induced to cross it when pressured by situational forces.
> — Philip Zimbardo

THE GHOST OF LYSENKO
SOVIET POSTER

Trofim Denisovich Lysenko was a Soviet Union biologist and agriculturalist under the influence of I.V. Michurin biologist, who had developed some 300 new fruit trees and berry plants based on his theory of acquired genetics (characteristics acquired after birth). When Michurin died in 1935, Lysenko transformed "Michurinism" into a campaign to produce bigger and better crops in the Soviet Union based on the theory that differed from that of Gregor Mendel's ideas of inherited genetics. Michurin and Trofim went so far as to state that genes do not exist.

Those that opposed Lysenko were removed from the scientific community and office, or imprisoned, at times executed for resisting the Communist Party. Trofim's policies and methods had set back the Soviet Union's agriculture for 20 years. His "grasslands" system caused a famine that killed millions of people in the Soviet Union. He was supported by comrade Stalin until Stalin's death in 1953.

Then Nikita Khrushchev came to power and continued to hold on to Trofim's ideas with the Virgin Lands campaign. The Soviet regime became more tolerant of criticism under Nikita Khrushchev and soviet scientists exposed Trofim's errors in a *Letter of Three Hundred* in 1955. However, Khrushchev kept Trofim's policies until he was removed from power in 1964.

These policies were adopted by the People's Republic of China causing widespread famine in China from 1952 to 1962 that some believed to have killed as many as 15 million people

1948 On a Soviet State Farm (Sovkkov)

He looked out over the station's vast size with the buildings and broad streets for the huge tractors to move. He was glad he was assigned to the Sovkkov for it was provided with new and better machines. He was here to see that the farm ran with no disruptions. Comrade Stalin did not trust the collective farms (Kolkhoz) for their capitalistic motivations for they were allowed to share the profits from the harvest each year.

Andrei's family had lived through the Ukrainian famine (The Holodomor) and then the Great Purges of the 1930s. His mind had drifted to the recent purges when he heard his name called.

"Andrei, come over here and see the beautiful new tractor the state has sent to the farm. It is a beautiful thing!"

"Georgii, the farm has twenty of these new machines. We get one every time we send one of the old tractors to a collective farm. Soon there will be no young people on the collective farms and those farms will soon all become state farms. Then we will get fewer new machines to do our work."

"What do you mean?" asked Georgii.

"It is a simple fact of the collective Soviet system. There are two ways the state gets workers to work, one is by fear and the other better way is by better tools and working conditions. The collective farms were Lenin's plan at the time to replace the poor working state farms after the Civil War. Then our great comrade Stalin helped re-establish these state farms with better tools and work conditions. Now, he wants all the farms to be state farms and to remove the collective farms.

He is encouraging the youth in the collectives to leave for better conditions on state farms or in our new industrial factories. The collective farms only have old equipment and their old equipment is replaced by old state farm units. Each year more collective farms become state farms. Then all the new resources will be spread over a larger number of state farms and that will reduce each state farm's allotment of new equipment. It is simple economic math, my friend," said Andrei.

"New or old equipment does not matter as long as we follow Lysenko and his ideas on farming. We have followed his ideas and only in the first year did the crop production increase," said Georgii.

"Georgii, be careful! That kind of talk will get you sent to a Gulag if you are lucky and if I am with you when you say it, I will be in the same cart with you. I know we have these talks when we are alone, but please be careful you never know when someone will turn you in for being a Trotskyite."

"Why are you saying this now?"

"Last night Doctor Solomon told Vitaly that Stalin was planning to remove the Jews from the Soviet Party soon by attacking the Jewish doctors. Olga, who hates Vitaly, overheard the conversation and then informed the KGB that he was speaking of Comrade Trofim and Stalin in negative terms. This morning Solomon and Vitaly were escorted to a room by the KGB. We must be very careful of what we say," said Andrei.

"How did you find all this out?"

"I heard Olga telling a Soviet officer last night what Solomon told Vitaly,"

"Olga, she is Yakov's wife, and everyone thinks Yakov is an informer. Do you think they are both informers?" said Georgii.

"Ha! In this country, every family is filled with informers for one reason or another. That is the best way and reason to get a step ahead of the others in line. We just need to do what work they demand and nothing more. There is no need to call more attention to us. Trofim may be a fool and every farmer thinks his policies are, but that will not change his policies.

Remember he told us about how to produce rye seeds by putting wheat seeds in an appropriate environment and they would become rye. Then there was his 'Jarovization' idea to make winter cereal seeds to become just like those of the spring seeds. We had to chill the wheat seeds in water and moisture to make them produce a better and faster crop and how did that work out?" asked Andrei.

"Ha! That was a massive failure and cost the farm a lot of seeds!"

"Remember what I said about loose talk. Just remember when Trofim was here and Boris spoke up about this failure. He went on and told Trofim that his theory of genes did not stand up to any scientific reasonings," said Andrei.

"Yes, I remember that comrade Trofim asked him if he had a degree in biology or any science and Boris said he held a biology doctorate from the

Berlin University. Then comrade Trofim asked him if he was a Trotskyite?" said Georgii.

"Yes, and what else happened?"

"Boris said he was not a Trotskyite!" said Georgii.

"Then?"

"Comrade Trofim shook his head and told Boris that his degree was sadly from a western bourgeoisie university whose aim was to keep the workers in their place with the writing of Charles Darwin, Gregor Mendel, or Herbert Spencer, and others who used the nonsense of natural gene section. That the gene theory was misinformation to keep the workers down. I remember that because the workers then gave cheers to Lysenko. They had been watching the whole exchange take place," replied Georgii.

"Yes, and where is Boris now?" asked Andrei.

"He was promoted and asked if he would like to go to the Moscow University to improve his knowledge in good Soviet biology," said Georgii.

"Have you ever wondered why nobody speaks of Boris or the gene theory?"

"No! Why should I?" said Georgii.

"Think about it. Do you remember the day Boris was promoted?"

"Yes, Why?"

"Just try to remember that day. Did you see him leave?" asked Andrei.

"Not really, he left late that very night. We were told he had impressed comrade Lysenko and was needed in Moscow."

"Yes, nobody talked about him after he left that night, and the theory of genes was never brought up by anyone again. Comrade Lysenko's 'grasslands' system was in full production, and we have not met our farm production quota for the last two years," said Andrei.

"What is your point?" asked Georgii.

"We were coerced into following the party line. The Marxists deny reality and Lysenko's scientific evidence. That night Boris was tortured and taken to a gulag or shot at some place on the farm."

"How can you say that?"

"Because I saw and heard Lysenko speaking to Boris before his bloody body was being dragged to the car that night. I heard Lysenko telling Boris that he wanted Boris to know that. Competition and mutual assistance were the keys to evolution and that created the different species and not some idiot inherent genes theory.

Then Lysenko walked away, and Boris was dragged to the car in the tractor barn by two KGB agents. Lysenko walked over to Olga and said that Boris would have been a good lesson to the others who dared to challenge the Soviet system, but that comrade Stalin had other plans in the fire. So, Georgii remember Doctor Solomon and Boris and we shall never speak of this again," said Andrei.

The next morning Andrei was seen leaving the farm by Olga on her way to the milk barn to watch the milking of the cows. She smiled to herself at how she had been able to arrange everything. She, and not her idiot husband, was now the chief KGB agent on the farm. She had made her husband the target of the community's fear and terror. That simple fool did not even understand why the workers treated him with fear and respect.

Now, she had been able to remove her competition with a simple recommendation. Agent Andrei left the farm with his promotion within the KGB. It was true that Andrei was smart and did her a favor by getting Georgii to stop his gossip. She would still have to watch Georgii and maybe she would make him her lover. He was just a little smarter than her husband.

Three days later at a meeting held in Moscow at Lubyanka Square building that afternoon the same day.

"Comrade Andrei, you did good work at the farm. Comrade Olga said you were a very bright agent and able to persuade people that things were in their best interest. That is why we are going to send you to America after some special training at a new school we have set up. You, comrade, are now part of a new operation to remove the West from power. This plan will undermine the West from within. We are calling it 'Winter Seeds'. The reason is that warmongers like Churchill and his 'Iron Curtain' speech and President Truman's Marshall Plan are starting what some are calling a Cold War against the Soviet Union.

"This new operation will not be part of any of our Leftist movements in the west that we now have in operation and it will not be any part of our spy network. So, you are never to have contact with any of those operatives. They are being watched closely by Western intelligence.

"The "Winter Seeds" operation's function will be to undermine the

Western culture over time by making them ask questions about their culture's history. Comrade Lenin said he could change the world in one generation and we plan to do just that! Do you have any questions about the plan?" asked Lev.

"Just one, I understand, I am to join the academic community as a student and support their Democratic ideals; however, I believe it will not be easy to enter their academic class system in America. They are not as class conscious as the English but my readings of the academic world in America show that it is a very close network of elites."

"We have considered that and that is why we have the special school on American culture. After you take the course you will be ready to make the move to America. There you will be considered an academic refugee from the Soviet Union, which will make you a fashionable anti-Soviet scholar.

The American elite universities will give you special consideration as someone who knows the evils of the Soviet Union. They will fast-track you once you finish your doctorate degree. The Americans love to believe they are superior in their ideals of freedom and their ability to show all sides of issues. They will start by having you as a special speaker on the failures of the Soviet system. Then offer you a teaching position and that will be your opportunity to develop what we call the 'New Left' thinking in the academic world," said Lev.

"I am sorry, New Left?"

"Yes, over the next few weeks, you will have a full briefing about the New Left. It is the idea of a world community or what we will be calling globalism of free independent nations working together."

"Is that not our soviet goal in the Party already?" asked Andrei.

"Yes! It is simply restated as a goal of freedom and democracy. The arrogance of the Americans with their 'City Upon a Hill' idea and their understanding of democracy will be the way to undermine their ideas about their cherished institutions. Their open society is filled with groups that want to be the new leaders and they will want to remove those in leadership. We will play on these desires and plant more of those seeds to increase the chaos," said Lev.

"Don't we have people helping to undermine the American society already? What about individuals like Paul Robeson and others who support socialist views? He is an intellectual with other artists who are already undermining their cultural identities by attacking their racism. These people are also challenging American institutions and speaking well of the Soviet system," said Andrei.

"Yes, you are right, but our efforts to get the black Americans and other minorities to join the communist party are less than favorable. Some blacks are sympatric, but not ready or are not joiners. Individuals like Robeson have shown us a way to divide the culture with the race issue, but it is not going to work on a wide political level by itself. So, we will tie the idea of race with the idea of imperialistic conquerors and occupiers that over time weaken native populations. We will link the American expansionists as the predators over innocent victims and this will cause some doubting of their history and its values.

That is what the New Left will represent — Globalism over Nationalism. It will take time to develop over time for those like yourself to build the New Left in the universities. The beauty is that many of the American academic scholars will pick up your ideas of universal freedom without understanding the total implications," said Lev.

"I am not completely clear on what you mean?" said Andrei.

"It is a simple fact that language can be used to change thinking. For example, the Elite in America sees their rise to the top as part of social evolution. They are the best because they made it. Many see the Soviet system as an advantage to help the less gifted. For example, touting the number of women medical doctors in the Soviet Union as marvelous.

The Left in America praised the Soviet Union's medical system for the number of women doctors. Yet, all they look at is the number of women doctors. They just see the word doctor and accept the number as a real value. Yet, a closer look at Soviet doctors shows that women doctors here are just low-level general practitioners and not considered a choice occupation. The choice occupation is the specialist surgeons and they are 99% male.

Changing the word can change the meaning or value. The language will be a way to undermine the system in the West. Our ultimate goal is a free society run by the workers and no government to control society. Replace Socialism with the term globalism and it shifts the image. The New Left is that society of free people working together. "

"I am starting to understand. When do I leave?"

"After you complete this training at the new school city we have built. There you will have several days of instruction on the ideas of the New Left and American life. We have a 'sleeper' family in California that will support you and help in your education at the university. Once you have your Doctorate you and others will slowly introduce our version of the New Left," said Lev.

"How will I get to America?"

"Berlin!"

"How? There is the Berlin blockade?"

"Yes, Andrei, remember never let a situation go to waste. This will be the best and perfect escape route. The most talented East Berliners are always trying to get to the West. In time we will have to stop this flow, but for now, it serves us an advantage.

You will be given a Soviet Army recruit uniform and then sent to a station across from the American Check Point Charlie in Berlin. Then one day you will cross the distance between the checkpoints to the American side. Once you are at Check Point Charlie you tell them you want to defect and want to go to America. You will be interrogated and then sent to your relatives in America.

Your instructors/controllers say you are one of our best operators for the New Left project. Just remember you are a new American who sees the Soviet Union for what the Americans see as an enemy. As an anti-Soviet refugee, you will want to right the wrongs of the imperialistic past and integrate into a tolerant global world. The Americans tolerate differences of opinion to a fault."

"Yes, I understand."

"Good, Then off you go for your preparation," said Lev.

As Andrei walked away he once more said thanks to his father for his wisdom. During the 1930's his father was a member of the communist party and had protected the Party from the greedy kulaks (rich peasants) who had hidden their crops from the workers and Soviet people.

He remembers the stories of great patriot heroes like the young comrade Peter Pavlik, whose unselfish loyalty to the party caused him to turn his anti-Soviet father into the authorities, and that of the comrade worker Alexi Stakhanov whose own work effort produced 102 tons of coal in just five hours of work.

Andrei's father had been a member of a Troika (three-member team) that saw that the kulaks paid their fair share of the crops to the workers. His father would tell Andrei how his team was able to triple their quota that was sent by Moscow. He would tell Andrei the stories of how Bukharin and Rykov finally confessed to being Trotskyists and the little part he played in the elimination of Trotsky in 1940 with his contacts in the Thieves-in-Law (criminals).

He told Andrei to be friendly to all and never trust anyone. That the Party always looked for the Greater Good

MAY 1949

"Over there is Check Point Charlie and when the guard is changed in a few minutes you can start your journey to the west," said the Soviet Colonel.

"Should I run or walk?" asked Andrei.

"Start by walking. The guards have been told not to fire their weapons which would most likely cause a shooting war over a deserter or civilian. There will be shouts and demands for you to stop — just keep moving. You will be listed as dead in the record and your family will be notified."

"My mother was all that was left in my family and she died last year. So there is nobody to notify." "Good, I do not know your mission, but good luck comrade. Now, the guards are changing so start your walk."

Andrei was halfway across the 100 yards when the Soviet guards began yelling and running after him with more shouts for him to stop or they would shoot. That caused the guards at Check Point Charlie to draw their weapons and point them toward Andrei. He raised his hands and yelled, "I am a soldier and I want to defect! Don't shoot!, Don't Shoot!, I want to defeat!"

One of the American guards went back into the hut and called the Officer of the Day, "Sir, we have Soviet soldiers saying he wants to defect."

"Detain him there, I am on my way!"

Andrei had reached the checkpoint and was taken into the hut just as a Soviet Colonel drove up in a leased America jeep. I am Colonel Zinoviev of the Soviet Union and I demand you turn over that Soviet soldier NOW!"

"Sir, I am just a sergeant, and you will have to wait for my officer to arrive."

"I am a Colonel in the Soviet Army and you will turn over that soldier to me right NOW." Yelled the colonel just as the American office drove up in another jeep.

"Colonel I would ask you to not yell at my troops!"

"I am a Colonel in the Soviet Union and I demand to speak to someone of equal rank."

"Very well, Staff Sergeant speak to this Soviet Colonel!" said the Major.

"You are insulting a member of the Soviet Union. What is your name and rank?"

"I am Major Richard K. Whittemore of the United States Army and you sir are in the American Zone of Berlin! If you want this soldier, then I suggest you go through the proper channels. Now, I suggest you get back in your vehicle and return to your side of Berlin."

The Colonel turned his back and climbed into the vehicle as he mumbled "American pigs!"

"Enjoy your ride back in that American-made jeep, Colonel!" Yelled an American soldier.

"I think you upset him Major!" said the Staff Sergeant.

"I hope so, he was an ass. Now let's get this soldier to HQ for interrogation."

1950 at an Airport in California

"Welcome to California Andrei. My mother has always talked about her sister. My mother was always sorry your mother stayed behind to care for your father. How is he?" asked Anna.

"He died five years ago and my mother last year. I had just graduated from Moscow University when the Army demanded that I join and since I did not volunteer I was not made an officer. My luck turned when I was stationed across from Check Point Charlie I decided to defect."

"Well, my boy, we are glad you did and now the family is coming together with the three of us. We will let you settle in a bit before you decide what you want to do," said Greg.

"I have already made a decision to go to an American University and get a doctorate degree in the study of history."

"That should not be a problem. In fact, I had requested for you to come a be a guest lecturer at my campus. So, once you get settled we will make the arrangement for you to enroll and make an appointment to speak on the Soviet Union," said Greg.

Three days later the Korean War started and Andrei was in demand as a guest lecturer.

CHAPTER TWO

Baby Boomers
1946 to 1965

> But a lie is a lie, and in itself intrinsically evil, whether it be told with good or bad intents.
> — Immanuel Kant

The American national population in 1940 numbered 132 million then between 1946 and 1964 the number of new births helped the population to reach 196 million. That generation became known as the Baby Boomers. The population growth caused Los Angeles County CA to open a new school every month during that period.

As that generation grew, consumerism and the youth market opened in full swing by 1958. The Boomer youth was looking for a share of the post-war wealth and power. Leaders in industry and politics began to see not only a new market but protests by the youth as a threat to the balance of power in American society. The Free Speech movement began in universities gave the youth a cause to rally and came to a head at the Democratic Convention in 1968.

1965 University of California at Berkeley

A University Biography on Professor Andrei – History Department

Professor Andrei had come to America in 1950 after defecting from the Soviet Army in East Berlin. In the Soviet Union, he had obtained a master's degree in European History from the best university in Moscow before the Soviet Army called him up for active duty. The army sent him to East Germany and was assigned just across from Check Point Charlie in Berlin. One day he decided to walk across the gap between the checkpoints and ask for political asylum. After months in detainment, he was allowed to come to America to relatives in California. He became a minor celebrity as a Soviet defector during the McCarthy Red Scare period.

He enrolled in one of our best universities to pursue his doctorate in European History. There he became a research assistant to a noted American scholar and within one year became an associate instructor in the history department. He was seen as a rising academic star. Then another university offered him a position as an Associate Professor, which allowed him to skip the process of being an assistant Professor.

He published three acclaimed books on European History and several articles on American and European influence and their impact on world history. He also wrote two books on the First Amendment and the rights of free speech.

1961 JFK and the Buildup of American Policy in Viet Nam

President Eisenhower began helping the French control their territory of French Indochina to prevent the spread of Communism. The Domino Theory became the cornerstone of American foreign policy.

Then as the French were defeated at Bien Dien Phu, America supported the South against the North in Viet Nam. By 1961 President

Kennedy was sending more advisors and troops to help the South fight the Viet Cong forces directed from the North.

The Free Speech Movement began in 1964 just when the Vietnam War was becoming the focus on many of the campuses around America. The Black Power movement had many in the Civil Rights movement move to the antiwar movement with free speech at the core.

Professor Andrei is a leader of a movement in the classroom to encourage a better America through free speech. Professor Andrei's class discussions included the countercultures of Hippie, the civil rights and anti-war protest movements, and feminism to understand the change in the American social, economic, and political institutions. Professor Andrei and New Left's ideas will give America a free and secure America.

In a University Lecture Hall 1965

"Good Morning Class, I am Professor Andrei, and this is the second half of the course on the important influences of great trials in American History. I only say this because, in my first year as a student, I made the mistake of taking the second section of a course first. So, if you made my mistake you may want to reconsider this class. However, it can be taken either way without much-lost information.

"Now, let's get started with today's class. Our first case centers on the trial of Sacco and Vanzetti, who were accused of robbery and murder. But first, let me start with some historical background on the judicial system in this country until recently. There was an unbalance towards the wealthy. Those with money could afford better defense lawyers. Those in the working class at times were left to shift for themselves until the Warren Court in the 1960's. The Gideon *vs.* Wainwright the Supreme Court ruled in 1963 that all individuals charged with a crime required a defense lawyer. Until then if one did not have the funds they were not represented by a lawyer.

"The civil rights amendments (13th, 14th, and 15th) shifted the interpretation to a more liberal one by the Supreme Court of the U.S. Constitution. The Due Process clause in the 14th was interpreted to expand the Bill of Rights to State laws. The court ruled on the Powers of Congress, Reproductive rights, Free Speech, and Voting rights all before 1964.

"Then the Great War increased government encroachment in civil liberty by reducing those rights. The Red Scare and race riots in the early 1920s had the U.S. Supreme Court addressing the civil rights of the working class. The Warren Court removed some of the restrictions. You can read some of those cases in your assigned readings.

"Now, let's get into this famous trial of Sacco and Vanzetti. On December 24, 1919, when there was an attempted robbery in Bridgewater, Massachusetts at the White Shoe Factory by what was described by witnesses as a group of foreign-looking men, gunfire was exchanged and cartridge casings were left on the ground.

"Then on April 15, 1920, in South Braintree, Massachusetts a robbery took place at the Slater Morill Shoe factory killing the paymaster, Mr. Parmenter, and wounding a guard, Mr. Berardelli. Once again witnesses said foreign-looking men drove off in a Buick with the $16,000 payroll.

"Then on April 17, 1920, the Buick was found abandoned in the woods. After some investigation, the Buick was found to have been stolen in December. Witnesses had said that a guy named Boda was seen driving the car and he stored at the Overland Car Garage in Bridgewater. The garage owner was told to call the police when Mr. Boda showed up at the garage. When the police showed up, Boda and another man jumped on a motorcycle and rode off. Two other men ran off down the street on foot.

"Later, the police stopped a street car to question two foreign-looking men, who were Nicola Sacco and Bartolomeo Vanzetti. They both denied owning a gun when first questioned; however, when searched Sacco had a 32-caliber pistol on him and Vanzetti was carrying a 38-caliber Richardson revolver. Both men had anarchist literature on them and their stories varied over time.

"Sacco had worked at a shoe factory and Vanzetti was a fish peddler with a street cart. Sacco had an alibi for the White Shoe Factory robbery and witnesses identified Sacco as the shooter at the Slater Morill factory and that Vanzetti was sitting in the car at the time. They were placed on trial.

"The presiding judge was 63-year-old Webster Thayer, who made comments against anarchists and communists. This trial was a political victim of the Red Scare of the 1920s. The defense attorney Fred Moore was busy writing news articles for the local newspapers...."

The professor continued to list more facts about the trial with inference. He spoke at length on Celestino Medeiro's jailhouse confession. He was part of the Joe Morelli Gang in Rhode Island that had committed the robberies. Then the professor pointed out that this confession was disregarded. Later a Blue-Ribbon Commission found the trial was fair and the Death sentences were upheld.

The Professor ended the lecture with the fact that in 1979 Massachusetts Governor Dukakis issued a proclamation that stated Sacco and Vanzetti were treated unjustly. Then he turned off the overhead and thanked the students for their attention and left the lecture hall.

Betty turned to Randy, "I like Professor Andrei's approach to history. He always gives us a balance."

"Are you sure about that? You were just given the defense side of the case without all the holes in the defense case," said Randy.

"What holes?"

"For starters, we were not told who paid for their defense or that Fred Moore was writing news articles to the press every day of the trial. Then he went into great detail on the jailhouse confession linking Joe Morelli's gangs to the shoe robbery and murders. In fact, we heard or learned more about the national climate during the Red Scare and A. Mitchell Palmer raids than we did about the trial. No Betty, we were given only one side of the case."

"For what purpose?"

"To make a point that the government is not working for the working class. That the elite is running the country and justice system. Ever since the trial, the left has complained that the trial was unjust. They have said the same thing about the Lindbergh Baby and the Rosenbergs. If you say something enough, people start to believe some of it. Your professor Andrei ended his lecture with the Dukakis proclamation. That should tell you something!"

"So, there is doubt about the conviction and death sentence."

"Yes, if you only look at the defense side, the Supreme Court of Massachusetts investigated the confession, The Lowell Committee looked into the confession and the then Governor interviewed Celestino Medeiros and found that he could not remember any simple details of the robbery. He was just unbelievable in his confession. The fact is there was evidence against them. The focus of the case has not been on the evidence but on community emotions."

"Again for what purpose?" asked Betty.

"Simple, just look around. Most of these students are starting to see the American culture and this nation as just another racist and imperialistic nation taking advantage of poor nations," said Randy.

"Why? Can you not think of anything positive? You always want to see the other side even if it is not there!"

"You say I am negative, and I say I am being open to other points of view. Plus, Betty we stood side by side when the Board of Regents decided on free speech and Rule #17. That rule is now gone from the university. So the question is what do we do now?" said Randy.

"You are right we did stand for free speech and it was a good cause, but there is a more important cause, and it is civil rights. That is the most important cause our generation will have to face and answer. I hear that James Meredith is going to walk through Mississippi and I think I will go and join him on his walk. What about you Randy?"

"I just got my draft notice. I think I'll go home before I have to report."

"Why are you going to join?"

"My dad did. He was a Marine and I could not look him in the face if I did not do my share for this nation."

"Are you kidding me? For god's sake! What has this country done for you?"

"I am at this university for one thing and that is big in my opinion. See you are beginning to express the liberal professor's views like Professor Andrei that America is a war and imperialist colonizer. They have influenced you and others in the country that America is a racist imperialistic capitalistic society. Did you ever stop to think that many of the individuals telling you that the poor have little to no chance are also those members of the elite most likely from the group that they say is oppressed and are being held down?

"Yet here they are teaching and studying at this elite university that they claim to have been told is holding them down from joining. If they were right, how did they get here? No, our government has had its problems, but we are addressing those problems and at times it has been slow to change."

"You surprise me. Randy don't you remember Joe McCarthy and the Army hearings or the Hollywood ten writers that were blacklisted. When the government violated their First and fifth amendment's rights of free speech!"

"You have a point Betty, but you forget to remember that there were eleven original members of the Hollywood Ten, and that eleventh member ran to the eastern world and was celebrated as a hero. Or the fact that they were accused of being members of an organization that advocated the overthrow of the United States government and not their free speech. In fact, it was the use of their free speech when they used their Fifth Amendment right.

"But you are right, that McCarthy was on a hysterical witch hunt, but it was free speech that stopped him during the Army hearings and that was when Joseph Nye Welch said, '...you've done enough. Have you no sense of decency, Sir!'.

"You also, do not remember that one of your current heroes is Robert F. Kennedy who had worked for that same Senator McCarthy. The photos of RFK with Joe are hard to find and I am afraid that your free speech advocates today will soon want to censor other free speech as hate speech."

"Well, I agree with what Professor Andrei said, we need to fight extreme elements like the paternalistic corporation leaders of today that have us fighting in Vietnam and keeping people of color and women from their full share of the American life," said Betty.

"Then I ask you what Professor Andrei's answer is to stop what he calls hate?"

"By removing hate from speech and preventing those that advocate hate."

"Who decides what is hate?"

"The People will."

"Which people is my question?"

"There you go again being negative!"

"NO, Betty I see your professor Andrei and those like him are removing faculty members like Professor Miller from the academic scholarship committees. Tenure has been denied to Professor Stewart for his conservative views. We seem to be exchanging one group of leaders for another group that will be more repressive of our rights. Your professor Andrei has freely cited the Nazis as an explanation as an example of the evil to humanity. Yet, he ignores the millions killed under Stalin and the Soviet system. The very system he escaped from. He has also spoken of Chairman Mao as a great leader who is moving China into the modern world. It is like he thinks the communist in China is different than that of the Soviet Union."

"It is true Chair Mao has made many reforms in China to improve the Chinese people's daily life. Women no longer are forced to bind their feet," said Betty.

"Let me ask you Betty have you done any reading outside the assigned class textbooks?"

"NO! I do not have enough time to read what is assigned now!"

"That is part of my point. You are discouraged from outside reading or should I say reading opposing viewpoints by the workload or selections of readings. You read about land reforms and reduced economic inequalities, but nothing about the persecution, starvation, forced labor, humiliations, and executions during the reform in China."

"The reforms are important!"

"True the end of opium production and its consumption in China was a good thing but at what price to human rights?"

"What cost could there have been?"

"Did you ever think of what happened to the growers of the opium? The dealers of the opium? The addicts of opium? The land was converted into other crops for the growers and dealers who were executed or sent to forced labor camps or the addicts who were forced into compulsory treatment centers at the forced labor camps. The nation's drug problem was taken care of by ignoring basic human rights that you express."

"You can't make an omelet without breaking a few eggs!"

"So, human rights can be ignored for the right cause?"

"Yes! You only cited one example of how reforms did not work in China. There were other reforms."

"True, so here is another one and it had the same effect on the vast majority of the Chinese population. The Great Leap Forward followed the Trofim agricultural policies that ruined Soviet agriculture which Professor Andrei spoke of as one of the reasons he fled the Soviet Union.

"I sat in another classroom when he praised the Great Leap Forward and did not mention the millions of Chinese that died because of the crop failures. Nor did he speak of the Communist Party weeding out party members by the Three-anti's and Five-anti's policies. Those campaigns were worse than the Great Purges conducted during the 1930's by Stalin. No, Betty, you have been influenced by the new Left and do not understand what it is doing to American society."

"Randy, you are so negative. We are living in a time of change, and I hope you do not get lost clinging to the past."

"It is not the past I am worried about Betty. It is tomorrow," said Randy.

"What is that supposed to mean?"

"I remember you supported LBJ against Berry Goldwater by calling Goldwater a warmonger that would start a bigger war. Remember that Daisy commercial sealed the election for LBJ. He was the candidate of peace. Only to have the Gulf of Tonkin and the following resolution that took us deeper into a foreign war. Then he began Operation Rolling Thunder and now I have received a draft notice. Your President of peace has us in a war that nobody voted for."

1966 MEETING ON THE STREET

Betty stopped and took a second look and then said "Randy you look so different! How was boot camp?"

"Let's just say that Marine Corp boot camp and Infantry Training will get you into condition. I am shipping out soon. So, I came by to see some friends and a couple of my professors."

"Well, it is lucky for me to see you. I came by for the same reasons, but I am sure for different professors. I stopped by before I am off to Mississippi to help finish the walk that James Meredith started," said Betty.

"I hope to see you again Betty. Just try to remember there are other points of view not just two. You take care on your walk for the tensions are high in the south and it only takes a few of the extreme segregationists."

"The world press will be covering the walk with the eyes of the world on the walk this time and you also be safe over there Randy,"

The next day Betty was on her way to support the civil rights movement in the walk James Meredith started with his one-man march (220 miles) from Memphis to Jackson, Mississippi. He was accompanied by friends and supporters who were monitored by State Police and FBI agents. The press covered the walk with reporters from the major and local news networks.

Before the walk started in a local bar two young men were talking. "Billy you know that uppity colored boy is on his walk and he will be lucky to get across Mississippi," said Eugene.

"So what? Colored folks need to know their place!" said Billy.

"You were in the army and worked, ate, and slept in barracks with colored men! How did they compare to the other soldiers?" said Eugene.

"What do you mean?" asked Billy.

"Were they poor soldiers?" asked Eugene.

"No, in fact, some were pretty darn good," said Billy.

"Then what is your problem with trying to move integration in the South?" asked Eugene.

"Well! They are different!" said Billy.

"That is not what you just said!" said Eugene.

"I did not say they were the same!" said Billy.

"You said some were pretty darn good just like us. There were poor soldiers and there were good and then some that were better. So, I do not see any real difference," said Eugene.

"Eugene what happened to you at that big university up north when you got that Doctorate degree in law? I heard you have taken on some colored folks' cases. Now you are telling me that the colored folk are my equal. What is wrong with you?" asked Billy.

"One thing for sure was that nothing happened if I used or drank from the same drinking fountain or any other segregated conditions that are enforced here in Mississippi and the rest of the South," said Eugene.

"Eugene, I am done talking about this with you. There are men in this place that might think it was a good time to educate you on good polite Southern society," said Billy.

"You know you go to church twice a week and still do not understand what the message is! Do you Billy?"

"I understand the message, Eugene and I understand the devil is in your head. I feel sorry for you!"

"Billy it is easy to follow without thinking!"

"Now, you are calling me dumb! I'm out of here," said Billy.

The next day just outside Hernando, Mississippi, Aubrey Novell a white salesman waited in the woods to ambush James Meredith. He fired shots in the air and yelled James' name to warn the bystanders. The police and FBI officers slowly failed to respond. Meredith was hit in the neck, head, and back. He survived the attack. Later Aubrey was arrested and then confessed to the shooting and was sentenced to two years in prison.

The Civil Rights leaders including Martin Luther King Jr. responded with an organized march to continue the journey that James had started. Then during the march at a rally one night the young Black leader Stokely Carmichael stepped up to the podium and used the term Black Power. That phrase was picked up by the crowd, who began shouting it 'BLACK POWER! BLACK POWER! with their hands in a fist raised in the air. The mood became more militant. Soon, after that night white civil rights supporters moved to new protests of the anti-war movement. That year saw 6,000 Americans die and 30,000 were wounded in Vietnam.

That minorities suffered the highest cost in life is a myth. In fact over 85% of the deaths were Caucasian and 12% of Blacks with the rest of other groups.

1968 Democratic Convention, Chicago:

The country was in turmoil over Civil Rights and the Vietnam War and the youth were demanding a part in the political discussion. The Democratic Convention saw the upheaval boil over with Hippies, Yippies, Black Panthers, Nation of Islam, Chicanos, and just plain every other protester movement.

The Democratic party was divided between Hubert Humphrey, Eugene McCarthy, and Robert F. Kennedy. Just before the convention Robert F. Kennedy was shot and killed by Sirhan Sirhan at the Ambassador Hotel in June just two months after the assassination of Martin Luther King Jr. and that added to the already national chaos.

In Chicago, the protesters asked for permits to camp and rally at Lincoln Park, Soldiers Field, and Grant Park in Chicago during the convention. Mayor Richard Daley, 'The last of the Big City Bosses', approved only one permit at Grant Park.

The Protest and political chaos started when the Yippies got the ball rolling by nominating a pig (Pigasus the Mortal) for president outside the Convention Hall. Inside the Convention, the floor was divided between Peace and War delegates who were contesting the various delegations. Outside the protesters were battling with blue-helmeted police and the Illinois National Guardsmen. The coverage inside and outside showed the television audience that chaos and mayhem was the Democratic Party's answer to the national problems. In his hotel room, Hubert Humphrey watched from his window and watched his election hopes fade in two different battlefields.

AT A CONVENTION PARTY AT THE UNIVERSITY:

Please turn the T.V. off Michael," asked Andrei.

"Look at what is happening in Chicago," said Sandy. "This was to be a party to celebrate the nomination of the Democratic candidate for President and Senator McCarthy will win!"

"No! I do not think so. This has made the progress of civil rights and the anti-war movement look bad. The people outside have given the nomination to Humphreys and 'Tricky Dick' will win the next election and that will lay at the feet of Chicago," said Professor Andrei.

"Well, I got a draft notice yesterday and I will not go. I am going to Canada. I will not be like Muhammad Ali last year and go to prison for my beliefs in anti-war," said Howard.

"That is your choice Howard but what remember Henry David Thoreau said about bad laws," said Michael.

"What did he say?" asked Sandy.

"That one should break bad laws and then who would be the jailer if everyone broke the bad law? Or something to that effect," said Michael.

"Well, he had someone pay his fine to release him from not paying his tax. Talk is cheap," said Howard.

"Alright everyone it is time to wrap this meeting up. I will see you all when classes start," said Andrei.

"Thank you for the invitations to view the convention party. I can stay and help clean up if you like?" said Sandy.

"Thank you but that will not be necessary. Tomorrow the lady comes and cleans the place but thank you."

"Come on Sandy I will walk with you," said Howard as they walked out the door.

"Howard, you do not need to walk with me!" said Sandy as they reached the sidewalk.

"I know that I was trying to save you from embarrassment with the professor."

"What are you trying to say?"

"I think you know and have a good night," said Howard.

Sandy stood there and watched Howard walk away. She knew he was right and that made her even more mad.

CHAPTER THREE

Iranian Revolution
Nika Escape

> Very few people see their own actions as truly evil.... It is left to their victims to decide what is evil and what is not.
>
> — Laurell K. Hamilton

Shah Mohammad Reza Pahlavi left Iran on January 17, 1979, and the Cleric Ayatollah Ruhollah Khomeini returned from exile in France on February 1, 1979. By March the Islamic Republic referendum passed and Khomeini became the Supreme leader of the nation.

The ex-Shah of Iran entered the United States for medical treatment on October 29, 1979. Then on November 4, 1979, the American Embassy in Iran was taken over by the Islamic extreme. The females were released and the male hostages were held for 444 days.

The Ayatollah revolution was added in part by Iranian women being in the vanguard of the revolutionary movement. The female activists were only able to voice their opinions in the streets. The Majlis (the Parliament) began passing laws restating women's rights.

The State Iran was in change away from American support and Iraq saw an opportunity. On September 22, 1980, launched a full invasion of Iran that ended in 1988 disrupting the balance of power in the Middle East.

1991 IRAN

The two men sat having coffee. "You know that Ruhollah Khomeini was the cause for the Revolution that removed the Shah and then turned this country into a religious nightmare with killings. He is also the reason behind the Iraq War because of that small-time thug in Iraq who believed we were weak. He might have won if the Americans had not secretly sent needed materials for us to combat the aggressor next door," said Azar.

"Be careful Azar for talk like that can be heard by the wrong ears. I agree and I am sorry he waited to die one year after that war ended. Then that massive 7.4 earthquake killed thousands in the northern part of Iran last year. That has caused financial troubles for the middle class in this country," said Cyrus.

"I agree these events have caused the social and political life in the Islamic Republic to become a de facto state of poverty due to living expenses and government mismanagement. The middle class is disappearing in this country," said Azar.

"The Imam have added new subjugations that added to the repression of women's rights on dress attire and any violation is subject to monetary fines or floggings. Censorship, executions, and limited political parties kept the Republic under tight religious control. They are afraid of the young who are demanding more freedom," said Cyrus.

"Thankfully, we are old my friend, and do not have that much longer on this earth. I lost both my sons to that war," said Azar.

"Both?"

"Yes, Abbas was 15 and Bahman was just 12 when the military took them away to go to the front. I told the soldiers the boys were too young to fight in a war and they looked right at me. I could see that if I said anything more I would die," said Azar.

"I did not know that happened to your family I was away at the time. I am so sorry. I just returned last month," said Cyrus.

"A government official came to my home to tell me both of my sons died in combat on the same day. That I was to honor them with silence and pride in the Republic. Then after the funeral, a wounded soldier with a missing arm came to see me when my wife was away. He said he had waited until she left the house," said Azar.

"Why?"

"He said that what he wanted to tell me was hard to tell and he did not want my wife to know the horror of this war. Then he said if I spoke of what he was telling me I and anyone I told would die. He was not scared, but I had never seen someone that worried. So let me ask you now should I go ahead with this story?" said Azar.

"How much longer do we both have to live anyways? Go ahead and finish your story," said Cyrus.

"He told me the young boys were driven not told to move towards the enemy. That if they did not move there was gunfire behind them to get them moving. The young boys ran into the enemy fire to clear the minefields. It was a blood bath and then the soldiers were able to move through the minefield," Azar.

"What, minefields?" asked Cyrus

"The minefields in front of the enemy lines. Our leaders used the young boys to clear the minefields in front of the lines. He said the boys were given a uniform jacket and a large stick then told them their job was to go and beat the enemy. If they did not run at the enemy, the soldiers fired at their feet to force them towards the enemy lines. The boys would run at the enemy and when they stepped on a landmine that path was cleared for the soldiers when they were ordered to attack," said Azar.

"This is outrageous! We need to get this guy and report this to the press!" said Cyrus.

"That soldier took his life after he left my house. He told me he could not live with the shame of allowing it to happen, He said he had gone to a dozen other families to inform them of the policy. He said most did not want to talk to him and did not want to hear what happened. He walked out of my house walked into the street and was hit by a truck. He died on the way to the hospital. May God be with him," said Azar.

"May God help us! We should have left this country with the Shah and those others. This country was better economically under him. He had his problems, but he started OPEC to get a share of the profit of oil that the nation deserved. Life was free and the middle class was growing. Now, I see and understand he was fighting these very people that are restricting and killing people for minor issues," said Cyrus.

"I have enjoyed our talk and now I must leave for my wife needs help around the house now as we get older," said Azar.

"Yes, we are getting old my friend. Peace be with you."

A mile away two women were speaking in the garden.

"We have been friends before the revolution Nika, and we both had worked to remove the Shah. Now, I am coming to you for a visit and I see that something has happened to you. When and who did this to you?" asked Sarina.

"Rashid, yesterday afternoon, I stepped outside the house for one second without my hijab, and he went crazy. It was not the first time he had done this. When I went home the first time, my parents told me that it was my duty as a wife. A good husband needs to beat his wife now and then for family unity. They said I should be thankful for Rashid," said Nika through her tears.

"This republic would not exist if it was not for the women who got the men in this country to join the revolution. We supported the revolution for our rights and now they ignore us and make us prisoners in our own homes. We were wrong and you must leave this country and Rashid!" said Sarina.

"How? His family is powerful and my own family refuses to interfere. His family's position in the security service makes it impossible for me to do anything. I am trapped in a horrible situation, and I have even thoughts about ending my life."

"NO, NO, you must not do that! I know someone who can help you. If you are willing to leave the country."

"What do you mean?"

"It is what I said, if you are willing, I will see that you get a chance to leave this country and this life. I cannot tell you more, but you can be out of the country in a very short period. But you must do it now or the window will close for good. So, if you are willing to leave meet me outside my home at noon tomorrow and bring only the clothes you normally wear."

"Yes, Yes, I will be there,"

"Do not do anything that will cause attention, you just do what you normally do. You shouldn't know anything about our plans. I will see on tomorrow," said Sarina as she hugged Nika. "Remember you must just act normal."

Later that night Rashid walked into his home and started yelling at Nika "You have not produced a child in the ten months that we have been married. My mother and I want to know why you are not pregnant?"

Nika looked at him and said, "You should ask yourself."

"What are you implying, are you saying it is me?" as he slapped her hard enough to knock her to the floor. "You listen to me! Things are going to change in this house. I do not have time tonight for I must leave right now tonight and go to Nishapur, but I will be back late tomorrow night. Then we will have a longer talk about your failure to produce a child and other things," he walked out the door.

Nika went into the bedroom and picked out what she would wear tomorrow. She knew if she stayed, she would die at the hands of Rashid, and he would get away with her murder. The next day Nika met outside Sarina's apartment where Sarina was standing by a car. "Oh, Sarina I was worried I was late!"

"Nika you are not late, but we are in a bit of a hurry get into the car and change into these clothes as we drive."

"How? Who is this driving? How can I change clothes in front of him?"

"I will draw the curtain. He is a friend who has contacts that will help both of us get out of the country by tonight. How long before Rashid will miss you."

"He we be back late tonight, so I think we have at least eight hours before he gets home. Then he will search for me at my father's house. I think he is planning to kill me if I do not get pregnant."

"Why do you say that?"

"His mother is complaining. He asked me why I was not pregnant. I told him it may be a problem with him. Then he slapped me and knocked me down again. He said he had to leave but things would change when he returned and he walked out for his trip. I do not think he will be happy when he gets home, so this better work."

"It will work. I called in a big favor to get you out with me."

"What do you mean out with you?"

"I work with some people that do not like the government here. My position is in danger of being exposed so I was ordered out of the country. I told them you are an asset that risked a lot and that you also need to leave tonight. So, by the morning we will be free of the mullahs. What you do is up to you once we get away from here. I will go home to America and if you want you can come with me. I feel you are like my sister and my family will love you. But if you know others someplace else you will be free to go there."

"I have no family or friends outside of Iran. My life will be so different. I do not think I can handle it on my own. I will go with you!"

"Nika you are more prepared for life outside Iran than you know. Besides you are young and have a whole life to live. My agency will give you a new name."

"What about my husband? He will not accept that I ran off and his honor will demand revenge."

"Do not worry about him. When he returns from his trip he will be arrested for crimes against the state. Plus, it seems that he beat up and raped the wrong women last week."

"What?"

"I was told this just before you showed up at my place. They told me that the SAVAK were going to pick him up along with his father and his brothers for they all are being accused of spying for the Russians."

"That is not possible! He hates the Russians."

"That is what he and his father wanted everyone to believe. They were running a large operation to provide women and young boys to the Russian mob for the Eastern European human prostitution market and selling information. I would be surprised if he even makes it to trial. A public trial like that would be a huge embarrassment to the nation's mullahs."

"I cannot believe this! Who was this woman that Rashid beat up and raped?"

"She was the daughter of a high-ranking Republican Army general. I was told that Rashid grabbed her off the street raped her and beat her up and then left her laying in an alley. The whole thing was caught on a camera behind a store. So, I do not think you need to worry about him or his family anymore. If you want, you can get out of the car now and go home. You will be safe."

"No, I have no life here. My own family was willing to throw me to the wolves. No, I will go with you. You are more of a family and a sister to me."

CHAPTER FOUR

Re-Education Camp

What is dangerous about extremists is not that they are extreme, but they are intolerant. The evil is not what they say about their cause, but what they say about their opponents.

— Robert F. Kennedy

The modern practice of the Falun Gong Buddhist was started in 1992 by Mr. Li Hongzhi. He taught that one should follow a morality existence of truthfulness, compassion, tolerance, and self-discipline. The movement grew into millions by the year 1999. The Chinese Communist Party outlawed the practice as an enemy of the state and at the same time, the Shen Yun that revised ancient Chinese culture was also outlawed.

The Communist Party has suppressed many spiritual movements in China. The Uyghur Muslims have been persecuted in China since 1949 when their moment for independence was ended by the communist. Then in the 1990's Separatists and anti-Han resistance used violence and the government accused the Uyghur of being behind the violence. When a bomb exploded in 2009, more government resistance was directed at the

Uyghurs. President Xi Jinping ordered that all religions in China should be Chinese in orientation to prevent this terrorism. Reeducation camps that started during the Cultural Revolution continued to violate human rights.

2010 China Mainland Re-education Camp

In 2009 China increased its crackdown on journalists locking up those that questioned government policies. A new code of conduct was issued for Chinese and foreign reporters. Confessions of the quilt were often tied to torture. That year also saw a conflict between the Uighurs at a toy factory explosion between Han Chinese and Uighurs.

The government then rounded up Uighur men and boys in whole neighborhoods to relocate them to camps. The Chinese government was tightening its control on the South China Sea, Hong Kong, and within China and denning any human rights violations. The Western leadership and business did not want to upset the Chinese leadership and said nothing about these issues.

Relocation Camp in northwestern China:

He was led through the gate escorted by two guards with rifles. They walked along another fence through another gate and into a building with a guard outside. The building looked temporary and was a poorly constructed building of wood and some kind of paper to seal the crack.

Inside he was taken into a room with two chairs and a small table and told to sit. He was told that his sister would be brought into the room with instructions and when she arrived they were not to touch or pass anything to each other. Ten minutes later she was escorted in with two guards.

The clothes she wore were old and dirty with holes in several places. She had bruises on her arms and one side of her face. Her hair was cut short and uncombed. He was shocked at her appearance.

"You look tired my sister. Are you being treated well?" asked Tao trying to keep the shocked expression off of his face.

"I am fine. They say I only have a few more classes to take and then I must take a test before I can come home," said Zhi, as she moved her eyes to the man and woman guards watching them.

"I was planning on getting you out of this re-education camp, but the corrupt official I am dealing with said that it was not possible for any amount of money. I am sorry Zhi," said Tao in a language they both had made up as kids. She looked at the guard and they did not appear to pay any attention.

"Tao, you must leave this county. They will know you came here and that will be all they need to arrest you. Most of those people here are Uyghurs and it is only their religion that had them sent to this hell on earth. Muslims and Christians are not wanted in China. You must leave for the family."

"How can I leave you in here? You are my family!"

"Look at me Tao, I am lucky to have survived this long. I have endured so much and I am tired. Please go and save yourself and the family's honor. I will contact you when and if they release me. After I get up and the two guards follow me, be careful not to look down right away. Make sure they have turned around before you look on the ground. There is a record of what is happening here. Be careful Tao and only trust Li Jie." Then she returned to Mandarin "Thank you for coming my brother Tao. I love you."

"Zhi, study well for the coming test. I love you," said Tao as Zhi stood up and walked to the guards. Tao waited and when the guards turned their backs he then picked up the small packet of notes on thin papers placed it inside his shirt under his arm and waited for his escort.

The very night that Tao left the camp he began making plans to escape from China by going to the person his sister said he should trust. "Hello! Mr. Li Jie my sister has sent me to you."

"Who is your sister?"

"Zhi Cheng!"

"Zhi Cheng is in a re-education camp and not allowed any visitors. So, I do not believe you are who you say you are! Leave now!"

"You both were at the demonstration at Tiananmen Square with other students who were named Fang and Wei," said Tao.

"That demonstration was a long time ago, but if I was there that night and if I was right in the head I would not be talking about that night with you. We could both be arrested as enemies of the state."

"I know you were part of the planning group and that you were missed in the round-up of the leaders. I was very young at the time and my sister made me stay home. The rumors were spread that you worked with the government before you protested, I know this is not true and I know this for a fact. My sister told me before she was arrested and that if I needed help to contact you. Now, she tells me to trust only you. You can help people to leave the county and I need your help," said Tao.

"If what you say is true. How do I know this is not a setup to trap me and my group?"

"I say again my sister Zhi told me to trust only you. She is the one who told me to see only you."

"How did you see your sister? She is in a re-education camp that is being filled with Falun Gong Buddhists and Uyghur Muslims. Very few ever leave that place. I am sorry. I cannot help you! The government will not let you go and are most likely watching you now. That makes this meeting dangerous for me. You must go now!"

"No, wait! I saw my sister bribing a high official for me to get in to see my sister. He will not report this meeting right away and he did not put the meeting down on paper. The report will take a few days for the meeting to work its way through the bureaucratic paperwork. She took a real risk to give me a detailed report on what was happening at the camp. This report must get to the Western news media to expose the evil being committed in the so-called re-education camps. Read the report and see that these re-education camps are no better than the North Korean camps."

"Why do you not just get on a plane and go to another country?" asked Li Jie.

"We both know that my sister is in a camp and that means my passport is flagged for watch."

"There are other escape ways."

"You know the rate of success is low! Occasionally some fool makes a spectacular exit that the Western news media will focus on for a few days and then turn to other news stories. I remember the guy who went 200 miles on a jet ski pulling gas cans behind him to South Korea. Then there was the guy who paddle-boarded miles to Taiwan. No, I need to get to Hong Kong and then the United States. This is a story that their press will cover and get world attention."

"May I see the report?"

"Yes, Yes, please be careful the paper is very thin."

Li Jie read the report and gave it back and said, "Sit here and talk to no one. I will be back in less than one hour. You are not to take anything but your sister's story. You will be provided with a new identity once you are in Hong Kong and another identity in Taiwan. You are never to discuss anything about the journey that you are about to take. There are others who will need to make the same journey. My network has been in place since that night in 1989. Do you understand and agree?" "Yes!"

CHAPTER FIVE
A Family Escapes from Mainland China

> People like to say the conflict is between good and evil. The real conflict is between truth and lies.
> — Don Miguel Ruiz

The 1911 Chinese Revolution did remove the Imperial family and then saw a period of warlords controlling various parts of China. The War Lord Chiang Kai-shek gained control of the nationalists and was opposed by the Communist Party. During the next few years, the nationalists pursued the communist party in what was called the Long March. During that march, Mao rose to become the major power in the leadership.

When the Japanese invaded China a somewhat truce was called between the communist and nationalists. Then at the end of the Second World War Stalin increased support for Mao in China. Mao shifted the communist focus on workers to that of a better life for peasants and won support over nationalist corruption. The Nationalists were soon pushed off the mainland and moved to the Island of Formosa in 1949 as a temporary reorganizing period. The island was renamed Taiwan.

Until 1972 the United States recognized two China's. Then in a change the One China policy was put into place and the U.S. did not recognize China's sovereignty over Taiwan. The Chinese refused to recognize Taiwan as a separate country and worked to change that.

2012 Zhou Family leaves Guangzhou

He came home walked into the house looked at his wife and said, "Beijing is moving much faster than we thought to dismantle the agreement on Hong Kong," said Sun Zhou.

"What have you heard?" asked his wife Li.

"The 'Arab Spring' last year was created and increased the party leadership fear and they are worried about civil demonstrations here. At the same time since the Olympics, the leadership has become more bolder in its plans to move into the Western world of business with the economic zones. The old communists and the modern economic communists disagree on the direction of the country. That is on hold for now. But the economic side is winning for they see their world of wealth growing. They are using Hong Kong as a bargaining chip," said Sun

"How?" asked his wife.

"By bringing Hong Kong back into China's complete control the business leaders think the old communists will be happy. They are thinking beyond the present. The economic group is slowly buying off the old guard with luxuries.

"How are they planning to move Hong Kong faster into control?"

"They think it will be simple with new laws. The Moral and National Education law they have issued in Hong Kong. They believed this simple change to the curriculum to increase nationalism would reduce the separateness feeling in Hong Kong. Only for now, it has caused mass demonstrations on that island city," said Sun Zhou.

"What does that curriculum have to do with Hong Kong?"

"Right now, the people of Hong Kong think of themselves as citizens of Hong Kong and not part of China. The government wants to change that. They did not expect any demonstration to be this massive or this long.

The Youth in Shifang, Wukan, and Zhenjiang began protesting corruption by local officials. What the protesters were claiming were government attempts at thought control by Beijing. The protest spread to Hong Kong and has many in the party worried that another Tiananmen Square will happen. That mass movement is always on their minds."

"Yes, yes, I see, now what the women in the market were talking about it this afternoon. Now, I understand why Jiefan was so upset with the older woman. She was standing in line listening to the women in front of her and then suddenly just interrupted their conversation. She was rude and scolded the older women for their old way of kowtowing to the government."

"Are you serious?"

"Yes, she told them that the government has become more authoritarian since the Olympics and that an 'Arab Spring' was needed for China. The new moral law is designed to remove any opposition to the Han Chinese. That the government is violating the agreement they made with Hong Kong of *One Country Two Systems*. She was very passionate saying that the government wants only one way of thinking. The Han way!

"Then when one of the older women said that the youth did not know what they were talking about. Jiefan then just stood right up in her face and said that if the older women paid any attention they would understand."

"Who is this Jiefan woman?"

"She lives in this building, and I think she works for an Australian finance company. She is very intelligent, and I think she is very active in the protest movement."

"How do you know she is in the protest movement?"

"She spoke of the Uyghurs, Falun Gong, Shen Yun, and the 6-10 Office in her argument against the government and the government's efforts to control alternate ideas. She said the young are willing to stand up and speak their opinions at any cost, unlike their elders."

"That was very rude! What happened to her?"

"The store security came and took her away. What surprised me was the women were shocked that one so young was so rude. They did not hear what she was saying about the government. They all agreed that the young ones who were taking part in these protests should be severely punished for their rudeness. There was no comment on any of the ideas the young woman had just expressed."

"Let us hope that the young woman is not going to disappear in this small protest demonstration, and you must be more careful. You could be exposed to questioning just for standing and listening to the young woman complaining about the government. Now, for my news.

There was talk of expanding the economic zones to more of the coastal areas. I was told today that I am being promoted to our office in Hong Kong as a V.P."

"What? That is wonderful when will it happen?"

"I start there on Monday and we have housing provided along with a car and driver. So, we can both pack up and start a new life in Hong Kong. When we are there, we will have to be more careful. Hong Kong has its system and Beijing, as I said, they are trying to erode that system."

"What about Xiu and her schooling?"

"I have already taken care of that before I left the office. I enrolled her in a British International Baccalaureate school. That will fast-track her into the American University system."

"I will be glad to leave here," said Li.

"So will I, but remember we need to be more careful in Hong Kong. We will be under the Party security service that has informers everywhere."

2014 Hong Kong

Sun Zhou walked into the small kitchen turned the T.V. on and said, "Beijing has issued a White Paper stating that Hong Kong's autonomy is not inherent and it is only allowed by the central government's willingness. It has caused more demonstrations of the youth in the streets here in Hong Kong.

I had a problem getting home tonight. They are using umbrellas to block the pepper spray used by the police. The press has given the protest the name of Umbrella Protest. I am afraid that scheming little fool Fai Zhang at the office will use the protest to undermine my efforts to reform the bank's organization. I am making plans."

"What are you planning?"

"It is time for the family to take a vacation to Thailand. We have us a flight booked for tomorrow morning and I have reserved a room in Bangkok. We must be careful and only take what we need for a five-day vacation trip. We may be in Hong Kong, but we are watched by the central government. That mouse Fai has been looking into my files and records. His main ambition is to remove me and take my place. It is my fortune that his ambition is not linked to any degree of intelligence by him. However, nothing can be kept a secret forever, and sooner or later he will stumble onto something he can use against me."

"What about our work? We have commitments!"

"Our controller has permitted us to abandon our station here. This trip is perfect for our move to Taiwan. I have moved our funds around the international banking market with another friend."

"Why have you not told me about Fai and of this move?"

"I did not want to worry you about Fai and his sneaking around the office. I was told to keep a lid on the plan to leave. Our controller will take care of everything once we land in Thailand and I know nothing more. The decision to remove us from here was being made far up the chain of command before I brought up the subject. We will be met at the airport and given our next arrangements. We are to go straight to our next flight once we land in Bangkok."

"What about the hotel room?" asked Li.

"It is part of the plan to throw our minders off. The political condition in the United States and its position on Taiwan is in some doubt. The People's Republic is making economic gains in the world with the 'Belt Road' plan. They are building roads, railways, ports, and pipelines in over 70 countries. The CCP is economically trapping many poor nations in China's political influence with money. Once these countries take the money, the debt will follow and China will take more control. That debt allows the CCP to gain control over those nation's economic institutions. As the economic power of the CCP grows it weakens the world's leader's ties to Taiwan and moves closer to China.

The Americans have moved to an international or global economy and moved much of their manufacturing overseas and a lot of this business has come to mainland China. That economic tie is going to influence the political and business leaders in the States. The leadership in Taiwan is concerned about the next election in America."

A week later Fai was visited by the head of security. "Sun Zhou was due back yesterday. Do you know why he is not here?"

"He went on a trip to Thailand with his family and was approved to go."

"Yes, You were to keep an eye on him and notify us of anything out of his ordinary pattern. How many trips has Sun taken in the last two years?"

"Just this one!"

"You did not think that was out of the ordinary?"

"Yes, but it was approved!"

"By his manager! We are not his manager! We are responsible for the security of the country. Now we have lost an individual who was an important key to our economic system and we do not know what he took with him. You as the assistant manager have failed the country!"

"What was I supposed to do? What is going to happen to me?"

"If it was up to me you would be shot! However, you as the assistant manager are going to be transferred to the interior and work in a village that is underperforming. If you can turn that performance around, you and your family's life will improve. If not, I think you know!"

Fai sat at his desk and wondered what had happened to his life. He had married into a highly connected family in the CCP. Now he was in disgrace and the only reason he was still alive was the family connection. His wife had not been happy for months and this would most likely be the last straw and end of the marriage. He made his decision and got up.

CHAPTER SIX

Lavatory Fire

Evil is the plague of the soul.
— Edward Counsel

1866   2016

1866 2016

The field of Philately has changed today with fewer individuals mailing letters. Instead are using email and texting. The first-class mail in the United States had fallen from 2001 to 2016 by 40%. Plus, the postal service in many countries had begun over-issuing printed stamps as a source of income.

Philately the stamp values have changed along with this changing stamp market. Stamp values have dropped across the board with a few exceptions in places like Asia and Africa with new interest in collection. The market in these areas has increased.

However, there are still stamps that are offered for high value. An 1856 British Guiana stamp that value was one cent, sold for $9.5 million in 2013 and in 2016 a U.S. Air Mail *Inverted Jenny* stamp sold for $1.175 million. The fewer the collectors will also shift the values of the stamps.

January 2020 C.E. at Home

They had just walked into the house from a morning walk when C.E.'s phone rang. "Hello?"

"C.E. give me a call at home when you get a chance. Do not call the office I will not be there! Call my personal number." C.E. put the phone down and wondered what was happening for Nick to make that call.

"What's wrong C.E.?" asked Elaine

"That was a call from Nick, and he wants me to call him on a personal phone. Let me call him and then I will come back in and tell you all about it." He walked out of the room and called Nick.

"C. E. I do not have much time. Things have gotten out of control here with two different competing groups in the agency. What I called for is to tell you that the agency will be reaching out to you on a firebombing. You need to be careful about who you talk to and about what you discover. Trust nobody and put nothing in writing but the simple facts. I am being sent out of the country," said Nick and hung up.

C.E. walked back in and Elaine asked, "What's the matter?"

INIQUITOUSNESS

"Your guess is as good as mine. Nick answered the phone and just started talking and when he finished, he just hung up."

"What did he say?"

"Not to trust anyone and not to put anything in writing but simple facts. That the agency is in some kind of internal split with sides being drawn with Nick being sent out of this country. Plus, he said, I was going to be asked to investigate a firebombing. I know more and even less now than I did before I called Nick back."

"What do you think?" asked Elaine.

"My best guess is the politicization of the agency has reached a breaking point. Political lines have been being drawn and it looks like Nick is on the outside group in this process. That also means me."

"How can this happen in a government agency?" asked Elaine.

"You'd be surprised. This is not new for it is just more out in the open now. The FBI was under J. Edgar Hoover for 48 years and he built an empire that at times violated many of the nation's laws. He conducted wide-ranged illegal electronic surveillance. This was all done under the cover of developing the FBI into the premier investigation agency against terrorists and organized crime to protect the public during the Red Scare and the KKK of the 1920s. Then in 30's the FBI went after organized crime and violent criminals by developing new technology laboratories. The high-profile case of John Dillinger allowed J. Edgar Hoover to get into the picture as the best agent on the ground.

By the late 1930s to the 50's the FBI turned to fighting Nazi and Communist espionage with the arrest of Ethel and Julius Rosenberg as spies for the Soviet Union after the war. As society changed Hoover changed and during the 1960's the FBI began targeting civil rights leaders as communist sympathizers. He even sent a letter to Martin Luther King Jr. that threatened to expose his extramarital episodes if he did not leave the Civil Rights movement."

"I know that he was not popular and there were rumors of him having files on everyone to keep everyone in line and there were other rumors also about him as well. I guess Lord Acton was right when he said, 'Power tends to corrupt, and absolute power corrupts absolutely,'" said Elaine.

"That being said, let's you and I go to breakfast," said C.E.

"I am with you."

LATER IN THE DAY:

Two men walked up to C.E. as he was leaving the house, "Mr. Hall we have been sent to ask you to come to the university with us. We have a car and will bring you back," said the taller man.

"And who are you two?"

"We are with the FBI and you were personally asked for by the regional director."

"Can you tell me what this is about?"

"There was a fire at a university lab. Director Edison would like your opinion on the fire. That is all I know currently," said the taller agent.

"I am afraid I do not know this director, Edison. Will agent Nick Thomson be there?" asked C.E.

"I am sorry, I am Agent Greg Peterson, and this is Agent Benjamin Barns. I do not know any agent by the name of Thomson. We were just posted here from Washington D.C. Shall we go?" said the taller agent.

At the university, C.E. was greeted by director Edison. "C.E. want to thank you for coming down. I am sorry we are meeting like this. I am aware of your skills on the recent stamp case and I feel you can be of some help with this situation."

"This is very unusual, what is going on? Where is Nick?"

"We'll talk about that later. For right now, I have either a crime site or an accident. This lab is very sensitive for a Military program and there was a small fire after an explosion or the other way around. I am not sure! There is a young female who suffered second-degree burns at the incident," said the director.

"Do we know who she is?" asked C.E.

"Fang, she is a researcher assistant who worked part-time between Professor Zhang and Professor Harrison," said Agent Barns.

"Was anyone else in the lab at the time?" asked C.E.

"Yes, and no, another lab researcher." Agent Peterson looked at his notes and said, "Her name is Xiu. I have her sitting outside."

"What do you mean, yes and no?" asked C.E.

"There were three people in the lab, but two were gone at the time of the incident," said agent Peterson.

Outside the building, a crowd was forming and there were a few anti-war signs being handed to anyone who took one. "That crowd out there is getting big. Peterson, you and Barns go out and get the campus security and try to control that mess that is gathering out there. Someone has spread that the military lab is testing weapons and the doves are rallying," said the director.

"I am still unclear why I am here?" said C.E. as the two agents walked off.

"Join the club. I was told to get to the office last night to meet the two agents I just sent to do something with the crowd. These two showed up from D.C. without notice last night with orders for Nick to report to an office in Guam and then change to New Mexico. This COVID is just going to make things worse I'm afraid. As for you, being here, the office in Washington asked for you personally as an impartial pair of eyes."

"Impartial eyes?"

"I know, this does smell like a political hot potato. So starting right now, it is CYA time. The less you say and write the better. Just remember responsibility for problems flow downhill to the lowest person," said the director.

"I believe there is a different wording for that phrase!" said C.E. and stopped and looked at the director. He did not say that Nick had called him.

"This pandemic has set off a turf war in government or should I say brought it into the open in the government. Those on the far wings of the bureaucracy feel they can now make major changes. The election emboldened the marginal elements and COVID has given them an opportunity for action and radical change. This is just a gut feeling I have and it is nothing new. Only now it has legs, so be careful. Plus, I did not say any of this," said the director.

"Is this why Nick was transferred?"

"My best guess is, yes! C.E. this radical group in the department is ruthless and will turn and twist anything so that down will become up. Last week Nick pointed out a flagrant violation of the bureau's policy to the Washington Office. Then these two new agents showed up last night at my office door with orders for Nick. The duty officer called me at home and told me I was needed at the office.

"I am letting this play out for now. I do not know if my head is also on the block. So it is best we focus on the job and keep all comments limited to absolute facts. I think Peterson and Barnes are also outcasts, but only time will tell.

"I can tell you this, that some recent investigations have been closed down that did not support a current leadership policy and individuals have been removed or retired for pushing views outside the desired results."

"What about this investigation?"

"I do not know what we have! It is a military issue so it may be outside the battle line. So, all I can say is to do the best we can and keep the record short and solid. Limit the discussion to as few as we can. This is a critical military lab and I have no idea what the powers in D.C. want. The fact that they did ask for you personally must have some meaning. I just do not know what! To tell the truth, again, I do not know how I stand in this mess. I just want to do my job," said the director.

"O.K. then let's go look at the lab. I am guessing that I cannot ask any question on what this project is about - Right!"

"You can ask, but I know nothing about it either. We will both have to ask questions and that may be cut short soon."

"Why?" asked C.E.

"Like I said the pandemic. There is talk of a complete lockdown for the whole country to check the spread of the pandemic. The medical so-called experts and others are pushing to go into a complete Draconian mode to combat the spread and will only allow the essential people to work. That will mean little independent movement. So, we better work fast," said the director.

"Who are the essential?" asked C.E.

"Those that the leaders say! I have no idea at the moment! That is what I am saying about the shift in power. If you noticed the source of the virus has shifted away from the original source and to say different is an attack against the Lysenko-type bully in charge." said the director as they walked.

"Lysenko bully?"

"He was a Soviet genetic scientist who set back Soviet agriculture 20 or more years. What I mean is that the people in charge are covering up or are just poor at their job."

"You just told me where you stand on this battlefront. I have noticed that our government funds have a connection to research in that lab in

China and that information is pushed aside by most news networks and the government leaders," said C.E.

"Like I said C.E. we are in the middle of a political struggle and need to limit any discussion beyond the two of us. Here we are at the lab."

There was yellow tape crisscrossing over the door. C.E. ducked under it with the director and walked into the lab taking some photos and samples as he moved around the room and the source of the fire. Then did the same where the young woman with second-degree burns had been found.

Something in the room did not fit together and C.E. could not put a finger on it. He turned to the director and asked, "Who found the burn victim, and where did she get moved?"

"That would be Professor Zhang who found her, and she was taken to the medical station downstairs. Professor Zhang is down the hall with Miss Xiu and Professor Harrison and before you ask. Yes, they are in separate rooms. I also, see that you have that puzzled look."

"Yes! Something is out of place and I cannot put it in place right now," said C.E.

"You are wondering how the fire is close to the door and Miss Fang was behind the lab tables several feet away. I asked Professor Zhang and he said that he put the small fire out with a hand extinguisher and then started to check the lab for anything missing when he heard Fang on the floor whimpering. He said she must have run that way before she fell."

"That may be the missing piece, because most people run to the exit they came in at any emergency. So why did she run the other way away from the exit!"

"I see, we are both on the same page," said the director.

"O.K. let's talk to this Xiu person first," said C.E. as they walked out of the lab and down the hall to another room. They entered the room and a small woman in a lab light green coat stood up. "Miss, I am C.E. Hall, and this is Director Edison of the FBI and we need to ask you some questions."

"Yes, of course! May I ask how is Fang?" said Xiu.

"She is being looked at by the medical team. That is all I know for now. We are trying to understand what happened here. I would like you to start with your day and end at the time of the fire. If you would please," said C.E.

"I do not think it was a fire it was more like an explosion." Both men stopped and looked right at her.

"Why is that?" asked the Director.

"My field is in explosives and explosive materials researcher and in the lab, if I remember right, the area around the test area had more of an explosion pattern and not a spontaneous fire pattern."

"That is part of what I could not place," said C.E. as he smiled at the director who nodded his head in agreement.

"This lab is a top security lab with high-security procedures. I had stepped out of the room no more than three minutes when I heard a whoosh sound and came back to find Professor Zhang carrying the fire extinguisher around the room. He was screaming something as he collapsed behind the table. I guess it was when he saw Fang. The room was filling with people, and I had to get them out of a secure lab. Someone had spread out the important documents on our research all over the lab tables." Xiu continued.

"You mean they were not spread out when you left the room?" asked the director.

"No, I was busy setting up the experiment and had looked at the notes and was missing one document. That is why I left the room. So the papers were in one stack when I left the room."

"Did you notice anything strange or different today around the lab?" asked C.E.

"No, we were working on an experiment. Fang and I were setting up the experiment and I needed to get the missing document from Professor Zhang's office."

"Tell me about Fang, if you can," asked C.E.

"She had recently started to work with us as a part-time assistant. I do not know her all that well."

"I have to ask is her clearance the same as yours?" asked the director.

"You are asking if I have high-level clearance. The answer is yes. We both do and I have been working with Professor Harrison on this project for two years in organic chemistry. Then recently Professor Zhang and his assistant Fang were asked to join our team.

Fang said she was from Hong Kong, but I do not think she lived there very long. She knew of the big things and some of the small things special to Hong Kong, but she did not know the tiny things that one would know if one grew up young in Hong Kong. She was nice, but not friendly. I spent a number of my younger years in Hong Kong before my family moved to Taiwan."

"If I may, can we jump to your knowledge about explosion patterns?" asked C.E.

"As I said my expertise is in explosives and how to prevent damage in an accident explosion. That pattern in the lab looked like an uncontrolled explosion. That is, it looked like there was no direction with the force of the explosion. Fang must have been hit by part of the device or something that was dislodged by the explosion," said Xiu.

"O.K. I may want to ask you more later. Do you have any questions director?" asked C.E.

"None for now, but as C.E. said we might have more questions later." Both men turned to the door.

"You could look at the camera," said Xiu.

"Camera?"

"Yes, I placed one in the lab. I had a feeling my notes were being read and I wanted to see who was doing it so I put a hidden camera in the lab last night. It is hidden in the back of the lab and has a full view of the lab room."

"Alright, we will need to look at that footage a little later. Wait here until I send an agent to go with you to get the camera if you will," said the director.

"Of course."

"Well, this just took a turn," said C.E.

The two men walked into the room and C.E. said, "Professor Harrison I am C.E. Hall, and this is Director Edison of the FBI, and we are conducting this preliminary investigation. We were wondering that outside of the fact that this research is top secret do you know of any reason this has happened?" asked C.E.

"No, our research lab is a top-secret, but there are as many twenty other labs around the world working on the same things we are working on. How is Fang? She is a good researcher, but kind of stand-off socially and did not join in outside of work. I was to supervise today but had a family problem and Professor Zhang agreed to cover for me. So, I am sorry I cannot be of more help," responded the professor.

"As for Fang she is being cared for in the medical unit is all we know for now. Do you know anyone who might want to hurt her?" asked the director.

"No, do you think she was the target? I did not mean she was disliked by anyone. She is liked by everyone, but I do know that she does not trust Xiu. She told me on several occasions that Xiu was not trustworthy. I told her Xiu had been with me from the start of this project. The fact is kind of funny since they are both from Hong Kong and had no common friends or went to the same places. Xiu once told me that was strange."

"Was there a planned experiment for a small explosion experiment today?" asked C.E.

"No, not at all that is not what was planned. We were planning on a small burn test on a new lightweight material to test its resistance to fire."

"How did you hear that there was a fire?" asked C.E.

"I did not hear about it. My family problem was taken care of and I came to pick up some notes that I wanted to study at home and saw the police and fire department. The security people had me wait in this room."

"O.K., That's all for now and thank you for your time," said C.E. then turned back to the professor and asked, "What can you tell me about Xiu?"

"She has been a good research aid and will most likely be given an appointment as an associate professor next year. It would have been this year, but there were some minor issues that had to be sorted out."

"Minor issues to be sorted out?" asked the director.

"Nothing serious, it was just that Professor Zhang's research and my research overlapped. It was decided to combine the two together. Before that Xiu was questioning Professor Zhang's interest in my research. He reported Xiu to the academic committee. It was all settled with linking the two research studies together."

"Thank you," said C.E. as he and the. The director walked over to Professor Zhang just as the professor put his phone away. "Professor Zhang I am the lead investigator on this case, and this is Director Edison. Can you tell me how the lab looked before the explosion?"

"Explosion? I thought it was a fire?"

"You tell me! You were there. What did you think happened?"

"I had just stepped out to take a call from my wife. I had to hang up and rush back into the room to find a small fire and Fang on the floor. In fact, that was my wife I just talked to on the phone."

"The evidence suggests a small explosion and not a small fire caused the burn injuries to Fang. Do you know anyone who would wish Fang harm?" asked the director.

"No, No, everyone liked her. Well, maybe Xiu."

"Why do you say that?" asked the director.

"Fang did not trust her. In fact, she even implied Xiu was a PRC spy to me. I told her she was way off base that Xiu's family are vocal dissidents to the PRC. She has been with Professor Harrison from the beginning," said Professor Zhang.

"Did she give any reasons for thinking Xiu was a PRC spy?" asked the director.

"No, Fang just said it was a feeling."

"O.K. one last thing were you planning on a small explosion test today?"

"Absolutely not, all explosive tests are done at a different test location and are monitored for safety checks. I cannot believe this is happening! This was to be a small fire test on resistive material."

"That is all for now and thank you for your time, Professor Zhang," said Director Edison.

As the two men walked away Edison turned to C.E. "What are you thinking?"

"Things just do not seem to add up so far. This Fang was found at least ten feet from the location of the blast or fire center behind a lab counter. I have not seen her or her burns yet, but if they are second degree that would seem to be a light explosion if the blast tossed her that far or if she was that close to the ignition site. Then I think the burns would be more than second-degree. Let's go and talk to Fang and try to complete the picture," said C.E. as the two men walked to the medical aid station.

Both men entered the medical station, "Miss Fang, I am Director Edison, and this is our investigator C.E. Hall, we would like to ask you some questions about what happened in the lab."

"I am sorry, it happened so fast it is all a blur to me."

"Anything you can remember will help us understand what happened," said C.E.

"I will try. I am still a little shocked that this happened. We were just testing a heat-resistance material. I think Xiu must have been confused and used a white Pyrophorus instead of a nickel alloy compound before she ran off to the professor's office for notes."

"Pyrophorus?"

"I am sorry. I forget not everyone is a chemist. A pyrophoric is a substance that will combust when exposed to air, like white phosphorus."

"Is that chemical easy to identify?"

"Yes, by any good chemist. She has been Professor Harrison's assistant longer than I have. Yet, I have noticed she is prone to make mistakes on several occasions and for that reason, I do not think she trusts me."

"Why is that?" asked Director Edison.

"She is always looking over my shoulder and checking my notes. She said she was going back to the office to get some notes. Although, we had all the notes we needed."

"Any other reasons?" asked C.E.

"I think she has a resentment of my social class. We are both from Hong Kong and she is always asking me questions about my life there."

"What class would that be?" asked C.E.

"I was born in Hong Kong and Xiu considers herself a refugee from the mainland of China. Her family used Hong Kong to get the family to Taiwan. I think she resents me for not having a disrupted life like her."

"I see. You also said she ran off?" said C.E.

"Yes, she just finished setting up the experiment. Then said she needed some notes and ran out the door."

"Did she say what the notes were?" asked Edison.

"No, Professor Zhang had also stepped out of the room. The next thing I remember is a flash and a boom."

"O.K. thank you for allowing us to ask you questions so soon after this horrible experience. We may have more questions later," said Director Edison.

As the two men walked away from the room C.E. turned to the director. "I think we are both right. There is something off here. I starting to think that this Xiu is being set up. The stories we are told make sense until you consider that Xiu is an organic chemistry scholar. There is no way she would mistake white phosphorus for any other substance. Plus, the timing is off. If it was white phosphorus and I remember from the Marines it did not have a delay once air contacted it," said C.E.

"I agree, white phosphorus will spontaneously ignite the second it is in contact with oxygen. Xiu could not have placed white phosphorus in the open air and walked or run out of the door fast enough not to notice the flash. I do not think it was an explosion or boom. It was more like a whoosh; I think we will find a white phosphorus trace as a trigger source. Now all we need to do is find who did it!"

An Office in China

The meeting was held in the leader's office. "Why have we had Fang dealing with this Mexican drug leader?" asked Leader He.

"He was the conduit for getting the documents out of California. I was told that we were not to have Fang to have any contact with the Chinese diplomats. We have been moving our chemicals through Mexico with the Leocadio Blanco's network. He has been a successful informant between Fang and us. Also, he has a cousin that is a reporter that at times provides information to Leocadio," said Jiehong.

"Who is this reporter?"

"A childhood cousin that grew up with Leocadio before the cousin moved to the States. The reporter knows that Leocadio is a cartel leader, but family is family. The cousin lives and works in the States and has no cartel connections except the family," said Jiehong.

"What value is this Leocadio to us outside of being a conduit."

"He has informed us of the relationship with the people at the university. He told us that Fang saw Xiu as a problem and he offered to remove her from the table. But Fang said that would cause more problems and that she would handle the matter in good time."

"Alright, keep me informed," said Leader He.

CHAPTER SEVEN

Spies at University

Education is the most powerful weapon which you can use to change the world.

— Nelson. Mandela

Nathan Hale was a young officer. Colonies Continental Army of George Washington. He volunteered to gather information for the colonial cause and was captured by the British. After the capture, he was sentenced to hang without a trial.

At his execution, it was said he said, "I have but one life to lose for my country." A British officer who witnessed the execution wrote in his diary of Hale, "He behaved with great composure and resolution…"

The circumstances of his capture are unclear. One rumor was a Tory family member turned him into the British.

January 2020 University Lab

The two men stood outside the building that housed the lab. "What do you say we walk around the science area and do a little individual interviewing? It might give us some insight into the faculty and students in the department. Universities are like small communities with lots of gossip," said the Director.

"Great idea," said C.E.

"Should we split up or go together?" asked the director.

"Split up I think. The two of us from the government coming onto the campus will most likely cause a limited response from individuals. You look like an official that is very important and I am just a small-time fire investigator asking questions about a fire. You can ask the hard investigation questions and I can ask more personal questions about individuals with little cause for concern," said C.E.

"You mean I look like the police, and this is a university that is liberal, and I will get very little information. I see your point. Give me a call when you are finished with your information gathering. I will go and interview some faculty," and with that, the director walked off.

C.E. walked around asking questions of students about the school and the science department. When a student would say they were a science major C.E. disclosed he was a fire investigator looking into the small fire that injured a research student. The last student he spoke with gave him an interesting story. When he walked away from the student, he called the director and left a voicemail message. "I have an interesting item that may or may not lead to some answers. I will be at the student store."

The director walked up to C.E., "I am glad you found something. I found nothing of interest. These people do not like the government that gives them all that research money. What did you find?"

"Well, I was talking to the young grad student in the science department, and she gave me some insight into Professor Zhang. It is rumored that he had at times traded grades for sex."

"What is new? University Professors have been doing this since the Middle Ages. There is the tragic love story of Abelard and Heloise in the 13th Century. Heloise was forced to become a Nun and Abelard became a monk after Heloise's family took his manhood. They continued to write to each other."

"True, but what was interesting in this story was Professor Zhang according to the rumor, he has stopped his little ventures since Fang became his assistant. Not much later he began working with Professor Harrison. It seems Fang, our burn victim, has replaced Professor Zhang's outside attractions. A married man might be willing to do anything to keep his secret. What do you say we go and talk with him?"

"First, let's review the footage from the hidden camera," said C.E.

They watched the footage and both men sat there before the director said, " This just became an international case with the Chinese and we are in mud up to our necks," said the director.

"How so?"

"The power in Washington is not willing to call out the virus or anything else connected to China. We will have to keep this quiet until we find more to make any solid connections. We are going to need hard confessions on tape and then that may not be enough. I think we were put on this to get us out of the way. They were thinking that this was a nothing case. Who knows where this thing is going? Let's go talk to Professor Zhang again," said the director.

They found the professor in his office reviewing papers. "Professor Zhang we have a few more questions for you, if you do not mind," said C.E.

"Of course, I have these papers to review and grade but I can spare a few minutes."

"Professor, I will cut to the chase, so we can all get on with our day," said the director.

"Oh! This sounds a little serious. Do I need a lawyer?"

"That is fine if you feel that is necessary?" said the director.

"No, no, I was just joking. What do you want to ask?"

"You are a married man with children, I understand?" asked the director.

"Yes,"

"We have uncovered a rumor that you were trading grades for sex until Fang became your research assistant. That rumor is common knowledge within the science department's student body."

"That is outrageous!" said the professor as he became fidgety.

"Professor I feel I must remind you. That it is a federal offense to lie to the FBI. Now before we waste a lot of time investigating the rumor, if the rumor is true there may be a reason for you to want to harm Fang if she was going to expose you to your wife," said C.E.

"OH, My God! OH MY GOD! That Bitch has ruined me! I am ruined. I knew this would happen! I am ruined!" cried the professor as he slumped in the chair.

C.E. looked at the director who looked back at him, "Professor what are you saying? Why are you ruined? Is it that why you tried to kill Fang?"

"Are you kidding me? That bitch would rather kill me. She started blackmailing me once she got me into bed. I think she is a Chinese spy and she tried to remove Xiu from Harrison's research team before we started working together. I would not be surprised if Professor Harrison is not also on the Chinese payroll. I am ruined, I am just ruined!"

This outburst shocked both men and the director was first to take control of the room and lock the door. "Listen to me professor you are in serious trouble, but if you cooperate you may get out of some of the serious trouble you are in. So, get control of yourself and listen. We need to collaborate on what you are telling us about Fang and Professor Harrison. What I want you to do is to wear a wire and go into the medical unit where Fang is and talk to her about our visit.

"When?"

"As soon as we get you wired up, there is no time to waste."

"What will I say?"

"Tell her you are worried."

"What if she does not say anything?"

"Then tell her that we were also asking questions about Professor Harrison and we know about his bank deposits."

"What deposits?"

"It is just a guess, if he is working with the Chinese it is for money," said C.E.

"What if she still does not admit anything?"

"Then when you break down and say you can't stand it any longer and tell her you are going to confess, that should get her to react."

"C.E. wait here with the professor and I will get thing this into motion," said the director as he left the room on his phone.

"Peterson, here." picked up his phone.

"Peterson you and Barns go and detain Professor Harrison. He is not allowed to contact anyone. Stay with him in a locked room if you need to. This case just ballooned into something major. It is important to keep a lid on this for the next few hours! Plus, have someone watch Fang and keep me informed of any movement," said the director.

"Understood!" said Peterson.

Next, the director called the office and had a technician rush to the university to wire Professor Zhang.

"Professor, you are all set to go," said the technician.

"I am scared! What if I make a mistake and she knows I am wearing a wire?"

"The wire is hidden and she will only know if you tell her. Your nerves will add to your story. She will see you are worried and scared," said the director.

Ten minutes later Professor Zhang walked into Fang's cubical, "Professor Zhang why are you here?" she demanded.

"I came to see you. Why are you out of bed?"

"I have been released. Why are you here?"

"The FBI came to see me and were asking questions about you."

"What were they asking about me?"

"What did I know about you and Professor Harrison!"

"They were just asking and gathering information on the fire. Stop worrying."

"No, they were asking about more than just the fire. I think they know things about you."

"Professor, they will only know that if you tell them. Now, for your family's sake take a deep breath and relax. The FBI will do nothing if you keep your mouth shut."

"NO, I am going to tell them everything and confess that you are blackmailing me and that you are not just a research assistant. I cannot keep this up any longer."

"You fool! Do that and your family will be in real danger, and you will go to prison. I have important people who can make your family's life difficult. So, go to your office or home and keep quiet."

"What about Professor Harrison's bank deposits and their questions?"

"They are fishing those deposits cannot be traced! Now, get out of my way," said Fang as she walked and pulled back the curtain and stopped by two men.

"Fang, I am Agent David Lev and this is Agent Chen Russel. We would like you to come to FBI the office for some questions."

"Am I under arrest?"

"Only if you insist!" said Agent Russel.

"I insist! What am I being charged with?"

"Right now, an act of terrorism! Other counts will be added for blackmail and spying for a foreign government."

"What, you are kidding! What act of terrorism?"

"First the fire in the lab and second for the threatening of Professor Zhang and his family," said Agent Russel.

"I am the victim of that fire. I have the burns to prove it."

"Yes, we know. It seems that Xiu did not trust you and set up a hidden camera in the lab. We viewed the tape that had recorded everything that happened in the lab for the last 30 hours. You and Professor Harrison had a nice discussion on how to remove Xiu from the program. I will give him some credit he did try to talk you out of it. He admired her academic mind and said he needed her intellect to complete the study. You on the other hand are a piece of work."

"That little Bitch, we should have killed her months ago when Leocadio Blanco suggested it!"

"Thank you!"

"For what? You will never be able to use it. I have not been given my rights," said Fang.

"We'll let the courts decide the legality of your words, but we have you on tape talking and planning an accident to another person. Also, we can use the information you just let slip out in your anger."

"I never said anything!"

"You gave us a name. Now, I am placing you under arrest for an act of terrorism. You have the right to...." said agent Russel.

The director turned to C.E. and said, "This is another fine mess you got me into!"

"You guys called me," said C.E.

The director turned to the other agents and said, "Take this person to headquarters and we will interview her again tomorrow. I want her to stew for a while. Now, C.E. shall we go and ask Professor Harrison some questions."

"I am with you and I think we should have someone look into these Leocadio Blanco individuals," said C.E.

"You read my mind, Agent Russel when you get to HQ contact DEA for an agent Edward Wilson, and make an appointment for him tomorrow at 9 a.m. with me."

"Where should tell him where the meeting will be held? Here or the office."

"My office."

C.E. Director Edison turned across the campus to the room where Professor Harrison was being detained. He was sitting in a chair and stood up as soon as the door opened. "I demand to be released from this unlawful detention – Right Now! This is a violation of my constitutional rights. This is kidnapping and false imprisonment. I want a lawyer."

"Professor if I may, will you please sit down? I need to understand what happened in the lab today. It is standard procedure to isolate the individuals and to question them separately. I am sorry this has taken so long, but Miss Fang gave us some interesting information. We had to follow up," said the director.

"I guess I am overreacting. This has been a very long and stressful day." What can I tell you for I already told you what I know," said the professor.

"Well, first you can tell us about the payment you have been receiving from the CCP for details of your project here at the lab," said the director.

"What details are you talking about?" said the professor.

"See, that C.E. asked about details, not the payments!" said the director.

"Professor I am sorry to tell you that Fang gave you up and told us everything," said C.E.

"That is not possible!"

"I am afraid you are wrong. A team of FBI agents are at your home and office going through everything there. Plus, Fang gave us the bank where the money was deposited. You are toast right now but if you are willing to cooperate things might go better," said C.E.

"It is impossible she does not know which bank!"

"So, there is an account in a bank with your name on it from the Chinese," said C.E.

The professor slumped and shook his head, "I never trusted that little whore. She had Zhang tied in a sexual knot after she tried to get me in bed. Then I was told to make her a part-time assistance. I knew when she wanted to remove Xiu things were coming to an end. What do you want the know?"

"You can start at the being."

"I told her to let that Mexican thug get rid of Xiu, that this plan was going to be complicated," said Professor Harrison.

"What Mexican Thug?" asked the director.

"Some guy named Juan Art or something,"

"Do you mean Juan Alfaro or something like that?"

"Yeah, that was his name. He scared me."

"Alright professor these two agents are going to take you to a different location and get your full statement," said the director.

After the professor and agents walked out C.E. turned to the director, "What changed?"

"Juan Alfaro is second in command to the cartel leader Lecoadio. If he is here and talking to a Chinese spy, we may have a far bigger problem."

LATER AT FBI HEADQUARTERS:

"C.E. Leocadio Blanco and Juan Alfaro's characters were members of the cartel you and Nick helped to break up," said the director.

"Are you thinking the same people are tied to this?"

"The research program I was told is a very sensitive military program. I think it would be wise to collect a team and look into this deeper."

"There was a Chinese analysis who did some fine work on the banking in China in our case. It would be good to get him if possible."

"I will see that he is a member of the team. Now let's get to the leg work and see what we can find" said the director.

CHAPTER EIGHT
Pandemic and Lockdown

> Knowledge is power. Information is liberating. Education is the promise of progress in every society, in every family.
>
> — Kofi Annan

The pandemic of 1918 was a type of swine virus that jumped to the human population killing 21 to 50 million people worldwide. The United States suffered 675,000 deaths with a population of 150 million individuals. The virus was named the Spanish Influenza because the King of Spain was the first person on note to die from it. The pandemic came in four waves attacking the young healthy adults 20 to 40 years old the hardest.

A hundred and two years later a man-made various was allowed to get out of a Chinese lab. Politics outweigh science and the governments began issuing draconian rules and providing funds for relief for any death with the virus. Most deaths were considered virus deaths for the connection to funds and to support the rules.

COVID-19 swept around the world killing 67 million worldwide. The United States suffered 620,000 American deaths out of a population of

320 million. Most deaths were in older adults and people with pre-existing conditions.

The press and government made mischaracterization of the virus by failing to investigate or check other scientific information. They recognized just the information being fed to it by just one side. Any opposing view was shut down as misinformation by extremists.

Government officials lied to the public a number of times saying they did so for the public good. One person like Trofim Lysenko said to question him was to question science.

2020 MARCH

A door of the room in the FBI building opened and a tall Hispanic man with green eyes entered the room saying, "I am sorry. I was just told to get over here, that I was assigned to this unit. I have no idea why I am here. I am special ATF agent Joaquin Miller."

"Not to worry, you will be filled in and are just in time. This unit was just formed last night. This team has been formed to investigate a recently discovered connection between a Chinese spy network and a Mexican cartel with a possible connection to Iran. So why not introduce ourselves? I am director Lee Edison." Let's start by going around from left to right.

"I am Benjamin Barns an agent with the FBI."

"I am Greg Peterson also an agent with the FBI."

"As I said I am Joaquin Miller an agent with the ATF."

"I am Edward Wilson an agent from the DEA."

"I am Mary Jo Longstreet FBI from the cyber division."

"I am C.E. Hall part time consultant with the FBI."

"Wait a minute! You're the consultant that broke up that old Nazi ring!" said Mary Jo. "I was part of the cyber group that traced the international banking."

"Yes, but I did not break up anything. I just got the ball rolling. Nick Thomson and his team did most of the leg work…" Just then the door opened and in walked Nick Thomson.

"Nick?" said C.E.

"Good day everyone," said Nick with a big smile.

"Good, you made it Nick. We just made introductions," said the director as he introduced everyone to Nick. "Now about this assignment. C.E. and I discovered a connection with a Chinese spy network at the local university to a possible connection to a Mexican drug cartel. After some digging, we discovered a connection that goes back to the investigation C.E. and Nick worked recently about stamp forgeries."

"Not Diego's cartel, His group was taken over by two other cartels," said Nick.

"True, but one of the lieutenants under Diego has decided to build a powerful group of his own and is causing tension in the limited truce between the cartels. It was the part you played in that bust-up of Diego's cartel and my limited influence that has brought this team together. Everyone is here because of my personal direct selection. Do not thank me yet for this may be a rabbit hole we will all be running down. Well, let's just say we need to get on this quickly. Any questions?" asked the director.

"I still do not know why I am here!" said Mary Jo.

"Mary Jo you are the best cyber researcher and code breaker in the department and we will need your skills. I am afraid we do not have a lot of time for things are in such an influx," said the director.

"Am I missing something?" asked Edward.

There is a power struggle in the top levels of government and this case may not be in the interest of one side. What I am saying is this team connection could affect one's position. So, let us stay on the mission and ignore the outside and inside elements if we can. One last thing, like I said, I picked each one of you for your skills and if you want out, I understand. Now is your chance to walk away without any blowback from me or those above," said the director.

"I for one, am in!" said Nick

"Does anyone want out?" asked the director and nobody stood to leave.

"If this is connected to the Diego group, it is more than spies, drugs, and human trafficking. Plus, thank you for bringing me back!" said Nick.

"Nick you need to thank Diego. His name allowed me the pressure to get you back. All right let's get started before everyone goes off to do their thing," said the director.

"Wait, who is this Diego?" asked Wilson.

"He was tied to a case that C.E. and Nick closed on terrorism, drugs, and stamps that was tied to an active Nazi organization. That makes this case of some importance. However, those at the top do not think it is that important but want to cover themselves with our investigation. That is all I can say about that case at this time. If it appears that some of the same players have entered the picture, I will bring everyone up to date. Now I would like Joaquin to give a short idea of patterns of the cartels in Mexico," said the director.

"I will try to make this brief and understandable in the limited time frame today. These are not the cartels of the past years. Mexican cartels have increased their power and military strength over the past twenty years. At times they are better armed than the Mexican enforcement groups or our own Border Guards.

There are ten major cartels. The *La Familia Michoacana* Cartel that goes back to the 1980s (LFM), The *Guerreros Unidos* (GU) started in 2009, and the *Beltran-Leyva* (BLO) in 2008. The *Sinaloa* Cartel controls the west coast of northern Mexico along with the *Tijuana* Cartel. The *Gulf* Cartel has agreed to a truce with their old enforcers the *Los Zetas* Cartel that control the east coast of Mexico. The *Juarez* Cartel is in the north along the Texas-Mexico border.

The cartels are responsible for some 360,000 homicides in Mexico since 2006 along with some 79,000 other disappearances. They have expanded their drug operation from Cocaine, Heroin, marijuana, and methamphetamine to include fentanyl supplied by China. The fentanyl deaths have quintupled this year from the 2019 numbers.

There have been American joint operations with the Mexican government but each side has a trust issue. Real trust damage was done with the 'Fast and Furious" program that started in 2009. That was an American administration program placing small trackers in guns that were sold and headed to the Mexican cartels. The hope was to trace cartel leaders. Later, one gun was traced to the killing of a U.S. Border agent raising questions on both sides of the border. The bottom line was there were very few arrests and those were for minor individuals in the trafficking trade. The plan was a failure and an embarrassment to the administration. Any questions?"

"You said there was a truce?" asked C.E.

"The killing was out of control between the *Gulf* cartel and *Los Zetas* cartel. The *Los Zetas were* the fastest-growing cartel with their uncontrolled violence. Do not get me wrong they are all violent but the *Zetas* did take it to another level. Now, there is a truce between the *Gulf* and *Zetas,* but not with the government. To be honest, one cannot tell who is a cartel or who is a government. Mexican cartels rival the Russian mob for mixing criminal activities with government actions. That is a very simplistic statement, but I think you all understand what I am saying. Are there any more questions?"

"O.K. then everyone has their assignments and keeps the written reports to just the limited facts. Off you go to check with their various agencies to gather information. Let's meet back here tomorrow morning say at 8:30 to review and plan our next step. One more thing before the end of the month the administration is planning to close down the society with only essential movement in the country. Some states are already starting to shut down all non-essential business and travel. That will make our job more difficult. New York has closed their school and moving patients with COVID into nursing homes from hospitals and I heard that California is issuing a stay-at-home rule," said the director.

"That will cause panic buying!" said Mary Jo.

"It has already started. Elaine and I were at the store and the toilet paper shelf was half empty," said C.E.

"The White House is trying to address the pandemic at the same time arguing within itself on what to do and who is the blame. The whole thing is a mess without any public debate. So, everyone stays focused on the investigation," Director Edison.

"So, back to our investigation!" said C.E.

"My fault, I am sorry and cut the review short for I am worried that the Bureau is being moved into a bad position in the public eye. That should not be our concern at the moment. We all need to be on the same page and understand what is discovered and when. The floor is open for any input," said the director.

"This guy Leocadio Blanco has begun to build a small cartel with Chinese Belt Road initiative money. I am not sure how he hooked up with the Chinese. He was a low member of the Diego cartel that C.E. and Nick had a part in breaking up. I have a feeler out looking into his organization," said Agent Wilson.

"What is the Belt Road initiative?" asked agent Miller.

"It is the Chinese plan to dominate world trade in the next few years by land and waterways routes. It is the old Silk Road of the historic past of the Chinese Han and Roman Empire period. Anyways that is a short summary," said C.E.

"That stamp nerd does know his history," said Nick to the laughter of the group.

"O.K. So let me be a little more detailed in what needs to be investigated. Mary Jo this Mexico-Chinese connection should be a priority for you right now. See, if there is more than just a casual association. As a matter of fact, everyone makes a note of any connection you discover with China and Mexico," said the director.

"If I may suggest we include Iran and the Middle East, for the last case connected terrorist and drugs," said C.E.

"Is this another gut feeling or …" asked Nick.

"No, do you remember Agent Tao?" asked C.E.

"Yes, he did great work on Chinese banking. We were unable to connect them to the whole stamp counterfeit case. However, he did find the money for the stamps in a Hong Kong bank by using his contacts in Hong Kong. He was able to find out that the forged stamp we were looking for had been held by the bank and was sold to an unidentified person. Tao was told the men who bought the stamp were agents of the Chinese security service. I think we should get him looking into Fang!" said Nick.

"He is already on the job and going through all the records and computer files. That is why he was not at the meeting," said the director.

"If that is the case maybe we should have someone looking into the Iranians. They did play a big part in our case and it looks like the same players are in this case," said C.E.

"Good point! O.K. let's get moving before we are limited by the powers to be and their Draconian rules," said the director.

"Draconian rules?" asked C.E.

"The world is going nuts and instituting lockdown orders. The Chinese locked down a whole city and went so far as to lock people in their buildings to stop the spread of COVID-19 virus. Now there are rumors that other nations are going to do the same. If anyone challenges or questions the origins or policies they are – what's the term they use now?" ask the director.

"Canceled!" said Mary Jo.

"That's it! So, I say again stay on the case and do not get sidetracked in the political crap."

CHAPTER NINE

Protest or Rebellion

> The aim of education is the knowledge, not facts, but of values.
>
> — William S. Burroughs

In 1786 Daniel Shays and western Massachusetts men tried to stop the Boston coastal elite leaders from taking their property under new tax laws. Sam Adams, the firebrand of the American Revolution, had the State of Massachusetts pass a Massachusetts Riot Act that used the same words from the British Parliament used in the Riot Act of 1714. That act limited gatherings to 12 persons or less.

The small rebellion in western Massachusetts was slow in being put down by the state government. This alarm of rebellion causes the call for a Constitutional Convention to fix the weak Articles of Confederation. When the Convention met, instead of fixing the Articles it drew up the new United States Constitution and Bill of Rights with a strong central government.

The new Secretary of Treasury Alexander Hamilton planned on making the new republic solid on economic principles. His plan called for the federal government to take over the state's war debts into a national debt to build confidence in the new government. The plan called for the selling off of federal land to raise money to pay off the debt. Another part of Hamilton's plan was to place a tax on whiskey.

In 1794 western Pennsylvania men tried to stop the new federal government from taxing their whiskey. Whiskey in the west was the best way to transport their grain crops to the east without spoiling. This act of resistance was called the Whiskey Rebellion and President Washington personally rode out with the army to put a stop to the rebellion. This was the first and last time that an American President led an army in the field for combat.

Both Rebellions were localized. The first caused a change to a strong national government and the second solidified national power.

2020 Summer of Love?

Nightly news was no longer just at dinner time. The news became a 24-hour event with the development of the CNN network. The internet and blogs created a rush for being first with news. The blogs and networks divvied between liberal and conservative coverage for their desired viewers. They all tried to appear balanced in their coverage.

The program started with another 'News Flash' report "This is Chet Butler and this is the third night of rioting in the cities across America. We go first to our reporter in the field, Pete Blanco."

"Good evening, Chet. As you can see there are a few burned-out cars and some buildings behind me are on fire, but the mayor just gave an update and said for the most part this has been a peaceful protest for the last three days. The mayor also said there have been only a few arrests for looting and arson. But as you can see the large store in this footage has been completely wiped out of merchandise by looters.

Police abandoned the station just across the street a few minutes ago and we are running the footage now. You can see demonstrators shouting and hurling items at the police units as they retreat. If you notice, the whole block is burned to the ground. I interviewed some of the demonstrators earlier today. Here are those interviews:

An individual came into view with a headscarf covering his face, "Young man why are you here?"

"To help the people cast out these imperialist oppressors!"

"What oppressors?

"Look around Man! They are the government, the fascist police, and greedy capitalists that are forcing the people into workers slavery. They have kept us from moving ahead."

"How have these groups oppressed you and others? "

"With 500 years of injustice to my people and others! The business community charges high prices and pays low wages, the police beat up people for no reason and the government kept taking our money with their taxes for other groups. This is just another tax revolt like the Shays Rebellion or the Whiskey Rebellion."

"Where did you hear about these rebellions?"

"Man! Didn't you go to a university?"

"Did You?'

"Yes, I am a USC graduate with a master's degree in theater!"

"I see, so how were you oppressed for 500 years?"

"What do you mean?"

"If you were oppressed how did you get through five years in a prestigious private university?"

"I had to work my way with student loans and working odd jobs. While the rich were going to parties, I was working and studying."

"Thank you." The camera and reporter could be seen walking. "Let me ask this young woman why she is here. Miss, why did you join this demonstration?"

"For women everywhere! We have been held down since Adam and Eve. That is why I am here, not for the likes of people like you to come here and ask stupid questions."

"What questions should I be asking?"

"Not what you should be asking, but who!"

"Then who is the who? I should ask?"

"The elite that run the country. They are keeping women, the poor down with poor wages and the long hours of labor in the Good Old Boy network. They are poisoning us with carbon, chemicals, that are changing our bodies and the environment. That is who and what questions you should be asking," said the young girl.

"You know, that is a very nice handbag you have. Do you mind telling me where I can get one for my wife?"

"So you need to buy your wife her wardrobe like she is an object for you to own. Did your daddy give you this job? I am tired of talking to you get out of our face you capitalist tyrant," she yelled walking off.

"Well, Chet that was two interviews earlier and that young woman was wearing Hermes sneakers, and the handbag was also a Hermes." While the video was running, the police station behind him that had been set on fire was now totally engulfed in flames. "This is Pete Blanco reporting from the center of the mostly peaceful unrest," said people back in the studio who could be heard laughing.

"Thank You, Pete, We will be right back with the weather and traffic," Chet said smiling and a voice came over his earpiece. "Chet, I want to see

INIQUITOUSNESS

you and Pete Blanco in my office as soon as you are off the air. Is that understood?" said the station manager.

"Can I ask why?"

"No! Just get him here, Right Now!"

Chet looked over to the program director, "Get on the radio and call Pete and get his team back here now, we have a meeting in the front office after the broadcast."

Later as Pete and Chet walked to the station manager's office, Pete was asking, "Why was my team called back?"

"I do not think it was for congratulations on a very good piece of reporting. I was ordered to get you and me to his office immediately after the report. To tell you the truth I felt like I was being called to the principal's office in grade school. But let's just see what happens."

As they entered the reception area, "You two can go right in," said the secretary.

"Who the devil do you think you are young man?" asked the station manager before Pete the door closed.

"What do you mean? I am a field reporter," said Pete.

"Let's see! Do field reporters investigate sources?"

"Of course!"

"Then how? Did you think your putting down an important celebrity daughter in an on-air interview would advance your career?" demanded the manager.

"Who did I put down?"

"THAT Little Miss Hermes! That's WHO! You made her look the fool with her idiotic comments about climate and the oppressed poor. She was standing in her shoes with a handbag that most likely had cost a king's ransom. Twenty seconds after that started being aired the head of the network called me on my phone. On my phone! He demanded that I fire both of you, which he referred to as tabloid news hacks.

Pete, you are done at this network as of this very second. However, you are being offered a good separation package of six months of salary and a good evaluation after you sign a statement that you will not discuss the reasons for your leaving the station!"

"It was an on-the-street interview! How was I to know she was an important person's daughter?"

"Well, the fact that she was wearing more than a thousand dollars in clothes most likely! That could have been a clue. You did not even ask her for a name."

"No, most of the people interviewed on the street do not give their full name unless they are drunk. What if I don't sign?"

"Then your career in reporting will most likely be over. I just had my job threatened by your actions and now I am on the ledge myself. I hate this but other jobs are on the line over this."

"What does that mean?"

"The whole crew that was out there with you young man. Plus the crew at the station was heard laughing at Little Miss Hermes. There is some real weight behind this and I am forced to be the bearer of the bad news. So, take the deal and save what is left of your career and the careers of others. I was told if you do not take the deal that you and all the others go without a package. As for you Chet your laughing and smile at Little Miss Hermes on-air almost had you moved to the a.m. time slot."

"We could stand together and fight this!" said Pete as he looked to Chet for support.

"Pete, remember the weatherman that made a joke on air about a big celebrity. He is on the radio now given the weather in the early morning. I am sorry, we would not win and nobody is going to support you if you fight!" said Chet.

"Alright, I will sign and you can send my checks. I never want to come to this station again for it is apparent that I have no friends here!"

"Pete, that is not true. You need to understand the big picture," said Chet.

"The big picture are you kidding! This is wrong and you both know it! Reporting is about looking for the truth and this station is now allowing the news to be influenced by others regardless of the truth. This station is turning into a propaganda network for special interest."

"That is your opinion and I suggest you keep it to yourself. This is your nondisclosure agreement and my secretary will walk you out," said the station manager.

Pete signed the statement and left the room. "Chet you go back to the newsroom and collect all the footage of that interview and bring it back here. First, you need to sign this."

"What is this?"

"Your statement not to discuss this meeting with anyone after you leave this room."

"Were you serious about the morning slot?"

"Chet, I had to negotiate that part of the deal. The first part of the call was that you both were gone. I suggested Pete's package to keep you. It was agreed that if he signed you would stay in your present time slot, if he did not you would go to the morning slot temporarily."

"Temporarily?"

"Yes, and Chet he also saved your crew at the station."

"What am I to tell them?"

"We will just let the rumors fly and then die in a few days. Now go and get that footage before it is copied and put on the internet."

CHAPTER TEN

Cartels

The world is a dangerous place to live; not because of the people who are evil, but because of the people who don't do anything about it.

— Albert Einstein

In 2020 there were 93,331 overdose death in the United States. The history of all drug purchases in this country were over the counter selling until the early 20th Century when laws were passed to control the sales of harmful drugs.

1906 - The Pure Food and Drug Act
1914 - The Harrison Act regulated sales of narcotic for taxes.
1919 - The 1933 Prohibition enforced.
1937 - The Marijuana Act did not criminalize use but impose hefty fine if taxes not paid.

1960's - Any problem had a pill to treat it.
1970 - The Control Substance Act to control Marijuana, LSD and other drugs.
1971 - War on Drugs.
1977 - President Carter decriminalized Marijuana.
1984 - "Just Say No" campaign.
1986 - The Anti-Drug Act passed to set mandatory sentence for drug convictions.
2010 - The Fair Sentencing Act
2020 - There were 93,000 overdose deaths with 48 million individuals addicted.

2020 THE CARTELS

"I will talk to my NGO contacts and get them interested in the general good. Amazingly, the Americans give money to organizations that undermine their very interest."

"What do you mean?" asked Juan. The two men were sitting in a large room drinking Tequila from a bottle of *Ley 925 Diamante*. Each had taken out a Cuban cigar after the women left the room. The doors were open with a view of the patio that was filled with greenery and flowers.

"The election victory up north has provided us with multiple opportunities in a wide variety of areas from Human transportation to drugs. We will use their actions against them and defuse their simple attacks on us," said Leocadio.

"I do not understand what simple actions?" asked Juan.

"Remember the gun-walking episode back in 2009 that they called Fast and Furious. Who knows where or why the genius came up with the idea of putting trackers on weapons and letting them be smuggled into Mexico in hopes of getting into the cartel leadership. The simple plan was to use the guns to trace where the cartel leaders were or something like that. Then the whole thing blew up in their face when it was discovered that one of the tracked weapons was used to kill an American agent. The story disappeared because it made the Administration look bad. We had it pretty much normal until 2016.

Anyway, that was a bad year for us in our activities on the border. That administration made it more difficult to get into the states and the Mexican government had bowed to political and economic pressure and began holding back individuals.

This year's election in the states will soon make things return to our normal or even better," said Leocadio.

"How?"

"If the American border is open like this guy said in the debate then the next American president takes office, we will have a huge source of income from running immigrants through Mexico to the states," said Leocadio.

"But we already make a king's ransom on the drug trade. Why add to our burden with a brand-new source of goods to control?" asked Juan.

INIQUITOUSNESS

"Let me ask you Juan a simple math problem. Say that we charge a single individual 5 thousand American dollars to get to America. Then say we were able to move 100,000 individuals to the American border over the next year which would be close to $500 million in American dollars. Now I ask you how many individuals will be seeking a way to get into the States?" asked Leocadio.

"I do not know maybe a million or more!"

"Do the math my friend. There is money to be made and everyone will want into the game. The beauty of this plan is that I know that the NGOs of the care agencies will be helping us with the care and treatment of the individuals we transport up to the American border. Just think about the indigenous people in Latin America who are being put out of their land by mining and industrial farming companies. All those people will want a better life and we will tell them it is their future to be in America for a price. We have just a few weeks to get this organized."

"What has to be organized?" asked Juan.

"We need to expand the route starting at the Darien Gap. That is where the NGOs have set up their headquarters to provide the need for immigrant care. Those NGO fools will help us by providing food and care along the long journey. We will help provide them with maps on how to get north. Then at each stage of the route money is to be made.

You get to Panama look at the refugee camp there and see what needs to be done. The current U.S. policy has cut off a lot of the migration pattern and that is going to change with the new administration. We need to be ready at each stage of the migration for there is a huge profit to be made.

"Each election year both political parties in the United States complain about illegal immigration and then provide funds to NGO's that help support the very immigration that they want to control. The best they have done to help us control the flow of immigrants is they change the terms. They were not long ago called illegal aliens, just aliens, or undocumented immigrants soon the undocumented being dropped I think they will soon be identified as noncitizens. Half their country want cheap labor and the other half use cheap labor."

"On a different topic. I was talking to our Chinese contact from the past. I was contacted by the new Chinese link. They both want to reopen and expand this new operation with a banking source," said Juan.

"Then it is not, those stamps again!" said Leocadio.

"No, this is about people and drugs. He said they are willing to cut their price on the materials to make Fentanyl and Meth for the demand has increased. They have offered to provide a Chinese banking system they have in place to launder money for us. They also, see that the new administration will most likely open borders as a bonus. I said I would run their proposition by you," said Juan.

"Set up a meeting for next week and see if that network from the Middle East wants to reopen an arrangement. An unstable government is good for business," said Leocadio.

"But we will be back in business with terrorists?" said Juan.

"What do you think the Americans think we are? I am surprised they have not labeled the cartels to the list of terrorists," said Leocadio.

"I have heard a rumor that a UN agency in refugee group in Palestine has some terrorist sympathizers working with their humanitarian aid groups. They may be moving towards a more political approach to bring more people to their cause," said Juan.

"My cousin the reporter called my sister and while they were talking, he let slip the story he is working on drop about the NGO's and the terrorists. So, I think the rumors are true and we are working with the Chinese for Fentanyl. Americans cannot get enough of the drugs since 2016 the overdose rate has more than doubled. The great news is the profits from Cocaine, Heroin, and Morphine have stayed up.

Now, that we are mixing Pentenyl here with counterfeit pills we have increased our profits. My cousin wanted to do a story on the cartels and I told him about the NGO's and their involvement in the human smuggling. He jumped at that story of humanitarian organizations taking money to violate American and International laws is a more shocking story."

"What about him? It would be a good story for his career."

"We grew up together for 14 years and are like brothers. He thinks I am a low-level member of family protection. He has become more American than Mexican. He calls my sister to check on our Grandmother. He tells Guadalupe what he is working on and what is happening. I use her to put him off the cartel story."

CHAPTER ELEVEN
Election Interference

>The price of apathy towards public affairs is to be ruled by evil men.
>
>— Plato

The Election of 1824 was won by John Q. Adams after a very dirty political campaign against candidate Andrew Jackson, who did win the popular vote and lost the electoral vote. There was a possible call for a civil war and that was averted when Jackson told his supporters there would be another election and to just wait.

Andrew Jackson won that election in 1828 after another bitter campaign. The opposition had attacked Jackson and his wife with falsehoods and half-truths. His wife in ill health had died just before he took office and he never forgot the insults against his wife.

When political and social scandal attacked Peggy Eaton, the wife of a member of his administration, Jackson stood by her against the accusations and people who attacked her.

When the wife of one of his other cabinet members at a dinner party said she would not eat at the same table as that woman, Jackson turned to her and said that she would not be eating many dinners at the White House.

It was also said Jackson hated Native Americans. However, he did adopt a Native American boy as his son. He was also blamed for the Trail of Tears; yet, it was Martin van Buren that moved most of the eastern native American population west to Oklahoma.

What really upset the elite was that Jackson believed the 'Common Man' could run the government and the elites found this frightening and insulting.

2020 Election Results

"Nick, it's good to have you back and where did you go?" asked C.E. "You know I got back early this morning and where is not important. I am back because of you and the director Edison. It seems that the little spy group you uncovered has made new connections to our old counterfeiting case. Therefore, I was brought back to be part of the investigation."

"I do not understand, I am not clear on the connection?"

"When the agents arrested the Chinese woman, she referred to Leocadio Blanco. He has been trying to rebuild the cartel we broke up. He has been seen with individuals from the Middle East and Asia. Fang's information caused a deeper dig into the Leocadio network. My guess is this case is holding the bureau together despite being separated from the political divide that is forming. To tell you the truth C.E. I do not know how long things will be stable."

"I still do not understand?"

"Bureaucracy is being taken over by a group of globalists and they have placed like-minded individuals in leadership roles in government. At the same time, the political parties are shifting their customary roles and both parties are moving away from the center of the political spectrum. Those on the left see the pandemic as a way to control and grab more control.

The administrative bureaucracy has been growing and controlling more of every day in American life with rules and regulations by these non-elected bureaucrats. The globalists have seized upon this and used this to promote their agendas. For example, world trade was said to help the world and the American industries. In the last 30 years manufacturing firms and plants have declined 25% and the middle class has declined some 13%.

The globalists have attached themselves to climate change issues and used the bureaucracy to impose change. Remember the government loaned $535 million to a company called Solyndra as the next Solar industry. Two years later that company declared bankruptcy, and the American taxpayers lost.

Now they are trying to cut off the oil and coal industries. These are just two examples of government interference in economic development.

Supply and demand no longer shape the marketplace and that is being taken over by a bureaucratic government of rules and regulations.

However, today there is an active expansion of the active of government within the involvement in domestic elections with the news media and internet. The pandemic has caused 29 states to enact laws to expand voting access from mail-in voting, early and late voting, and voter registration, to rules at polling stations for the coming election. Where voting rights and methods were set by state legislatures in some states the court system has changed the rules because of COVID-19. Then there is an increase in government interference."

"What?"

"The bureaucracy of the CIA has a history of interfering in foreign elections from Italy, Greece, Chile to Israel. In 1996 the Clinton administration tried to influence the election in Israel and then the Obama administration also used an NGO that tried to influence the Israel election. This was done to a nation that is a friend and supporter of the United States. The CIA's history of election interference goes back to the late 1940's.

"What has changed is the government is now involved in domestic affairs by laws passed after 9-11. They are used to control American citizens by surveillance done by the National Security Agency under the code name PRISM to listen into phone conversations or by audit by the IRS on groups considered threats to America. All done in the name of a safe and secure America."

"Come on Nick, this is America! We have rules and laws. The press will report any government corruption."

"Yeah, tell that to the men who stood and waited for support at Benghazi or the members of the Tea Party. In fact, look at the press. It no longer reports news, it provides opinions from both sides by individuals out of the system. The left reports their opinions using the exact same words in newsprint and on every T.V. news station they control. Then on the right, the news is looped for 24 hours with the same story over and over by different individuals each hour.

"Look at this summer with government and private buildings being attacked and burned. People have been killed and injured in what the political left is calling the 'Summer of Love' and one reporter said on air the protest was basically peaceful with a burning building blazing behind him. The political right continues to show the violence without any real discussion of what is behind the rioting in depth. If one dares to step out of the narrative being presented, they are out of line and will be canceled. They do not seem to understand revolution eats their own. The left seems to do more eating."

"Now you are becoming philosophical, but just what do you mean?"

"Simply that revolution eat their own. Many of those who started the French Revolution went to the guillotine by their partners in the revolution. The Russian Revolution had Stalin remove all his fellow revolutionaries who did not agree with him. Even the Castro brothers had Ernesto "Che" Guevara de La Serna removed from Cuba for wanting to spread the revolution outside of Cuba. She was a thug who used brutality and ruthlessness to enforce his policies in Cuba. He was called by many the Butcher of La Cabana for executing prisoners without open and fair trials.

Now, today that murderous thug is held up by the leftists as a cultural symbol and global icon of popular revolution with people wearing shirts with Che's face. If you asked those individuals who were Che, they could not give a clear answer because the image has been romanticized."

"What has happened Nick that has set you off like this?'

"Things are changing the entrenched bureaucracy here is stepping into the political arena and forcing people to pick a side. This lockdown has given the globalists the opportunity to grab control. Do not get me wrong I do not think this was just a one side grabbing for power. During my time in government, I have not seen one single individual leave an elected government office poorer than when they went into office. Many come out millionaires. They all express ideas of liberty, democracy, and laws then ignore them at will. Many are just pure hypocrites."

"Just what are you saying?"

"That the far left going after their competition with the legal system."

"How?"

"We have all been watching both sides as it was happening. Change the word and you change the meaning slightly or completely and you have a change. A custodian becomes a sanitary engineer, a car wash becomes a car spa, or you can expand or decrease the definition of a rule or law to fit your objective. Reduce the crime level and you will reduce crime stats. In some states, one can steal almost a thousand dollars before it reaches the level of a criminal crime.

Recently, the illegal alien has become an undocumented person to unauthorized asylum seekers. The left and the right are masters of vocabulary. Remember Nicaragua Contras became freedom fighters.

Today a pro-communist/socialist senator is running again for president as a democrat/socialist. Yet, his form of socialism is closer to communism than capitalist democracy. He is a socialist who owns three homes and a wife who helped bankrupt a private school. The left could not believe they lost the last election. They won this one and are not going to allow a loss to happen again if they can stop it with political actions.

The Russia dossier has no feet. It was made up of others related to the intelligence agencies in the world. That is just one false flag the left is throwing out against the next election. Depending on how the public reacts in the next four years will depend on who will run the nation either by the minority elite or the majority elite."

"You are implying both are elites?"

"Yes, the minority disregards the rights of others while the major elite considers the rights of the minority. The Left and Right both used to stand for the rights of the minority. They were both in the middle of the political spectrum. Today the Left is moving to the radical elements on their political side. The reality is those that who profess this socialism are living in two or three homes as they tell us to share the wealth. They do not see they are part of the problems that they want to fix. That is not a crime but the racist police that are the problem.

The Left is attacking anything that connects the nation together in a common way. They attack the national history, national institutions, the Jewish and Christian religions, and the way of life is under attack as being part of the Imperialist colonializing Western world. But they do not attack any part of the Islamic world."

"Why?"

"Islam is a victim of Western and Jewish imperialism and is fighting for their rights. The 1960s saw the left gaining influence in our universities with radicals being given the opportunity to speak and at times given professorship. Then by the 1990s globalism and the left became a major component in our universities. The Chinese and Islamic world have been flowing funds into the universities for the curriculum they wish to push. We are losing a generation…"

"Nick, what has happened to you? You are more animated than I have ever seen you being upset with the system?" said C.E.

"You're right, I guess it was my memo on the Russian dossier that I submitted to the Office in Washington D.C. I pointed out that the memo was just hearsay of hearsay and had not one creditable source."

"You mean the dossier on Russian interference in the presidential election?"

"Yes, I think the leadership, the Bureau, and CIA came up with it to influence the election and there is also that laptop out there that is a real bomb. That is all water under the bridge. Let get focus on this case.

CHAPTER TWELVE
Chinese Secret Police Stations

We have placed too much hope in political and social reforms, only to find out that we were being deprived of our most precious possession: Our spiritual life.
— Alexander Solzhenitsyn

Freedom is the right to tell other people what they do not want to hear.
— George Orwell

During the Spanish Civil War, George Orwell fought as a socialist with POUM and saw the Stalinist of the CNT try to remove any member that opposed the Moscow view. The last year of the war saw a civil war within a civil war and the Stalinists won that war within the Civil War and Republicans lost the war to the Right. At the beginning of the war, the communists were a small part of the republican side by the end Moscow controlled the republicans with the Spanish gold sent to Moscow.

The Americans and other liberals who fought in the Spanish Civil

War were branded communist and not trusted. One English liberal was George Orwell who saw the communists for what they were and warned the world with his novel *1984* and many did not listen or believe. A small note is he wrote the book in 1948 and just flipped the date.

2022 Manhattan Chinatown, New York

The cell phone in her back pocket was vibrating, Nuan reached for it and answered it and just listened to whoever was on the other side of the conversation, "You would be safer in China and off the dangerous streets of New York!" said the voice.

Nuan dropped the phone like it was hot, "What's wrong Nuan?" asked Liu.

"Someone is intimidating me with horrible messages on my cell phone and by e-mail. I reported it to the police and they said they would investigate it last week. That was another message telling me I would be safer in China," said Nuan.

"Have the police told you anything?"

"No, they said it takes time and they are very burdened with such calls. So, I do not think the police have made any progress."

"What are you going to do?"

"I know that once I set foot in China I will be arrested and sent to a re-education camp in the north like my grandmother during the Cultural Revolution," said Nuan.

"Who and why would they do this here?" asked Liu.

"Who else but the People's Republic of China? It has no regard for other nations' rights or sovereignty. The dissidents I meet with tell me that the PRC is actively trying to remove any critical comments about the party all over the world."

"Are you safe? What if this harassment becomes more aggressive?" asked Liu.

"The good news is that I was told yesterday that the FBI is looking into the situation. So, maybe the police did investigate or turn my case over to the FBI. I hope something happens soon," said Nuan.

"You know my parents were born right here in New York after their parents left Taiwan. They always impressed upon me the PRC's flagrant abuse of civil rights. Then at the university, many of the professors spoke of the progress of China and how that nation is becoming a world power equal to the United States.

I would go home and tell my parents what the professors were saying. I have never seen my father get upset each time I brought it up. After a few times, he said I was to come with him the very night. He took me to a dissident Chinese meeting right here in the city. The stories they related to their time in China were very upsetting. They all told a story of abuse at the hands of the PRC and the Ministry of Public Security. Some would show the scars and point to broken bones. I now understand my parent's hate and fear of the Chinese government," said Liu.

"Is this country any different?" asked Nuan.

"What do you mean?" asked Liu.

"I was valedictorian when I graduated from highly rated high school and I could not get into an Ivy League school when many students that had lower SAT scores were admitted to those institutions. I ended up going to a good public university but even there we Chinese had to sue the university for institutional discrimination. We Chinese here are discriminated against because we study and are limited to only a few slots in the top higher educational system. Remember this country had its camps for the Japanese during World War II. We are not trusted here. We are seen as outsiders. My parents love this country and they do not understand my hostility towards the country," said Nuan.

"You have been educated in a system that has put their focus on the negative aspects of American and European History. That has led to the breakdown of the pride in the accomplishment of this and other European nations. The West has its problems politically, economically, and socially and yet that far outweighs the degree of freedom that is present in China," said Liu.

"Yes, but we are still seen as outsiders!"

"Nuan, everyone that has come here is at first an outsider. You still live in Chinatown with your parents and when the Irish, Germans, Italians, Polish, and Puerto Rican came they lived together in their separate communities with their parents. Many of those communities are still present. But after a few generations, the children married and moved outside their communities and in time married outside the culture.

Those groups have assimilated over time, and we will do the same. Look at the Asian Americans you just mentioned who have sued the university system on their affirmative action policies that denied Asian students based only on their race. The American legal system works slow and at times poorly, but it works," said Liu.

"How can you be so certain?" asked Nuan.

"As I said, the university faculty is liberal and it provides a Left-leaning view of America. I was lucky to have a professor who had been a Catholic priest who later married a nun. He was trained by the Jesuits and pointed out in every lecture the opposing views. I remember that when I asked about the treatment of Asians, he pointed out that it takes four or five generations to be completely assimilated. Then he made a point that Latin Americans are assimilating in two or three generations. I asked him why. He said he did not know, but it would make a good topic for research. So, what I am telling you, is to look at all sides of an issue. Why not come to a dissident meeting with me tonight?" said Liu.

"O.K. what time?"

"I'll pick you up at seven. You will have a good experience."

"Will I be able to understand what is being said?"

"Yes, most speak English to some degree and the others speak in your grandparent's Mandarin," Liu.

That night on the evening news:

"Good evening America, This is Chet Butler with the evening with a special edition news report. We have a breaking story in New York with the FBI tonight. Agents have taken into custody several individuals that we have been told were running an illegal Chinese police station for the People's Republic of China right here in New York City's Chinatown. The group was connected to the Chinese Ministry of Public Security. Now, we go to Jenny Zou our reporter on site in Chinatown. Jenny, are you there?"

"Yes, Chet, I am here in Chinatown outside the office that was said to be used as a cladistics PRC police station. One of the unidentified persons that I talked to told me that one secret police member who was picked up in the raid was an individual who had been active in this country since 2015. That year he was accused of harassing Chinese dissidents living here in New York. Then a year later he was an active participant in a counter-protest that attacked the pro-Falun Gong protest at the UN building. The protesters were citing the treatment of Falun Gong individuals who were being arrested in China. This PRC individual was arrested for assaulting members of the Falun Gong protest and resisting arrest.

My source in the FBI reported that the PRC and MPS have been trying to obstruct justice by deleting and destroying communications with the illegal police stations that have been operated by the MPS since 2014. The FBI operation I was told is called Operation Fox Hunt.

The PRC has set up police stations in foreign countries to repatriate or to keep quiet dissidents speaking against China. Then in 2015, the PRC started Operation Sky Net to collect dissidents. I am told by one of the dissidents that the PRC has over a hundred secret police stations in some 50 countries around the world. I have been told that there are other secret police stations in New York, Los Angeles, Houston, San Francisco, Nebraska, and Minnesota.

The report goes on to tell of fake accounts on the internet by the PRC to harass and intimidate Chinese dissidents. The agent said it was one of the most flagrant violations of American sovereignty he has seen in his thirty-three years with the bureau.

The MSP is part of the *TikTok Tok*controversy. My Chinese source a dissident went on to relate that the PRC is spying on the Hong Kong protesters and collecting data in the United States through *Tok*. The source said the PRC is collecting information by using backdoor access the PRC implanted in the program. He also, said that the *TikTok* version in China called *Douyin* is strictly controlled by the PRC and MPS. The accusation that Western *TikTok* is banned in China is not true because it is a separate identity. Although the American *Tik Has* the majority ownership in a Chinese company that is registered in the Cayman Islands.

The U.S. Congress is looking into *TikTok* as a security threat and as a source of disinformation. Back to you, Chet, this is Jenny Zou in New York Chinatown."

"Thank you, Jenny. On a little different subject, we have Edward Young an independent reporter with us tonight from his location in Panama. He has reported on the immigration and asylum seekers. What can you tell us about this global migration crisis," asked Chet.

"Well, first of all, most of the migration in the last three years is one of economic opportunity and not about political asylum seekers. These migrants that are flooding in from Latin America, Africa, the Middle

East, and Europe are disappearing into the heartland and are for the most untraceable.

This flood of immigrants is starting to have a backlash with arguments about an increase in crime and a burden on American taxpayers. Immigration is not just an American issue, many European nations are beginning to react to the impact on their resources. The globalist side denies the rise in crimes is due to immigration and the other side's response by citing examples. I will not get into the political debate between nationalists and globalists. But what I can report is that this massive migration is aided and, in part, funded by various NGOs from this country and others around the world."

"Wait a minute Edward can you tell our viewers what an NGO is?"

"NGO stands for Non-Government Organizations like the Red Cross, Hebrew Immigration Aid Society, World Refugee Organization, and Doctors without Borders to name a few. These NGOs provide care for the refugee's food, shelter, and medical aid to them with supplies for the trip as well as maps with so-called safe routes to the United States."

"They provide maps?"

"Yes, the maps provide the immigrants with a selection of different routes through Mexico to locations on the American border. The journey starts when the refugees get to Panama at a place called the Darien Gap they are provided with supplies and information for the trip north."

"What is the Darien Gap?" asked Chet.

"It is a thick jungle of mountains, rivers, and swamps in Panama. The Trans-Continental (Pan American) Highway, which the U.S. government mostly financed, runs from Alaska to the Darien Gap. That road stops or breaks at the Darien Gap, between Columbia and Panama, for the cost to build across it was considered too high at the time. That in itself should tell you how difficult the terrain is in the Gap for any form of travel and yet these people are willing to make the trip."

"O.K. that explains that, I think, but how do they get to Panama?"

"There are several ways to see the immigrants moving to Panama. Although not all the migrants are coming to the United States. There are two major routes for immigrants to get to Europe. The first is the Balkans route that is used from central Asia and the Middle East. That route seems to center on Serbia as the central destination before moving to Bosnia-Herzegovina as the gateway to the rest of Europe. Abandoned villages in the Balkan from the Balkan War are used by the NGOs to care for the refugees. The second route is located in Africa and smugglers will transport individuals at a cost to Greece, Italy, and Spain.

The route for the Americans is first to South American where individuals arrive in Brazil, Venezuela, or Ecuador. Many may stay there and for others, it is a stopover before the trip to Columbia to begin the journey through the Darien Gap to Panama. Once they are in Columbia those that have money pay the cartels for transportation. Those with less money pay in trade for the Walking Route."

"What is the walking route?"

"The Walking Route is just that a walking route. It became popular in 2020 when large groups were formed to walk across Mexico to the American border. The Chinese call it the *Zou Xian* and this is the most dangerous route. They go through the dangerous triangle of El Salvador, Guatemala, and Honduras. Where all the refugees are preyed upon by local thugs, the cartels, and government agents along the way."

"What about the cartels?"

"They run the show with the aid of NGO's."

"You mean the aid organizations are working with the cartels?"

"Not necessarily in a real sense they are, but they will deny it if asked. Once the refugees are assembled in areas in Panama they are provided with NGO aid. The refugees are then enlisted by cartel coyote guides to walk north across the Darien Gap and then on to Mexico for cash or alternate payments of work. During the trek north the refugees suffer all types of hardships. My team and I will be starting that walk tomorrow and will provide updates along our walk to the American border. This is Edward Young in Panama just outside the Darien Gap."

"Thank you for the report, and we look forward to the update. Be safe Edward," said Chet.

"Thank You, Chet."

"We will be right back after these few words from our sponsors."

CHAPTER THIRTEEN
The Lecture Hall

> Education is the passport to the future, for tomorrow belongs to those who prepare for it today.
>
> — Malcolm X

The American Civil War demonstrated the country's need and demand for engineering and agriculture studies. This was addressed by the Congress that brought back to President Lincoln a Congressional Bill that President Buchanan had vetoed in 1859.

President Lincoln signed this Bill which was named the Morrill Act. It provided for the development of universities to increase their studies in agriculture and engineering. Kansas State University was the first A&M state college to open on September 3, 1863. The goal was to provide agriculture, science, and engineering along with a Reserve Military Officer Training. These Land Grant schools were identified as Agriculture and Mechanics (A & M) schools. A few still have that title.

In 1866 there were just 300 engineers in the United States and four years later there were 866 engineers. Then by the year 1911, there were 106 Land Grant schools in the U.S. and they were graduating 3,000 engineers each year. This number of A&M Universities included 30 Native American schools and 17 African American schools.

In comparison Germany that year was graduating 1,800 engineers each year.

LECTURE HALL 2022

The lecture hall screen was filled with an image of a small ape sitting on a stool wearing a three-piece suit and the title above him read 'The Monkey Trial'. The lecture hall was filled with 300 students on their phones and most likely talking to someone in that very room.

Professor Andrei walked into the room:

"Welcome to the second-semester class on Famous Trials in American History. The reasoning behind this class is once again Free Speech. The background of our first semester and this semester's trials are during a period of drastic change in America called the Progressive Period. The period came to an end in October 1929. It was a period that accelerated industrial development with movies, communication in the telephone and radio, with transportation in autos, and airplanes. Plus, the social changes in the household with electric appliances. There were also political and religious shifts taking place in the world with the Bolsheviks and the Fundamentalist and hate groups like the Ku Klux Klan in this country.

"The Bolsheviks in Russia gave the working people of the world a cause to hope for a better life. Parts of this socialist movement use violence to achieve their goals. Two of these groups on the left were Industrial Workers of the World (also called the Wobblies) and the Anarchist movement. These two groups were willing to use violence that included assassination and bombs to make change. On the Right were the KKK and the Fascist movement in Italy and Germany which were also willing to use violence to achieve their goals.

"The reaction to the left actions was the Red Scare with the bombings on Wall Street and other places had the government take actions against the Left. The U.S. Attorney General Arnold Palmer set out to clean up the radicals with the Palmer Raids. These raids collected any foreigner who was suspected of Bolshevism and shipped many to Finland in what was called SOS (Ship or Shot). The reason for Finland was there was no American foreign relationship with the Soviet Union so passengers were sent to Finland so they could walk into Russia.

"On the right, the Fundamentalist saw the Bible under attack. New theories on evolution disrupted this biblical interpretation of Genesis. Evangelists like Billy Sunday, Aimee Simple McPherson, and the Chicago evangelist Dwight L. Moody spoke against Darwinism. The Fundamentalist ideas had begun to take shape in 1910 with the first of 12 pamphlets that were published by 1915 refuting Darwinism.

"Darwin's ideas began to run wild and produced the concept of eugenics that called for society to eliminate the defective genes from the human gene pool. Thousands of individuals were removed from society for no other reason than a genetic variation and many were forcibly sterilized, and the American Supreme Court ruled in favor of this treatment that violated the Constitutional Rights.

"Then in 1914, the Ku Klux Klan (KKK) was reborn as the Second Invisible Empire. This new Klan hated just about everyone except White Anglo-Saxon Protestants (WASP). The Second Empire used religion and patriotism to get people to fall into their new racist organization and soon they dominated the political systems of several states from Oregon to Maine. It was highlighted with the film: *Birth of A Nation* in 1915 and shown at the White House by President Wilson. This new KKK built its power using the American flag and the Cross as symbols of American values. Then in 1925, the KKK lost much of its support with the arrest, trial, and conviction for the murder of a Klan leader in Indiana for the brutal rape and murder of his secretary. The Klan's reputation declined rapidly in the following years outside of the Old South. That same year a different trial was playing out in Tennessee.

"The fundamentalist in the state of Tennessee passed a Bill that was introduced by Tennessee State Representative John Washington Butler. The Bill called for the prohibition of the teaching of human evolution in schools. His position was that the taxpayers should have a say in what was taught to their children. At the time the Tennessee high school textbook, *Hunter's for Biology,* did address animal evolution.

"The Governor signed the Bill thinking nothing would come of it. He could not have been more wrong. The American Civil Liberties Union (ACLU) saw a chance and stepped in with a plan to challenge the law. They were looking for a way to challenge the law in court. The business and political leaders of the city of Dayton and Tennessee sat together and came up with a plan. They wanted to draw people to their city and saw that a test case by the ACLU could be used as a tool to achieve their goal. They convinced a young biology teacher and athlete coach to stand in as a test of the law.

"This was all happening during the decade that the American urban population had become larger than the rural population. The public was adjusting to this new image of the average American. The trial would add to the shifting idea of a rural man from a Yeoman farmer to one of a "Hilly Billy's", "Hicks", Yokel's", or what many were now calling the country "bumpkins". The rural yeoman was now becoming considered one of less education than their counterpart urbanites elites.

"This image was exploited and helped to make the trial more of a circus. That image was done when someone dressed a monkey up in a three-piece suit in a chair drinking a Coke. The monkey was named Joe a common name. Next entered the well-known news reporter H.L. Mencken to add more fuel to the circus fire with his antics and articles.

"He was the first to coin the terms Monkey *Trial, Collective Ignorance*, and the *Bible Belt*. When the trial was moved outside because of the summer heat wave Mencken had the paper add the city leaders' faces to monkeys sitting in a tall tree watching the trial.

"The ACLU wanted a test case they take to the U.S. Supreme Court. Clarence Darrow was a lawyer well-known for his defense of the child murders of Lobe and Leopold in Chicago. Darrow's defense kept the two rich boys from the death penalty. The ACLU did not want him on the case for they feared he would use the case to attack religion. However, when Scoops heard that Darrow volunteered, he wanted Darrow as his lawyer. The opposing lawyer was also of note he was William J. Bryan a five-time presidential candidate. Bryan was a well-known defender of religion added to the ACLU's worries. Both Darrow and Bryan did not like each other and did exactly what the ACLU was afraid of and turned the trial into one on religion. The trial became a mockery and condemnation of religion that came to a climax when Bryan agreed to testify for the prosecution and defend the Biblical interpretations. Darrow made him look foolish with questions that denied well-known and established scientific facts. Questions like: Did Joshua actually stop the Sun from moving around the Earth?

"The trial made good national headlines and gave the public a good laugh. In the end, John Scoops was found guilty and fined $100. The ACLU went right to the State Supreme Court to appeal with the hope of being able to take the case to the higher court.

"The Tennessee Supreme Court sidestepped the trial's advancement to a higher court by dismissing the verdict and set aside the fine by saying the jury should have set the amount of the fine and not the judge. The question of should the taxpayer have a say in what professional educators teach in school went unanswered for the next 100 years. The question is now being asked today around the nation and that ends our lecture for today.

"If you have questions, put them in writing and I will answer them next class. Now, before we meet next time I have an assignment for you in the library. There you will find the film *Inherit the Wind* reserved for my class or you can view it on the net. Plus, you need to read about the Gitlow v. New York case. Thank you for your attention," with that the professor walked away from the podium and out the door.

"Well, Mary?" asked Joe as they walked out of the lecture hall.

"Well, What?"

"How was it being back in the classroom and what do you think of Professor Andrei?" asked Joe.

"To tell the truth the whole authoritarian lockdown, I think, was over the top. COVID was dangerous to the old and those with special conditions. Yet, we were forced to take what the big pharmaceutical companies were calling a vaccine, we were forced to wear a mask that was not going to prevent anyone from getting sick. We were told that we could kill our grandparents. In the process I lost some valuable education time with distance learning," said Mary.

"I asked about the professor!"

"Right, I like him and his free spirit of looking at both sides."

"Are you kidding me? That guy is anything but, balanced. He is the New Left and to the far left," said Joe.

"How can you say that? I think he just gave a very balanced lecture," said Mary.

"You have to be kidding! Every student in the room most likely walked out with the idea that the middle of the country is Hicksville in the Flyover part of the country. That it is gun carrying country of Klan members and religious Bible thumpers. Those who lived there hated anyone who looked or talked differently. That the new Left has little concern about the hard-working rural people."

"Wow, I can see your grade in this class already."

"Well, in the next class, he will answer the questions on the left with positive responses and those on the right with negative responses. I took a class from him last year and socialism was treated as a progressive movement and any movement not in line with that was fascism. I know this professor and what I tell you is not what I write in an exam."

"Why not express yourself in class?"

"That class I just told you about had a student who did challenge the professor in a heated debate. Then the student was charged with hate speech by others in the class. The student was warned that any more attacks on the professor would be cause for expelling him from the university. Less than a week later he questioned the professor's status as a Soviet dissident after the professor praised the Soviet biologist Trofim Lysenko as a visionary," said Joe.

"What happened to him?"

"He transferred to another college before the administration could process the paperwork. His major was law. So, if a law student knows he will not win, why would I think about challenging the same professor? The problem is the student was right about Lysenko."

"How do you know that?"

"I am a biology major and Lysenko is well-known and discussed in the field for not following solid science. His experiments have never been able to be duplicated or collaborated," said Joe as two men walked up.

"Are you Joe Tuner?"

"Yes, who is asking?"

"I am C.E. Hall and this is Director Edison, may we talk with you in private," asked C.E.

"What is this about?" asked Joe.

"We just have a few confidential questions about the university. We would prefer to do this quietly with just the three of us. The matter is of a very sensitive nature," said C.E.

"Am I in some trouble here?"

"Absolutely not! They are questions we would prefer to stay in a small circle for right now," said the director.

"Who are you guys?" demanded Mary.

"You are Mary Robinson Rush and, Miss Rush, we may want to ask you some questions later but for right now we would like a few minutes with Joe. If you would please give us some space for right now," said C.E.

"How do you both know my name? No! I will not leave Joe alone with you two."

"It is O.K. Mary. I know about C.E. Hall he is a famous fire investigator."

C.E. had a shocked look on his face, "You got to be kidding!" said C.E.

"No, in fact, it was your case that involved a claim for a dead racehorse. You proved that the fire was deliberately started to cover up an act of insurance fraud about a million-dollar racehorse. The fire was staged to look like the cause was from a stack of chemical sacks. The chemicals in the sacks reacted to water with a thermal dynamic reaction. The sacks were placed under a leak in the roof so that when it rained the runoff would leak onto the sacks. The fire would look like an accidental fire that killed a dozen racehorses and one multimillion horse.

"The problem was you had no real evidence of fraud until you had all the dead horses' DNA tested with the results showing that none of the horses that died in the barn were the million-dollar horse. The owner confessed to the insurance fraud case after you also found the missing horse. I remember the case because my dad also told me about the case. He was a big investor in the horse racing.

"So, I remember your name when the university class I was taking on the study and development of research used that case to express the need to look at every piece of information when doing research. If I remember right your name was even in the textbook in the footnotes."

The director was smiling at C.E. "Well this is good news to share with the rest of the team. We have a celebrity in our ranks."

"You better not start spreading this story. They already think I get special treatment!" said C.E.

Joe looked at Mary and smiled "Mary. It is O.K. I will call you later."

"Are you sure? You better call!"

"I will." He said dropping her hand. "Where would you two gentlemen like to go and ask your questions?"

"I hope we did not interrupt anything important," said C.E.

"We just started seeing each other and it is getting serious. I think!" said Joe.

"I think the way she looked and protected you is more than just getting serious!" said C.E.

"We can talk here. You were a student of Professor Zhang if our records are right," said the director.

"But, first, who are you guys? I know your names, but are you with the university?" asked Joe.

"I am sorry, we are with the FBI and this has nothing to do with you or Mary. We are looking into Professors Zhang and Harrison and who their associates were when they were here."

"I never had a class with Professor Harrison, but I did some research with his assistance Xiu. I had to suffer through Professor Zhang's class for my degree. He was a good chemist just a poor teacher and his female student always seemed to get the best grades. If I remember right that stopped when his new assistant Fang showed up. She was the real reason my grade suffered. The demands that she put on the class were the worst and she would yell at you if you missed a point and made a mistake."

"Did she have any friends?"

"Not that I knew of, I did see her once with a Hispanic guy. I remember that!"

"Why do you say that?"

"The guy had tattoos and he looked scary in the daylight. The tats looked like gang tats not just the everyday ones most people get."

"Do you think you would recognize him in a photograph?"

"Oh, yeah. He looked like the actor that is always playing the part of a cartel killer in the movies."

C.E. pulled out a few photos and gave them to Joe, "Is he one of these?"

Joe went through the photos twice and then gave them Leocadio's photo. "This is the guy. I remember this mark on his neck it was all scary. It looked like a brand you see on cattle."

"O.K. Joe what we have discussed here is to be just between us. I have a paper that I am asking you to sign. It just states you will not discuss this with anyone and that includes Mary. Your nation will be very grateful for your cooperation."

"Is this for real?"

"Yes, we are in a sensitive investigation and we do not want the information floating out there. You just gave us a big break in our investigation. You may not discuss this with anyone. Again that includes Mary! Is that understood?" asked the director.

"You know you have made my life miserable?" complained Joe. "Did you not see Mary? She will not let this go!"

"Then tell her it was about the illegal dumping on the athletic field. The FBI is investigating that and we think it was a fraternity prank," said C.E.

"O.K. she would buy that! But I do not like telling her a lie. If she finds that I lied to her it will ruin the relationship we are building."

"It is that serious with you?" asked C.E.

"I think so!" said Joe.

"When this case is over I will personally come and tell her that you were ordered to say what was told her and that if you failed to follow the instruction you would go to jail," said C.E. as the director looked at him.

"I guess I should ask are you in a fraternity?" asked the director.

"No, not enough time with my job and studying."

"Thank you for your time and the information," said the director.

"May I ask one last question?"

"Sure, What is it?"

"I was recruited for the FBI science lab last month. Is that why you picked me?"

"Let me just say if you want the job I am pretty sure you have it. Thank you again Joe for your time," said the director as he and C.E. walked away.

"O.K. tell me why you told the kid you would personally explain the situation to Mary?" asked the director.

"It is simple, I have someone in my life that I would miss and sometimes little things get in the way of relationships. I do not want to be the person responsible for any misunderstanding between two young people."

"C.E. you really are a romantic!"

"That better be another thing that is not spread around!" as they both laughed.

CHAPTER FOURTEEN
Secret Chinese Biolab

If you think education is expensive, try ignorance.
— Jeff Rich

Cuban epidemiologist Carlos Juan Finlay formulated a theory that an insect was the cause of the transmission of yellow fever. He could not prove this because of the level of biological evidence at the time.

Later Italian bacteriologist Giuseppe Sanarelli claimed to have isolated the Yellow Fever organism that he called Bacillus. Then the U.S. Army appointed Doctors James Carroll and Walter Reed to investigate the disease in Cuba using Sanarelli's *Bacillus*. They discovered that the *Aedes aegypti* mosquito was indeed transmitting the Yellow Fever virus by a bite.

This knowledge allowed Major William Crawford Gorgas to introduce mosquito control methods to prevent the spread of Yellow Fever and Malaria in Cuba. Later Major Gorgas was sent to Panama for canal construction, and he saw the eradication of the Yellow Fever disease and brought Malaria under control in the Canal Zone.

China and Trojan Horse:

China relaunched the *One Belt Road* initiative (New Silk Road) in 2013 of maritime and land routes to bridge the connections between nations. The globalization of commerce would all be tied to Beijing. They planned that geostrategic consequences would cause a shift in the geopolitical world towards China. Then the American involvement with world commerce and its security blanket to protect south east Asia and the rest of the world would be weakened.

The Chinese see world military security as too expensive and offer economic connectivity with investments in roads, bridges, airports, and ports that will allow their industry to grow. The funds that are saved from not providing military protection would be used to build the Chinese military at home and address regional goals.

Meeting in Xiamen Office:

The meeting was with just one man and the leader looked at him standing in front of the desk looking very worried and nervous, "What is happening in Canada with Guo?"

"Agent Guo who was there ran into some problems," replied Ying.

"What kind of problem or problems?" asked Leader He.

"Guo was caught stealing intellectual property and the Canadian government judgment against him for 330 million. Guo then fled justice there and crossed over to the States with a new identity. The Canadian government has him listed as a fugitive.

"What is our risk with him?"

"Little to none. Guo is a master of disguise and has already set up new companies in America."

"Then let us use this new source of business to set up a lab. The Americans are cutting funds on our research or should I say their bioresearch in this country. Fortunately, there are still those in that country who feel the price of genetic research is worth the cost and danger. Plus, make sure that any new lab there is outside the health network," said Leader He.

"It has already been done."

"Good, now I must get home. It is my wife's birthday."

2022 Closed meeting at a City Hall in Central California

The meeting was held with a small group of people with the city manager Casimir acting as chairperson. "This meeting is being held to understand and evaluate the potential danger to the local community from exposure to the illegal lab that was discovered two weeks ago. So, let's get started with this enforcement agent Williams."

"That would be me. I am the local code enforcement agent who was called to that warehouse just inside the city. I was called because of the complaints about parking violations. When I arrived, I noticed a foul smell and several obvious building code violations. I walked over and knocked on the warehouse door and it was answered by a woman in a lab coat, in gloves, wearing a breathing mask. Behind her were four other workers that were all dressed the same. I backed away and called for the fire and police chiefs to come to the location," said Inspector Williams

"Why did you do that?"

"The building is not zoned for that type of operation!"

"What type of operation was it?" asked Casimir.

"I did not know! But I do know that lab coats and gloves and breathing masks are outside anything I have seen in this county or city.

"Did you go into the building inspector Williams?"

"Not, the workers were in protective clothes, and I was not and I did not have any with me, so I just waited by the door. I did tell dispatch to inform the police and fire to come with environmental gear."

"Can you tell us anything more that would clarify the situation?"

"No, once the fire crew and police showed up, I was just left in the background outside of the building."

"Thank you, now Chief Young what can you tell us."

"I had the first fire crew suit up with me and we entered the building, I had the workers in there go outside to stay with the police. I thought all we had was an illegal drug lab."

"Why did you think that?"

"We have had a few Meth labs blow up this last year and the next county over just had a cartel marijuana farm busted. Once I was inside the building I knew that this was no ordinary street drug lab. That was for sure!"

"What made you think that?"

"Well first off, some of the containers were labeled hazardous biomaterial and ready for shipment. I ordered everyone out of the building and called the health department."

"The reason for that was?"

"I was almost scared to death with what I read. The labels were listed as various pathogens. You have the photos."

"Is that what these are?"

"Yes, you can see those containers that were labeled and identified as E-coli, SARS, HIV, Hepatitis, Herpes, Rubella, Streptococcus pneumonia, and Malaria. They were addressed to a location in Mexico. After the health department showed up, we did a complete search, and in the back was a freezer with a group of vials that were labeled Ebola. At that point, we called the CDC and FBI, and they might just as well have stayed home!"

"Why do you say that? Did they not take charge?"

"Just the opposite. They came and downplayed the whole thing. We asked them to test the contents of the warehouse and they said they did not have the manpower. They did not even test the items that were labeled to see if the labels were right. They just took the whole lot away. However, they did issue a three-page report that said there was no evidence of toxins and I do not know how they came to that conclusion without testing."

"Is there anything else you would like to add?"

"Yes, we also found genetic mice that had been developed over six years to carry pathogens. We discovered this when we interviewed the woman who cared for the mice."

"Who was that woman?"

"We do not know for the women in the lab were also taken away before we could ask any more questions."

"O.K. Now, for this private fire insurance investigator, is that right?"

"Yes, I am C.E. Hall and the fire chief called and asked me to investigate. I told him that since there was no fire I did not see how I could help. He said this was a special case that required my ability to get background information. I was in the area working on another case in the next county on a drug farm and told him I would do a little digging as a favor."

"A favor?"

"I have worked with him before, and he is a top-ranked man to work with and I was looking into that marijuana farm in the next county. I said I would investigate it for a day since I had some free time and planned to later buy some stamps from a local couple."

"Wait a minute you're the investigator that broke up the modern Nazi ring not too long ago!" said the mayor.

"I did play a small part in that, yes!"

"Can we get back to the topic? Did you discover anything?" said the manager.

"Yes, as a matter of fact, I found quite a bit of information on the company that ran the lab. The owner is a fugitive from Canada and the individual had fled from Canada under a new name. He then set up a new company in Texas where Texas officials closed it down. His next move was to California where he set up shop in four different cities before coming here. The company started selling COVID masks and testing kits with false CDC numbers.

The owner has a huge judgment in Canada for stealing intellectual property from China. I also found that the Bank of China has large investments in the companies of this individual. It is surprising what one can learn on the internet," said C.E. and did not mention his connection with the FBI and Leocadio's connection to the Marijuana farm. He realized that the director was right about certain cases being ignored or dropped for political reasons.

"Thank You Mr. Hall for taking on this small case. Now what is our game plan on what to do next and how to prevent this from happening again?" asked Casimir.

"Our congressman is going to have a House Committee Hearing on the lab and the CDC and FBI part and the lack of investigation. I find it deplorable that there was not a complete investigation," said the mayor.

"Well, that may get the mountain moving!" said the fire chief.

"This is no time for joking Chief!" said the mayor.

"I am not joking. Did you listen to what I said? The FBI and CDC did nothing until we finally arrested the owner. Then the FBI came in and arrested him for lying to the FBI and not for the secret lab. The government is worried that they will upset the Chinese government. So worried that they are willing to ignore a bio lab producing bioweapons right here in this country," said the fire chief.

"Alright, that is enough before we turn this into a local political battle, lets come back on Monday with some solutions. Thank you Mr. Hall for your time, " said Casimir.

"I was nearby and glad I could help unravel the mystery," said C.E. As he walked out the door he dialed the Director. "I think we have another connection to Leocadio. This lab case I helped on had materials addressed to Leocadio and ready to ship to his address in Mexico."

"Are you on your way back?" asked the director.

"Yes, and you can tell Tao thanks for the information on the Chinese bank and that he needs to dig into it a bit deeper," said C.E.

"Will do!"

CHAPTER FIFTEEN
The Walking Route

> The only thing necessary for the triumph of evil is for good men to do nothing.
>
> — Edmond Burke

In 1865 Edouard de Laboulaye proposed to build a statue honoring the American Declaration of Independence. By 1875 the sculptor Frederic-Auguste Bartholdi was given the commission to build the statue with the help of Alexandre Gustave Eiffel. The French would be responsible for the funds for the statue and the Americans were to be responsible for the funds for the pedestal.

The American fundraising had fallen behind and Joseph Pulitzer offered to publish the name of anyone who donated for the pedestal in his newspaper. The funds were collected and the pedestal was designed by Richard Morris Hunt. The dedication took place in 1886 and included the poem *The New Colossus* by Emma Lazarus on a plaque at the base of the pedestal.

This idea of Liberty and democracy was young in the 19th Century and to many it represented violence and revolution to many in the 19th Century. Revolutions in Latin America and 1848 were behind these fears. Edouard was a supporter of liberty and the American Revolution. He had spoken out against the rioting in France in 1871 and felt that the statue was a way to help bring back the idea of Liberty.

2023 Wyoming on Interstate #15:

The man walked across the border of California then hailed a taxi and went directly to the San Diego airport to a car rental agency. Then he drove to a motel and met a Mule and was given his shipment of meth and fentanyl they both loaded into the rental car.

He had made this trip a dozen times to Montana, Wyoming, or Idaho. His bosses had made huge profits. On this trip, he used the same route he had taken before using Interstate #5 to #80 to #15 into Wyoming listening to Mexican music. It was hot and he was tired and thirsty. When he finished his beer, he tossed the can out the window.

A minute later he looked into the rear-view mirror and saw the flashing lights of a Wyoming state officer's car. He pulled over and waited with both hands on the steering wheel as he watched the officer approach the side mirror.

He noticed the officer called in the plates and make of the car before he exited his patrol car. Officer Davis got out of his vehicle, as he approached the car he radioed once more and told dispatch that he had pulled over a California car with a Latino driver. The briefing earlier that day had told the day crew to be on the lookout for a drug dealer in a California registered vehicle. The warning came from the FBI.

The State had been hit with a large amount of meth and fentanyl and one of the local dealers held in custody by the FBI claimed that he was getting the drugs from a Mexican cop that worked for the Tijuana cartel. He was to deliver a new shipment of drugs today.

Since 2020 the Fentanyl drug has become an epidemic in this part of the state and lives were lost and ruined by that and other drugs. Officer Davis had first-hand knowledge of the effects for his sister's youngest son died from fentanyl. He walked up to the driver's side of the car and said, "Good morning, sir, do you know why I pulled you over?"

"I do not think I was speeding, so no I do not officer!"

"At first it was for littering the highway, but then I noticed the litter was a beer can. So, now I have stopped you from drinking and driving. Please, get out of the car."

"You are right it was a beer can, but it was empty and rolling around in the rental car, so I did not think and just tossed it."

"I need you to step out of the car, sir! I need your driver's license."

"O.K. I am sorry on vacation from Mexico and wanted to see the Black Hills," said the guy as he handed over his Mexican driver's license as he stepped out of the car.

"Still, will need to have you take a sobriety test."

"Sure, no problem," he started to take a step toward the officer just as a second unit drove up behind him.

"Officer Davis is everything O.K. here?" asked Sergeant Phillips.

"I stop Mr. Perez for littering. He tossed a beer can out his window. He said it was empty and, rolling around in the car, it was there when he rented the car and he just got tired of it rolling around in the car. I was just getting ready to have him take a test. Would you check his car out and make sure there is no other alcohol in the car."

"Now! Wait a minute here! You have no right to search my car!" said Santiago Perez.

"I can smell the beer on your breath sir, and I am sure you will test above the legal level and the fact that you were stopped for littering and smell of alcohol is enough of a reason to search your car. Is there anything in the car you do not want to be found?"

"No!"

"You might want to rethink that Mr. Perez. It looks like there are close to fourteen pounds of pills scattered in the back seat from one of the brown bags under the blanket," said Sargent Phillips.

"You had no right to open anything in my car."

"I did not open the bag. You did not seal the bag and it must have rolled around and the pills spilled out on the seat and floor. Cuff him and put him in the back of my car. Good work Davis."

"More luck than good work. This guy was not paying attention He tossed the beer can right in front of me."

"Regardless, good work. There is an FBI agent Nick Thomson who will want to talk to this guy.

FIVE HOURS LATER:

"Santiago, I am Nick Thomson and this is C.E. Hall we have you for violations of transporting and selling of controlled substances. The State of Wyoming I am afraid wants you for murder. I believe they have a half a dozen counts," said Nick.

"That is a load of crap! I murdered nobody!"

"Well, the State of Wyoming has five witnesses that are willing to testify that you sold the pills that killed citizens in this state. Plus, once we had you in custody we discovered you had a relationship to an illegal marijuana farm factory in California. Our cybercrime unit is going through your phone as we speak. So, I would say your best option is to work with us so you can lose some of the charges."

"I'll take my chances!"

"I forgot! We were tipped off of your run. There is a leak in your organization and I am not saying you will win your case but your organization just might think you are the leak," said Nick.

"You may not know or remember agent Nick Thomson and myself, but we were part of the group that broke up the old boss of your new cartel. That may not look good in your favor back home or in prison here. Your new boss has a reputation that is filled with violent actions against those that he thinks have betrayed him. That violence does not stop with the individual it goes to the family and at times to those near to the family members," said C.E.

"If what you say is true, then I am a dead man already!"

"Did you notice you were not booked when you came into the station? That was at my request. Your window of opportunity will close when I walk out that door. Then the State and Federal government will begin processing you for various charges. So what is it going to be?" asked Nick.

Santiago sat there staring at the two FBI men. Then C.E. got up and said, "Nick this is a waste of time." Nick stood up and turned to the door.

"Wait, I have one request if I provide you information."

"It depends on the information if we grant your wish," said Nick.

"My wife is all I have. Both of our families are gone. She has no idea what I do on my trips. She thinks it is police business. I want you to bring her to the United States and give her a new identity."

"That is possible, but first we need information then you will get what you want!" said Nick.

"What do you want to know?"

"Tell us about Leocadio and who he has meetings with within the last month," said Nick.

"Listen I am a local police officer and not that high up in the organization. I have seen Leocadio only twice once when a shipment from China came into town and the other when I was part of a security detail for a big meeting."

"Who was at the meeting?" asked C.E.

"This Iranian character they called Rashid and some Chinese guy in a suit. He looked like a diplomat."

"What? Did they talk about it?" asked Nick.

"I could not say I was at the perimeter of the house but when they came out the Iranian was smiling."

"That shipment what did it contain?" asked C.E.

"Mostly chemicals the cartel turns into drugs and part was in crates that were not identified."

"O.K. that is enough for today. We are going to transport you to another location and your questioning will continue there," said Nick.

"What about my wife? She will be in danger if they find I am in custody in the States!" said Santiago.

"That will be taken care of as soon as I leave this room," said Nick.

Outside the room, C.E. turned to Nick, "We were walking a line there with threats."

"You mean when you implied that his family was in danger either way he decided or the murder charges?"

"Both, I wish we knew what we were chasing with all the players that seem to be popping up!" said C.E.

"Yeah, now we have an Iranian tossed into the mix. I will put a feeler out on this Rashid character," said Nick.

CHAPTER SIXTEEN

Refugee and Asylum

Evil draws men together.

— Aristotle

World War II displaced millions of individuals just in Europe and between 40 and 60 million worldwide. These refugees were listed as Displace Persons (DP's). They were made up of POWs, foreign workers, survivors from concentration camps, and refugees who fled from war zones. Many of these individuals were continuing to seek asylum from persecution. Many of the Soviet returnees were executed as enemies of the State by Uncle Joe Stalin.

Today there are still some 50 million migrants moving around the world to obtain better economic conditions with several million flowing into the United States illegally as undocumented aliens. There have come some 30 caravans of immigrants marching through Mexico with government and NGO aid given to the migrants.

2023 Darien Gap, Panama

The Gap is 66 miles of difficult terrain in tropical forests, swamps and marshlands, and rivers with strong currents. Flash floods are a constant danger along with tropical diseases are present. These were some of the reasons for the TransAmerica Highway to end at the Darien Gap. One official reason given was to protect the indigenous people in the area. Then in the 1970's the Drug Cartels began using the Gap for their trade.

Inside the Darien Gap:

The couple were tired, and the children did not make the walking easy. One needed to be carried half of the time the other would run ahead and had to be watched. The woman finally tied a rope around the child's waist to keep him close.

"Maria, watch out this path is not safe for the children. We need to stay closer together. Once we get out of the jungle the path north will be easier," said Hector.

"Why do you think I had the boy on the rope? Besides, why do we have these two kids anyway?" asked Maria.

"Give me the little one, I am sorry. We are taking them as part of the fee we are paying the smugglers to get us to the United States," said Hector.

"You told me they were your uncle's kids?"

"Yes, I did not want to upset you. Look, the truth is this trip is costly and they offered me half price if we took two children with us."

"Now you are telling me this! What happens to the children when they get to the States?"

"I was told they have relatives there to take care of them," said Hector.

"Do you trust them?" asked Maria.

"What choice do we have?"

"We can return to our village," said Maria.

"What would we do then? Watch the chickens scratch the dirt. We are going to America and get rich. You have heard the stories of wealth."

"Yes! But they are stories. I have never seen anyone come back."

"What about the guy that organized this group? He drove into the village in the big American jeep," said Hector.

"Yes, with two men with guns. Hector that guy is part of a drug cartel. You have agreed to take these two young ones north for the cartel, not their relatives. Now, we are trapped!" said Maria.

"How are we trapped?"

"You made an agreement with a drug cartel and if one or worse both of these children die or get lost before we reach the States the cartel will demand the other half of the passage you bargain for with them and then they will add the price of the two children on top. No, we are trapped," said Maria.

"Look at the people with this group do they look trapped? No! We are going. So let's just do what we can until we get to the states."

"Hector, do you see the two men there that are guiding us through this jungle? They are dressed in good clothes and backpacks with new weapons. Half the people in this group have sandals old shoes and old clothes. I do not want you to leave me alone at any time. I see the way they look at the young teenage girl. The other women have been talking. They do not feel safe either. Are these guides or guards?"

"Maria, this they say is the hardest part of the journey. Once we get to Bajo Chiquita the trip will be easy. There we will have a rest before we start north again. They said the UN and NGO agencies would provide us with assistance for what we will need for the rest of the journey.

A week later at Bajo Chiquita, Panama.

"Hector, I will be glad to leave this place. I thought the jungle, with all the rain, mud, deep streams, crocodiles, and snakes was bad. This place is worse off than our village back home. I counted three international aid organizations and that Panama government official who took our names in the last three days. They all said they were out of supplies and that there would be more at our next stop."

"Just remember to keep the children close!" said Hector.

"Why are you telling me this again?"

"A young aid worker told me that children get lost on this journey and that we should not show that we have anything of value. That the trip the rest of the way is filled with dangerous people that will murder, steal and rape those in the caravans. He said to watch the Arabs he believes some are terrorists sneaking into the United States," said Hector.

"We all are!"

"No, we are going to the American border and turning ourselves over to the border guards. He said that there are a number of those in this group who will break away from the group and join the cartel as drug mules to enter the States without being stopped. He said the American news crews are there talking about the invasion of their country."

"What invasion?" asked Maria.

"This invasion, how many people are in this caravan?"

"I guess 5,000."

"Yes, and we are just one caravan just starting out. There are those in the United States that want to stop us from coming. Look at how we are leaving this place. There is trash and junk just thrown around. What would we call it if this came to our village?" said Hector.

"But we were told to come by their President and we must go through a half a dozen countries before we get there. I heard at the Red Cross station that the President of Mexico said he was seeing that we passed through Mexico orderly to make sure it is legal. So, it is not an invasion," said Maria.

Weeks later:

"Stay close and do not let the Americans separate us. I am glad we moved away from the people that took the children. I felt sorry for them that man and woman were not parents," said Maria.

"How can you say that? How do parents act?" asked Hector.

"Not like those two. I wish you would have asked me about bringing them along before you got us in this mess."

"What mess? We are in the United States now and they will take us to any place we say we want to go and provide us with essentials. I think we are in good shape."

"Time will answer that once we get to New York and my cousin," said Maria.

"About that Maria, I was offered a job in California doing farm work and I told them yes."

"Hector, I have had enough. We plan on coming to the States and then getting married and working with my cousin's family. Now, you have this new plan to go off in a country we do not know with most likely and Cartel drug farm in California. NO! I am done and you know where you can find me. I would suggest you do not take too long."

"But we can't go to New York!"

"Why NOT?"

"California was part of the deal I made. Half of the money for the trip was for bringing the children and the other half was an agreement to work for two years in California until the passage was paid in full."

"Hector! What did you do with the money I gave you?"

"I loaned it to my uncle because I would not be there to help him."

"YOU DID WHAT! You gave my money to your uncle. My family gave that to us as a wedding gift. Hector, we are done get away from me."

"I can't. You have to stay with me. I have made promises."

"Then break them like you have with those you have made to me. I guess I should feel lucky that you did not offer me. Wait, did you trade me!"

"No, No, I would never do that just come with me you will see everything will be fine."

"Hector, you can go the HELL!" said Maria as she walked away.

"They will find you Maria you will be safe with me!" He yelled after her.

Maria saw a man with a jacket with DEA on it and walked over to him. "Excuse me, my name is Maria and I need to talk to a government official."

"Miss, you need to talk to the border control officers. I am Officer Wilson with the Drug Enforcement Agency. So please go back to your group."

"I have information about a cartel member called Leocadio that I need to pass on to someone in authority."

"What name did you just say?"

"Leocadio, I think Blanco is his full name."

"Miss, will you come with me? We are going to skip this line and you will come with me for a long interview. Is that acceptable with you?"

"Anything to get me away from here. I do not feel safe."

"Prefect that is my vehicle over there. We will take care of any paperwork later," said Wilson as they started toward the car.

"Maria, Maria, where do you think you are going," yelled Hector as he was shoved into the back of a pickup.

"Is he a friend of yours?"

"More of a disappointment and liar and cheat," said Maria.

In the car, Agent Wilson called the Director. "I am bringing in a link to Leocadio. So get the team together. I think we just had a big break walk up to me at the border," leaving a voice message.

CHAPTER SEVENTEEN
Golan Heights

Whoever fights monsters should see to it that in the process he does not become a monster.
— Friedrich Nietzsche

In 1967 Syria lost the Golan Heights to the Israeli army in the Six Day War. The Muslim Brotherhood began increasing its activities against the Syrian government and by 1982 President Hafez al-Assad sent the Army to crush the Brotherhood in Syria killing more than twenty-five thousand people.

The Syrian Army occupied parts of Lebanon until 2004 and The government was fighting the Kurds in the north. These and the internal stiff between the Sunni and Shia Muslims along with the Radical Islamic groups of Al-Qaeda and Hezbollah caused the government more problems that broke out in 2011 with a Civil War.

In 2020 the Turkish government began attacks on the Kurds in Syria. The Middle East was drawing new lines of alliances. When the Russians brokered a peace agreement between the Turks and Syrians while the U.S. had troops in Syria to protect their interest.

2023 The Kurds in Northern Syria

The Kurds are the largest group of people in the world without a nation. Their homeland had been overrun countless times during the centuries by Persians, Greeks, Romans, Mongols, and Ottomans, and today they are divided within different nations living in Iran, Iraq, Syria, and Turkey as unwelcome individuals. Their lives are in a state of conflict.

In a Kurdish Camp:

"Sherko where is Soran?" asked Jiyan.

"Dead, he was wounded in last night's attack and died this morning," said Karwan.

"We are under siege from all sides the Syrians, Iraqis, Iranians, and Turks refuse our independence," said Jiyan.

"How do you think we can win independence when our people are spread in five different countries and with us divided into over a dozen different political groups? When Turkey joined NATO there has been little support from Europe and the U.S. governments for our cause. The Turks were important to stop the Soviet Union during the Cold War and today they are seen as a block on the radical Islamic states. The West is willing to allow the Turks to attack us as terrorists," said Sherko.

"What about the UN?" asked Jiyan.

"You must be joking! That organization has done very little except fill the pockets of their own governments and political leaders. Every relief shipment that is sent has lost a portion each time. I went on a relief convoy and we had to pay bribes at each checkpoint. We even had to pay the head relief worker at the start of the convoy," said Sherko.

"Why were you on a relief convoy?" asked Karwan.

"We were using it to smuggle in weapons because the Turks are preparing to renew the attacks against us," said Sherko.

"Where did you hear this?" asked Jiyan.

"When I was at the UN relief center there was talk of the Turks intensifying their operations in Syria with the Russian's preoccupation in the war in the Ukraine. So, the Turkish leadership is turning more to smuggling to hide their actions from the Americans and Europeans. Do not want to upset their Muslim ally."

"Everyone talks about the Israel and Palestine conflict with both sides claiming the territory as their homeland. The Kurdish homeland is ignored by the West. The PLO, Hamas, Hezbollah, Al-Qaeda, the Taliban, and the Muslim Brotherhood get noticed and supported by the Left in the West. While here we are locked in a political power struggle with oppressors on all sides each waiting for their chance to grab our land. The pandemic allowed oppressors to expand their reach into power. The Russian used in the Ukraine War, Turkey has and will use it more to crush the Kurdish people in Syria," said Jiyan.

"Jiyan, we are seen just as the Armenians during the Great War, and their genocide was ignored by the world for a hundred years. That genocide is still lucky to get a paragraph in a history book. While the Holocaust gets a chapter in history books with pictures. Who has heard of the Kurds?

KURDS IN IRAQ

"Rebaz, I was helping unload U.N. aid and heard two aid workers talking about Palestine and a connection with a drug cartel in Mexico. They were standing just outside the building after unloading a shipment from China. I did not hear all they were saying but it was about drugs and Chinese chemicals. They also, said something about Palestine but the driver of the aid truck walked up and wanted to get moving." said Zilan.

"Do you have a name?" asked Rebaz.

"One worker said there was a Mexican cartel guy named Leocadio waiting for a shipment. I did not hear which drug Cartel. The conversation was also about something to do with Hamas and Hezbollah," said Zilan.

"I will pass this to the Americans."

"Why tell the Americans? They had abandoned us for the most part!" said Haval.

"Information is what the Americans need in the Middle East. Now more than ever after they left Afghanistan and the way they abandoned everything and everyone. We can now build on that and win favor with the leadership," said Rebaz.

INIQUITOUSNESS

That afternoon Rebaz found the foreign contractor James and asked if they could talk in private. "I always have time for you Rebaz."

"That is very kind of you to say. I have some information that may or may not be of interest to the American government. Do you know who I might talk to so I can deliver this information?" said Rebaz.

"Rebaz, we both know how this works and who we both are, so just tell me and I will see what I can do for you. I know we have lost sight in this part of the world and there is very little I can do about it. Things are what they are!" said James.

"That is true. This information came by way of a conversation overheard between two UN aid workers. They were talking about a connection between China, Mexico, and Palestine. My individual only heard parts of the conversation between the two before she was interrupted.

Most of what she heard was about drugs from a Chinese chemical company and something being planned for Palestine. They kept mentioning some Mexican cartel guy named sounding like Leonardo or Lecoadio, but she could not be sure. Like I said the conversation was between two U.N. workers and just in bits and pieces."

"Did they mention any other groups?"

"One UN worker said something about Hamas and Hezbollah when their conversation stopped by the truck driver that wanted to get moving."

"Thanks for the information. Now what can I do for you?"

"I want to build trust. This is the first step, I hope, in a new partnership."

"In that case you are right we need to rebuild the trust we have lost."

James went back to his office picked up the secure phone and made a call, "There is a rumor that Hamas and Hezbollah have people working with Humanitarian groups. I need to pass this information to an agent Nick Thomson."

"Hold the line."

At An Office in States

A woman stuck her head into the room and said, "Agent Nick Thomas you have a call."

Nick picked up the phone, "Hello, this is Nick Thomson."

"You may not remember me, but I was with you on that detail that broke up the international banking laundering scandal. My name is James Wallace."

"Yes, I do remember. You were with the detail in Germany, if I remember right."

"Yes, I played a small part in that part of the plan. Now I am in northern Syria with the Kurds. I have received some information that may be connected to the cartels in Mexico. I remember the banking bust also had something to do with terrorists and Mexican drug cartels. The name Leocadio popped up and I remember he was part of that cartel. So, I figured I would give you a call. I am not sure it is anything."

"Your timing could not be any better. What do you have?"

"Not, a lot just a name Leocadio that was mentioned with a Chinese chemical company. I just remember the connections with the banking. This may not be anything but, there are rumors that something big is coming this year. The interesting part is what was heard and not heard. The conversation mentioned Palestine before it was interrupted. The informant also heard Hamas and Hezbollah mention," said James.

"It appears the Chinese and the cartels are back together, and I am with a team looking into that right now. The Chinese chemical companies are sending their raw product to Mexico and the cartels refine it and flood it into the states. I do not know of anything with a connection to Palestine but I will put it on our list of things to look into! I can say the cartels have added human transportation to their smuggling enterprise and the border is in organized chaos."

"Are you still working with that fire investigator? I believe his name was initials of some kind!" asked James.

"Right, C.E. and he is on this detail."

"Well, tell him he got me hooked on stamp collecting and if I hear more on the cartel I give you a call."

"James thanks for the information it may be connected to what we are looking into now and I will tell C.E. that he has ruined another good man. Be safe!"

"You do the same!"

Kurds in Turkey:

"Rivin, I hear that the Turkish military is moving more men into Syria tonight. You better call Commander Karwan and warn him that he is possibly the subject of this attack. Those idiot Russians in their invasion of the Ukraine have allowed the Turks to be bold in their action in Syria. They see us in Turkey as a security threat but in Syria, they see an opportunity with the civil war there to wipe out the Kurds by cutting off a safe haven for our fighters here," said Eylo.

"Where is Baran?" asked Soran.

"He was arrested this afternoon in town when he was hit by a kid's soccer ball. He made the mistake of yelling at the kid in Kurdish. Not only have we lost our homeland we are not allowed to use our one language in this country," said Naza.

"Why was he arrested?" asked Soran.

"The officer did not say it was for using Kurdish he said it was for causing a public disturbance and defiance," said Naza.

"What did he do that was defiant?" asked Soran.

"The officer came up behind Soran and grabbed his arm. Soran pushed the arm that grabbed him. Soran did not know who grabbed him and when he saw it was an officer he put his hands up. Another Turkish officer came up and they placed Soran on the ground and cuffed him. Those around the square cheered the officers," said Naza.

"Ever since 2002, this nation has been shifting to a more Islamic state with their radical party victory in the election that year. The only thing that is keeping them from full-out change is the European Union carrot of admission to the E.U. The government has loosened political restrictions on speech and the press but that has not stopped the fundamentalist from pushing their objectives.

The headscarf rule in 2008 was a start by the Islamic right. Today you can see their influence in Istanbul with almost a complete unofficial dress code in place. All the women wear long pants or skirts with sleeves that are elbow length with head scarves. There you can even see more burkas," said Rozerin.

"You are right but if you go to Antalya there the dress is more casual with t-shirts and shorts," said Rojan.

"If I can interrupt this discussion on dress codes. I have been asked to verify by an agent a connection between the Middle East, China, and Mexico in the drug trade out of Iraq," said Eylo.

"Why should we care?" asked Rojan.

"If you would think more globally we could get more aid from the West. Turkey is trying to walk a line in the middle of political conflicts. Our demands for an independent state and some of the Kurdish groups that used bombs and assassinations to force the Turks to give our people their independence only create more chaos between the West and Arab world," said Eylo.

"The Turks will never allow us our freedom. It is just wishful thinking by you! Look at the Turks and the Armenian mass deportation and murder in 1915. They still refuse to admit that it even happened," said Rojan.

"You are right but the Turkish people can change. Ataturk pulled them into the modern world after the Great War. So, I would never say never," said Eylo.

"Eylo, if we verify the connection, who do we contact?" asked Soran.

"That CIA guy Wallace over in Iraq. I think it is a priority with them so let's see what we can find," Eylo.

"The more we cooperate the better we build our weakened relationship with this American administration and begin to lay a solid foundation for the next administration," said Soran.

Kurds in Iran:

The door opened and the woman inside looked up, "Darya I have a message to send to the U.N. about the increased use of executions of Kurdish in the prisons here. I have verified 144 executions this year as compared to 52 last year," said Azad.

"I think that number is low for I know of at least two individuals that died a week after they were released and sent home because they were dying from beatings they were given. We cannot trust this government!" said Darya.

"Nevertheless, we need to get these numbers to the Human Rights Commission at the UN," said Azad.

"Why do you bother the U.N. is worthless the only thing it has stopped in its lifetime is Smallpox. The U.N. looks the other way when anything interferes with its interest and continues with their business as normal," said Darya.

"What you are saying is absolutely right but there will be a record for recorded history."

"These Islamic Republics care less about human rights than just about anybody. They do not follow the Islamic law. Kurds have been massacred for centuries because we are not just one religion. We are the largest group of people without a homeland of our own. The Armenians have a home, the Jews have a home, and even the Palestinians have some land they have authority over. Many of us follow Islam, maybe not as strictly as some, but we are followers of the faith. Our history can be traced back to the Jews and their Old Testament when we were called the Medes," said Darya.

"That is why this part of the world is in constant conflict over who owns what piece of land. The Iraqis want to recreate Babylon, the Egyptians want to reclaim their empire, and Iran seeks to rebuild the Persian empire. Now, the Saudis are seeking power with their oil money while some in that nation want to spread terror. Then many of the smaller empires during that span of time want the right to their own nations like us.

History is filled with people who want to recapture the past for various reasons. The most often reason is power or because of the discrimination and the displacement of their groups. I have simplified the whole issue, but the reason I bring it up is that these issues can be used to grab power, expand power, and control power by evil men. These men can always find good men to do evil things for the greater good."

"Azad, always the professor," said Darya.

"Yes, I forget and fall into the old professor habit now and then."

CHAPTER EIGHTEEN
West Bank

All concerns of men go wrong when they wish to cure evil with evil.

— Sophocles

For the Jews the site of Temple of the Mount is a holy place of the 1st and 2nd temple.

It is the site where Abraham was prepared to sacrifice his son Isaac.

1st Temple was destroyed by Babylon in 587 BCE
2nd Temple was destruction by Rome in 70 CE

That fragment of the second Temple that was left is known as West Wall which is 160 feet long and 60 feet high and is where papers of prayer placed in cracks.

Reasons for the Site today:

- God save a part of the Wall for the Jews
  or
- Rome saved it to remind Jews of the Defeat.
- For the Christian it is the site of where Jesus was crucified, and the resurrection took place.
- For Islam the site was captured in 638 and the Jews, Christians and Muslims see the city as their holy site.

The Dome of the Rock was built over the ruins of the Temple of the Mount in 691 and it is the spot where Abraham, Moses, Jesus and Muhammad gave prayers. Muhammad was said to assented to heaven from the spot.

2023 JERUSALEM

The cities of Jericho and Jerusalem are in the West Bank. When the Babylonians captured Israel and Judah, they carried off much of the elite populations for seventy years. During those years the Jews and new settlers left behind intermarried and continued many of the Jewish ceremonies. When the Babylonian captivity ended the Jews from Babylon returned and saw those that remained as unclean Jews called Samarians. They built separate Temples and disliked each other. Jesus would use that dislike in a parable of the Good Samarian.

AT A COFFEE CAFÉ

The Catholic priest sitting outside a small coffee shop stood up and when an Orthodox priest walked up said, "Father Nikolaos today is a blessing with the bright sun and few clouds on this fine day," said Father Giuseppe.

"Blessing upon you my friend and is Farther Usire to join us today?" asked Father Nikolaos.

"No, he has a meeting with his Coptic Bishop today in Alexandria. He said to give you, his blessing. The others will come. They are always late to our meetings," said Father Giuseppe.

"I think we are failing to make any progress any agreement between the faiths. I believe the Egyptian and Coptic are worried and that is why Father Usire was called to Alexandria. I was told by an Armenian Archpriest that things are happening with Iran and their weapons smuggling to the radicals in Gaza. He said the route has shifted and nobody knows the new route. He also said that Iran was testing small aerial craft and some of these technicians in Gaza," said Father Nikolaos.

"If Iran was the only problem! Evil never sleeps. It is within all of us, and some cannot control their evil desires of what others have or they seek power. I am afraid the belief in peace is never enough to stop hate. Our Lord Jesus Christ tried to explain to the Jews that kindness is better than hate with the story of the Good Samaritan," said Father Giuseppe as the waiter walked up to the table.

"Excuse me for interrupting your conversation. I have heard of this Good Samaritan but never understood what it meant. I would like to understand if you do not mind telling me the story," said the young woman.

"The Samarians and the Jews were very similar in their faith. The Samaritans were those that were left behind in Judea during the Babylonian Captivity. Babylonians settle in the area with the Jews left behind and began mixing the faiths. When the Captive Jews in Babylon were allowed to return, they saw the Samarians as unclean Jews and that developed into pure dislike.

To teach his followers compassion the Lord Jesus used the story of a Jewish man that was beaten and robbed of even his clothes laying by the roadside. All those that passed him ignored the injured man except a Samarian who did stop to help. The story was told to tell the people that kindness should come before hate."

"How?"

"Well, this Jewish man was beaten and robbed of all his things and left on the side of the road. A Rabbi and a Levite saw him lying there and walked pass. Then a Samaritan came along and help the man up saw that he was given clothes and food. The simple act of kindness is the tale of the Good Samaritan."

"Young lady you see before you two priest of different Christian religions who can sit a talk together. Yet, the Christian world much like the Jewish and Islamic worlds are divided on interpretations. All three major religions stared with the Old Testament harsh God and punishment, then Jesus came with the interpretation of the Christian New Testament with God of forgiveness and peace, followed by Mohammad and Islam a God of conquest. All three religions use the same stories with different outcomes," said Father Giuseppe.

"Thank you for explaining this to me. Once again I am sorry to have interrupted your conversation. I must get back to work."

"You know Nikolaos I wonder if we will ever learn to find our common grounds instead of those that divide us. The Golden Rule is found in every religion in one form or another. Yet, when a war breaks out good people kill other good people for evil power," said Father Giuseppe.

"You are right my friend. I see it is late and the others are not coming so I will see next week for our coffee and chats."

WEST BANK AT TOWN OF RAMALLAH

"Halima is Aya's family still divided between Fatah and Hamas?" asked Essam.

"I think they are divided more than ever since the marriage agreement had been broken between Halima and Mustafa he became involved with the Hamas military group in Gaza and started to make increasing demands on Halima to act more faithful. His demands were upsetting Aya's father. It had become so bad that he approached Mustafa's family and canceled the marriage agreement," said Halima.

"I did not think it was an arranged marriage?" said Raed.

"It was not. They met two years ago when they both worked at the NGO called Doctors without Borders. The two families were divided during the Brother's War back in 2007 between Fatah and Hamas. Aya and Mustafa did not care about the political differences until last year when he became radicalized. Then Mustafa became more dominant in his attitude towards Aya's behavior and dress. I am not sure but I think violence was involved and Aya's father did not let it go," said Salma.

"I would have paid to watch that confrontation. Aya's father is huge and a street fighter during the Second Intifada. Mustafa's family has always been corruptible little weasels playing both sides in any conflict. I do know that when Mustafa's father sees Aya's father he walks the other way in a hurry." said Essam and laughed.

"Anyway, the answer to the question is yes," said Halima. "Why do you ask?"

"There is something brewing in Gaza and it may spill over here on the West Bank. I would like to be ready for counteractions," said Essam.

"My mother cleans the home of one of the Fatah corrupted agency administrators. She is always telling me what they are doing. They seem to not care what she hears," said Raed.

"If you hear anything no matter how minor pass it along. Fatah and Hamas should be on the same page in this struggle for a homeland, yet here we are still at odds with each other," said Essam.

LATER THAT EVENING:

"Aya, what is so important that you need this meeting? Said Haviva.

"I need to disappear from here. Mustafa is becoming more threatened. He was unbalanced and threatened to kill me. My father cannot be at my side every minute. I am surprised that Mustafa is not following me right now."

"If you disappear it will expose your father," said Haviva.

"No, he said for you to see that I leave here tonight. He will accuse Mustafa of my disappearance. There is enough evidence to cause questions and direct everything from my father."

"I will check with Tel Aviv," said Haviva.

"Haviva, I do not think you understand what I am saying. I must leave tonight with the information my father is afraid to send by normal means."

"Alright give me an hour to step up the operation. Do not go home and stay here in this house. We do not want witnesses then once you leave this area there will be no witnesses so your disappearance will fall towards Mustafa," said Haviva.

Just after midnight, an unidentified vehicle left the West Bank with one passenger sitting in the back seat behind blacked-out windows and drove to a safe house just outside Tel Aviv. The passenger got out and was taken into the house to meet a Mossad handler. "Aya, you will have to leave Israel for your father's safety," said Rachel.

"My father explained all that to me. He said that he wanted me out of this business for good. That it was a poor decision on his part to have me seek out Mustafa for information on Hamas for Fatah as a cover. The plan got out of hand with Mustafa."

"Well, the operation to remove you from the West Bank went better than we planned. Your father has already started the search for you there and Mustafa is being questioned. It seems he has no alibi for last night which focuses on him even more," said Rachel.

"Good! That bastard knocked me down in my own home and kicked me and if my father did not come home right then I think I would have died. I cannot feel any sympathy for him." She pulled out a paper and handed it to Rachel.

"Do you know what this is?" asked Rachel.

"No! He made me swear not to look or read it. He did say he hoped it was not too late."

"Here is a new passport from the United States and we have provided clothes and funds for you. Your flight to London tonight is on a private plane for any possible chance you will be seen at the airport? Once you are in the States a place to live and a job will be waiting for you.

If you like the job is yours for as long as you like but you will not be required to stay with it. After you land your service with us is completed. Your name will be on the wall of departed agents. As you can see we gave you an American name close to your birth name for you to easier remember. Thank you for your service Aya."

CHAPTER NINETEEN

Drug Smugglers

It is much easier at all times to prevent and evil than to rectify mistakes.

— George Washington

Prior to 1937 marihuana was not listed as a major drug for its use in medical treatments by the Federal government. Many states and foreign countries had banned the drug by1930's. The United States government in 1937 began a campaign against cannabis. The Custom Agency wrote a report that stated that because cannabis was so widely cultivated and grew freely in the wild that it was therefore not expected to be a smuggling problem.

The Federal Bureau of Narcotics commissioner wanted to regulate cannabis and passed the 1937 Marihuana Act to help prevent the use as a recreational drug. The custom stamp was to verify that the revenue was paid for the importation of the product. By the 1970's marihuana was classified with opium and heroin. Smuggling of the product grew and in 2011 that three million pounds were confiscated at the southern border in a multi-billion-dollar enterprise.

2023 MEETING WITH THE TEAM

"Nick, what do we have that made you call the team together?" asked the director.

"I got a call from James Wallace who worked with C.E. and myself on the stamp case. He made the connection with the Iranians and the drug trail. I had him follow that up with contacts' sources with the Kurds. That got very interesting for not only did their tip make the link to Mexico and Leocadio but with some individuals in the Chinese of the Stamp case."

"Perfect." said C.E. "While I was looking into the Marijuana farm in California, I was asked to also as a favor to a local fire chief to look into an illegal chemical lab. What I found was a Chinese national who was on the run from Canadian authorities and in Texas for industrial and intellectual theft. What was most important was he was funding the farm with a Chinese bank and had the cartel shipping his product out of California. You would be surprised if I told you whose name came up in my investigation?"

"I bet it was our boy Leocadio!" said Nick.

"That is why I like working with you, Nick. You catch every slow ball I throw out," said C.E.

"Before you two start your Abbott and Costello routine can we get back to the point of this meeting," said the director.

"Right, I received corroborated information from two different sources. One from Mossad and the other from a Kurdish military commander. They both identified a Chinese agent by the name of Ying Wu who was used as a contact with the Mexican Cartel. He was seen with Leocadio in Istanbul with an Iranian. They held a meeting with an Afghan drug dealer. That gives us a solid connection of the old network is being re-established," said Nick.

"C.E. what about this Bio-lab and Marijuana farm?" asked the director.

"Last year a city inspector was sent to a warehouse to check on some parking complaints and instead discovered an illegal bio-lab run by a Chinese national in this country illegally. He also had an arrest warrant for him in Canada. This guy was into everything from money laundering to a wide range of illegal drug operations.

"The best I can tell is that Gou had a deal with Leocadio to put the front money up on this Marijuana farm in exchange for shipping lab products out of California," said C.E.

"How is this Gou connected to the old case?" asked Edward Wilson.

"I was able to get contact numbers off the phones collected at the illegal bio-lab and gave them to Mary Jo. She can update us on what she has learned," said C.E.

"Most of the emails went straight to a central place in China and I was unable to read any of the messages. However, one text went to a phone in Turkey. This individual Ying was upset with Gou's family. It seems that Ying's daughter is married to someone in Gou's family and Ying is not happy with her treatment. The message in the text pointed out that Gou's position was on dangerous ground because of recent stamp failures and he needed a friend. He would get support that support if the issue with Ying's daughter was resolved," said Mary Jo.

"Do we know what the issue was?" asked the director.

"No, but I found that this Ying is more than just a messenger. He is a major player in a Chinese company with close ties to the Chinese military. His company is buying land in a number of countries that are part of their Belt Road project.

"Just in the United States the Chinese own close to four hundred thousand acres of land. That is still only 1% of foreign land ownership in this country. However, they are buying in strategic areas close to military bases. Their U.S. land purchases have jumped 30% in the last three years.

"One little bit of information was at the end of Gou's text. He said the funds for the bio-lab and pot farm needed to be shut down and he was rushing back to take care of the situation," said Mary Jo.

"Well, he did get back in time to be picked up by the local police. While they were under arrest it was discovered there was a Canadian warrant out on him. I was impressed by that small police department. They had this guy bagged and packaged for the Fed within 36 hours," said C.E.

"What did you find at the pot farm?" asked Wilson.

"I first had to investigate cannabis agriculture farms in California. I was surprised that there are almost 7,000 legal growers of cannabis in California with a value of just over $5 billion dollars.

"The legal use was started to sell to the public in 2016, as a way, to control the illegal production of the crop. However, the lure of money has caused individuals and cartels to set up some 3,000 illegal farms in the state. The cartels have turned some farms into fortified camps.

"Turf wars have left bodies in the desert. Recent laws were changed on penalties and fines reduced to $500 and 6 months in custody. The illegal farms and some of the legal farms use pesticides and other toxins that stay with the weed causing a health hazard.

"Two names came up that are tied to Leocadio. One is Martin who runs adult clubs in the San Diego area and the other is Santiago known as an enforcer," said C.E.

"Were there any other Chinese individuals we can pull into question?" asked Nick.

"A woman named Hua in Los Angeles who runs a few coin laundry shops. I think she is laundering more than clothes," said C.E.

"O.K. Barns you and Wilson go and pick up this Hua woman for questioning. Mary Jo look into her and see if we have enough to get a search warrant for her work. Peterson you and Miller get some help and collect this Martin and Santiago. I want whoever goes after Santiago to take care if he is an enforcer he could be real trouble.

"Mary Jo you start looking into these individuals. I want C.E. and Nick to work with you and go over that old case and see if there are other connections to this case," said the director.

"Mary Jo while you are going into these individuals there might be a connection to shipping. The bio-lab had biohazards labeled just pharmaceuticals. The place looked like a bioweapon plant with the pathogens found in the building. We should check with the postal department and see if we can track the packages," said C.E.

"That is a lot for one person to look into in a short period of time. Director I know two other agents that can be of a lot of assistance," said Mary Jo.

"Give me their names and I will see if I can get them released to me."

"Joan St. Janes and Martha McKenna, they work with me and are I think better than me in tracing down details."

"Then if there is nothing else, let's go and catch some bad guys."

"How long have you been waiting to use that line?" asked Mary Jo.

"Pretty Good isn't it?"

"If this was a sitcom, maybe!" said Nick.

CHAPTER TWENTY

Sponsors of Terrorism

> Terrorism is the preferred weapon of weak and evil men.
>
> — Ronald Reagan

The Arab Spring began in 2010 when the Tunisian government confiscated a 26-year-old street vendor's fruit. In protest to the government, his self-immolation set off independent protest in the Arab world. Tunisia and Egypt saw regime change and concessions made to the protestors in Algeria, Jordan, Morocco, and Oman. Yemen and Syria turned into civil war while protests in Bahrain and Libya ended with foreign interventions. The Gulf Cooperation Council ended the protest in Bahrain and NATO interfered in Libya with air strikes.

The Iranian Spring saw widespread protest with protesters yelling 'Allah is Great and Death to the Dictator'. The leadership turned once more to tactics used in the Iraq-Iran War to control the protesters. The Obama administration held that the conflict was an internal problem and not in American interest. The leadership was splitting the baby, but not very visionary or bold. The new Leader in Egypt said the Arabs want America to stop supporting corrupted dictators in the Arab world.

Then President Obama gave Iran $150 Billion and reduced restrictions. This was followed by the Next administration cutting off funds and oil sales and those ended with the next administration in 2020. Iran then becomes the biggest backer of Islamic fundamentalists in the Middle East from Yemen to Gaza.

2023 Iran

"When is the Hizballah representative to arrive?" asked Darab.

"He is down the hall waiting now. I told him we are waiting for the general," said Arzhang as the two walked into the hall.

In the hall was a major general of the Revolutionary Guard, "*Salamu Alaykum*, I am Major General Hashem I was sent to represent General Ormazd. He had to go to Isfahan Nuclear Center."

"I hope it is nothing serious. I did hear there was a spy caught there last week," said Arzhang.

The general looked at Arzhang with a hard look. "It would be best if you did not repeat rumors, young man. I will let this side but you are warned."

"I am so sorry; it was very foolish of me to repeat a rumor."

"I would suggest you remind the person who gave you the information."

"I was at the site yesterday and heard the scientist talking when I delivered a report. I just heard it walking by and believed it was common knowledge at the time. I did not think. I am truly sorry."

"Yes, Yes, I will talk to the people there about where they should be having sensitive conversations. Now, where is the representative from Hizballah?" said the general as they walked.

"Right in this room," said Arzhang as he opened the door. "Peace be with you my brothers," said Kevork as they entered.

"Let's get right down to business. Why are the shipments to Hamas being delayed?" asks the general.

"The Israelis are increasing security and we have found a solution."

"What do you mean increased security? Are they worried that something is being planned?"

"No, not at all general. Last week there was an incident at the Sinai entry and they stepped up the new search methods. We found a new temporary solution with a humanitarian shipment. It added a little more in cost but they will have everything needed for the operation to go off on time," said Kevork.

"Excellent! Here are instructions for our Revolutionary Guard instructors with the Islamic Jihad group in Palestine. Please see that it is on the next shipment."

"It is my pleasure and it will be done," said Kevork.

"Then have a safe trip home and may Allah go with you!" said the general as Kevork walked out the door.

"General if I may ask, when did we start training the Islamic Jihad in Palestine?" asked Darab.

"You may ask and I cannot answer that question for I do not know. It was done far above my level. Now, May I ask you why?"

"Their reparation as being very violent and bloody. We do not allow them in Iran."

"I believe that is why the Council has decided to use them to create chaos in Israel. There is a belief that that things need to get done before the next election in the United States for if there is a policy change it will upset our economy once more. Plus, the Saudis and the Jews are close to a peace plan they have in the works," said the general.

"Yes, we have talked about that in the foreign department for the last three months," said Darab.

"Is there anything else we need to go over?"

"No, I think we covered it all."

"Then, I must be off for another meeting so peace be with you both," said the general as he got up and left the room.

"I thought I was ruined when I mention the spy. His look was of absolute evil," said Arzhang.

"You do not know who he is?"

"No, should I?"

"He is the grandson of a powerful cleric on the council. He was just a major until one year ago. The rumor was his men may have tried to kill him on a training exercise. When he survived the company was disciplined and the idiot major was promoted the Major General. The Army has refused to allow him around the Republican Guards. I think it may be because he may have made a poor decision and there is the rumor that there is a target on his back."

"You mean the soldiers will try to kill him?

"He did get five members of his unit of troops killed in that live fire exercise. He had a machine gun fire on an armored vehicle that was moving away from a group of men behind it loading on a truck. As the armored vehicle moved the fire hit the back of the truck killing three and wounding eight of which two later died. Now he has become a message carrier and nothing more," said Darab.

"So, he has powerful connections and no personal value."

"Yes, and I need to bring up a stumble in our Mexico connection,"

"What about it?"

"I was told last night that the Chinese are increasing their influence in the drug trade with Latin America. That has disrupted our trade avenues in Europe."

"How much?"

"In 2017 the Cocaine shipment from Latin America through the trans-shipment paradise of the Caribbean Islands of the French, Dutch, and British has jumped. For example, the amount of cocaine seized in Rotterdam jumped from 20 tons to 228 tons in 2018. That is a jump of 164% and that hurts our distribution and price and that is just one city. What should I do?" asked Arzhang.

"I will have to think about this. We are working with the Chinese and weapons shipments from North Korea and China for the Russians. Their army is not the Army they sent to Afghanistan in the 1970s. The Ukrainians did a real number on the first attempt at invasion. Give me a day or two and we go over this issue again," said Darab.

"One last item. Should I still release the funds to the educational fund on the study of Islamic world studies in the States?" asked Arzhang.

"Actually, I think we should increase them."

"May I ask, why?"

"The Americans have been undermining their culture for years during the Cold War. It started during the 1960s but those students were shaped by the civil rights and war protests to challenge and distrust authority and their own history.

The Russians were masters of seeding false information in America under the disguise of free speech. Many universities accepted communist sympathizers to lecture to students. Then these individuals wrote alternative histories to the American story the Americans as imperialistic aggressors and the native side as nothing more than the victims.

Then in the 1980s in the Islamic world, we began a campaign to educate the American students on the Crusades from the Islamic point of view of the Western world being the oppressors and occupiers. That carried into the conquests of native Americans, Pacific Islanders, and Asia, along with the slave trade helping reinforce our narrative of colonizers in Palestine.

Recently in 2020, the Chinese began to become more involved in the American educational system with Confucius Institutions. They are run by a Chinese company called Hanban and those that sign the contract must sign that both Chinese and U.S. Laws will be followed. The Chinese call it the soft power to influence the study of business, economy, and history. Hanban reviews all requests and speakers at universities.

The Chinese provide millions each year to the American educational system. The universities cannot wait to get their hands on these Chinese funds. The long-term game the Chinese plan has opened American investigations into the money sources. A recent report noted that 70% of the schools failed to report any of their donations that were more than $250,000 to the Department of Education."

"How can that help us?"

"We use it for the propaganda value. All the American student wants is answers for a test and not for more understanding. We will be able to mobilize their youth to support our cause. Education will be just another Trojan Horse for us to use. Remember what Vladimir Lenin said, *'Give me just one generation of youth, and I'll transform the whole world.'* Now, I have another meeting, so let's wrap this up."

"I will give to an update tomorrow."

"Good!" He got up and walked out.

CHAPTER TWENTY-ONE

Gaza Strip

No one becomes depraved all at once.
— Juvenal

The Second Intifada began in 2000 with uprisings in the West Bank and in the Gaza Strip with the capture and lynching of Israeli soldiers. A new organization called Hamas came into being and by 2006 the Hamas group took control in Gaza and began a campaign of sending *Qassam* Rockets into Israel each year. There was a brief power struggle between Hamas and Fatah with Hamas controlling Gaza and Fatah staying in control of the West Bank.

In 2007 Israel declared Gaza a hostile territory and the rocks still rained on Israel. That year Israel began major construction on the separation barrier between Gaza and Israel after suicide bombers increased their attacks. The Israelis cut off service to Gaza to bring Hamas to stop the rocket attacks. Human Rights organizations called the blockade illegal and barbaric. The Palestinians were seen as the victims of their acts of violence against Israel.

2023 GAZA STRIP

"Rami, I think Mahmoud has loyalty to Fatah and should not be trusted!" said Ismail.

"Why have you come to this conclusion?" asked Rami.

"While I was in the tunnel under the U.N building he was asking about the power supply and the connection to the U.N. generator that we get for our energy supply. This is not the first time he has been asking questions."

"Ismail, Mahmoud is not a Fatah supporter. He is part of the Brotherhood in Egypt. You must not tell anyone of your suspicions!"

"Why, he is a spy or traitor!"

"No, he is a tool we use for misinformation. The Brotherhood is filled with enemies of Islam, so we feed him information that we want the Western imperialists to know. That information keeps the West focused on other things while we finalize our plans. So, what else do you have to report?"

"The shipment of drones from Iran has been programmed and the training of the paragliders is going better than expected."

"This will be an invasion like no other for it will be done by people, not an army and we will video the whole thing for the world to see the power of Hamas. When it happens, it will unite the Arab world to drive the Jews off the face of the earth in every country."

"The Saudis, Egyptians, and those knee kneelers in Jordan will not support us. If it was not for Iran we would have any real support," said Ismail.

"You forget the help we get from the West. The United States and the United Nations have provided us with funds for relief and that has allowed us to take some of the money and shift it to other things. We have been able to construct our tunnels with that same money. They know we have been building and we tell them they are for access to food, fuel, and medicines. They ignore the weapons we smuggle in.

Since 2020 the West has allowed Iran to build their weapons system unhindered. They allowed the supply of arms to the true followers of Islam to fight the colonists and Jewish occupiers. The Islamic world has built up Islamic sympathy in their Western universities influencing the young. I heard the other day that one city in the United States has suggested Sharia law be the city law. Soon Sharia became the only law. But first, we need to remove the State of Israel. Now, how is the security of the tunnels going?" said Rami.

"There are 360 kilometers of tunnels and shafts under Gaza with everything we will need in the coming fight. It was built in part by the good-hearted liberals in the West. What were these people called during the Cold War?" asked Ismail with a smile.

"I think they were called useful idiots! We capture a lot of them on the Chinese thing called TikTok which is filled with disinformation and stupid things. It is surprising how lazy the Americans are in education. We spread a rumor and it spreads like wildfire. We were able to turn the Benghazi attack into an administration political and security blunder. It shows a weak administration unable to react in an emergency. Then the Secretary of State told Congress 'What difference did it matter' or something like that.

"We are able through our people in the States to turn any race incident into an attack against either party and or the administration.

"Now the Democrats are using foreign policy as a weapon against the Republicans. Russia and China are their foreign villains and it is incredible that white democrats are telling the people the biggest fear of terrorism is from White supremacists in their own country. While people of color burn down cities.

"No, Ismail our plan will upset the balance of power in America and Israel will lose the support of a strong allied power with our coming plan."

CHAPTER TWENTY-TWO
Israel Settlements

Don't be in a hurry to change one evil for another.
— Aesop

The First Aliyah (Jews returning to Palestine) began in 1881 with Jews fleeing pogrom in Europe to the traditional homeland of the Hebrew nation. One of these settlements was the kibbutz Kfar Etzion which was abandoned after 1948 and the War for Jewish Independence. This new state was not recognized by the Arab nations with continued conflict of killing, terrorism, propaganda, and at times war.

The Palestinians in 1964 formed a coalition to represent the Palestinian people. That organization was the PLO and was also engaged in acts of violence against civilian populations within Israel and outside of Israel.

Then in 1967, Egypt launched a war with Israel that allowed in the end the Israelis to gain more territory in the Sinai, Gaza Strip, Golan Heights, and West Bank. To protect the State of Israel from these continuous attacks the hardliners in Israel pushed for settlements in the new territories and Kfar Etzion was reestablished.

The PLO was removed from the Gaza Strip and Hamas filled the leadership role with popular support. Between 2000 – 2013 during the Second Intifada Hamas fired 8,749 rockets and 5,047 mortars into Israel. The Palestinians reject any settlement for peace except the removal of the State of Israel.

The right-wing Israeli leadership supported the building of settlements in the occupied territory. Although, the government started to withdraw from those built in the Sinai and Gaza Strip in 1982. There are some 127 legal Israeli settlements in the West Bank and then some illegal Israeli outpost communities.

INIQUITOUSNESS

2023 JERUSALEM ON THE WEST BANK

"Sarah come and join Shiloh and me," asked Rebecca.

"I would love to, but Jeremiah is going to see his mother over in the settlement of *Modi'in llit*. After I see him off, I will come back to visit for a spell," said Sarah as she hurried off.

"I did not know Jeremiah came from the city of *Modi'in llit*. He is not a Haredi or a Zionist!" said Shiloh.

"No, his family lived in Gaza until the government began the forced settlement explosions and removed the final four settlements in 2005. Jeremiah's mother lost her husband that year and married her husband's older brother," said Rebecca.

"What? Do people still follow that old religious custom of *yibbum*?" asked Shiloh.

"Yes, I forgot you are from California and follow the reform community beliefs. Anyway, that is why Jeremiah's mother is living in *Modi'in llit* today. He and his father do not get along very well. They had an argument about military service and Jeremiah left the home," said Rebecca.

"What about military service? Everyone is required to serve in. Israel!" said Shiloh.

"No, that is not true. There is an exception for those in the Haredi community so they can study and keep their faith alive. Jeremiah told his father he was not going to become a rabbi and would do his military service," said Rebecca.

"O.K. so what is the big deal?" asked Shiloh.

"Jeremiah's father is the son of a rabbi that was the son of a rabbi. It is a family tradition to be a rabbi. So, Elijah, Jeremiah's father has turned his back on Jeremiah. That is all I will say, and Jeremiah can tell you more if he wishes to share more. You are Sarah's sister, and she is marrying into an important religious family," Rebecca was interrupted by Sarah.

"I see that when I am not here you talk about me. What is this about an important religious family?" said Sarah.

"I was told that Jeremiah's mother followed the custom of *yibbum* and was, I guess, a little shocked that it is still being practiced. Rebecca told me that Jeremiah and his father do not talk," said Shiloh.

"Well, I guess now is a good time," said Sarah.

"A good time for what Sarah? Is there something you are hiding?" asked Shiloh.

"No, Well yes! I guess so! Jeremiah's mother Naomi and her first husband fell in love and their families did not like each other like the McCoy's and Hatfield's in the States."

"You mean they were feuding and killing each other?" asked Shiloh.

"Not killing, but enemies. Jeremiah's father's family put a lot of pressure on his mother to marry Elijah. She agreed against her mother and father's wishes. She thought that the marriage would bring the families together. It only divided them more if that was possible," said Sarah.

"What was the feud over?" asked Shiloh.

"Jeremiah said it goes back a hundred years or more to Russia. Naomi's family left a village in Russia before the Great War of 1914. They left the village because of the pogroms and one family that had profited from the Russians. That family moved to Israel in 1946 and began to move up in politics with the radical parties and religious influence. Elijah's grandfather voiced the radical demands for land and used the Jordanian government expelling Jews in 1948 as the right of Jews after the Six-Day War in 1967. He was one of the men behind the settlement at *Beitar llit* before the foreign minister Yigal Allon issued his Allon Plan for Palestine territory taken in that war.

"Jeremiah has said his father is a religious man, but the family is corrupt and will do nothing unless it brings in money to the family," said Sarah.

"That is horrible! If they are corrupt why not arrest them?" asked Shiloh.

"You cannot arrest people on rumors and corruption that hides behind rules. Elijah's family hides the corruption within their construction company. There are some 132 legal settlements in the West Bank plus several outpost communities that have no legal status. Each community needs materials to build and Elijah's family owns a small construction materials company. They are a voice for more settlements to hold the Palestinians at bay. Their spokesperson keeps saying the population demands protection at the same time the Haredi are exempt from the very military service they demand," said Rebecca.

"Why are the settlements allowed?" asked Shiloh.

INIQUITOUSNESS

"Israel has been under attack since 1948 with rockets, mortars, kidnappings, murders, and other terrorist attacks. The War of Liberation saw a reaction to some 900,000 Jews being expelled from Arab countries with seventeen thousand just from Jordan. The Arabs that left from Israel were told to come to their Arab brother and they would return and kill the Jews to take back the homeland. In those neighboring countries, the Palestine refugees were placed in camps and not allowed to assimilate into the populations. Those camps became breeding grounds for hate over the years. The problem is that the extremes on each side kept the discussion for a peaceful solution from taking place," said Rebecca.

"What discussions?" asked Shiloh.

"Well, for one, the population of the settlement is not growing at the rate that it used to grow," said Rebecca.

"So?" said Shiloh.

"Before 2000 the growth rate in the settlements was 16% by 2020 the population of the settlements grew at a normal 2.5%. The opinion in Israel is changing with more moderates making their voice heard. Both sides have made mistakes and committed violent acts against the other and when peace seems possible the extremes create a roadblock and put the extreme parties back in power," said Rebecca.

Adam walked up and smiled at Shiloh, "I see I am interrupting I…"

"Don't be silly. We were talking about the settlements. I would like your opinion!" said Shiloh.

"I think that this could end up being bad for me. When a young woman asks a guy for his opinion it usually means she has the answer and he better give the right answer. I would rather keep my opinion and my options open."

Shiloh smiled at Adam, "Oh, Adam I have no opinion and I would like to understand and you were born here. So, give me your honest opinion!"

"Against my better judgment, the Middle East is the birth of the three major religions of Jews, Christians, and Islam with Jerusalem as a holy site for all three. The Jews were removed a number of times by Babylonians, Assyrians, and Egyptians before the Romans came and began the Diaspora in 70 A.D. By then Christianity started to grow and became a power in Europe. They saw the rise of Islam and then Islam's capture of Jerusalem as a sacrilege and came to retake the Holy City in what was called the Crusades.

"When the Crusaders captured Jerusalem, they slaughtered Moslems and Christians in the name of God. Anyone in a robe was an enemy of the Roman church. When Islam retook the Middle East the Jews were allowed to live in peace for a tax.

"By the time of the Great War events were upsetting the political balance in the Middle East with the European powers giving Arabs and Jews false promises. Then the antisemitism in the Western world grew to a malignment level in Germany in the 1930s and the Holocaust from 1941 to 1945 happened.

"The world's guilty of their lack of action to stop the killings they created the State of Israel in 1948. The Arabs never accepted this and told the Palestinians to leave, and they would return to reclaim their land. They did not allow the Palestinians to assimilate and held them in camps that were breeding grounds for hate of Israel. The Palestinians turned to terrorist methods that have been used since the beginning of civilization to force change.

"The PLO and their actions became a threat to other Arab governments. The King of Jordan went to war against the PLO to remove the Black September group from Jordan when they tried a coup. Today Israel is surrounded by hostile nations and various groups within those nations. One country is funding the resistance against Israel.

"The theocratic Republic of Iran has vowed to eliminate Israel and is providing funds to the various terrorist groups that attack Israel on a daily base. Israel responded to this with force to keep the wolves at bay.

"The Islamic right then used this Israeli response to make Israel look like the aggressor. Just look on the web and you will see most of the articles are about the killing of Palestinians and not the Palestine attacks that caused the attacks. When peace is possible radical Islamic leaders provoke an incident to derail the process. So, there you have my opinion!"

"No, Adam, I just had a history lesson! I want your opinion," said Shiloh.

"I knew it! I am trapped," said Adam. "But then again you are right. I do get carried away. So, I feel that the extremes on both sides are controlling to direction of the policy. The extremists in Gaza cheer with every rocket and celebrate in the streets when every mortar lands on civilians in Israel.

"Then we respond with precision-targeted spots where they feel that they are being attacked for no cause. It is a never-ending cycle and Iran and other hard Islamic leaders continue to provide support and refuse to compromise because for them the only solution to the problem extremist is the complete destruction of Israel.

"The extremists on our side fall into two basic groups. Those who want to expand the territory of Israel and those who want protection from terrorists. This last group is a little harder to separate for the many different reasons for obtaining some kind of protection."

"The Zionist?" asked Shiloh.

"No, Zionist is a term of the past that is misused today just like antisemitism."

"What do you mean that antisemitism is misused?" asked Sarah.

"The prefix means against the Semitic and is a reference to a family of languages that include Hebrew, Arabic, and Aramaic. So, if one is to be antisemitic the Islamic world is filled with self-haters. The word Zionism for the re-establishment of a homeland for the Jews of the diaspora of 70 A.D. by the Romans.

"Theodor Herzl in Switzerland developed the idea of a Jewish homeland that would be someplace in the world. There were several suggestions from Africa to South America. Palestine became the focus of a homeland for Jews fleeing persecution in Europe. Some five Alias of Jews who came to Palestine. The first Aliya was supported by the Rothschild banking family. Many of those who came to Palestine during that period left after a year or two. The second Aliya came from Poland and Russian pogroms. That was followed by Russian Jews fleeing the Great pogroms in Russia. The fourth Aliya were Jews fleeing Poland after the Great War. Then the fifth Aliya was the German Jews fleeing Germany and Holocaust actions and memories. See, I cannot help giving history lessons."

"Adam, that is why we love You!" said Shiloh smiling and taking his hand.

He looked at her and smiled.

IN THE TOWN OF RAMALLAH ON WEST BANK

"You know George this town was a majority of Christians when my grandfather was alive. Today there are only 50,000 of us in the West Bank and this town has a majority of Muslims," said Salim.

"I know this town is an old Biblical town and was reestablished as a Christian town back in the 16thcentury with Arabs and Christians living together under the Ottomans That changed with the European mandates, then once more with the Jordanians, again with the Israelis after 1967 war, and now shared power under the Palestine Authority. Yasser Arafat made the West Bank the *de facto* political, economic, and cultural capital of Palestine. We are lucky the Muslim population here stayed with the PLO and did not join the radicals of Hamas in Gaza," said George as Samyah and Suzan walked up.

"What are you guys discussing so intently?" asked Suzan.

"I just happened to mention that we Christians are no longer the majority in this town and were given a history lesson. Thank you for my rescue!" said Salim.

"Why were you bringing that up?" asked Samyah.

"I guess I was thinking about my grandfather and the stories he told about growing up here. They seem to be simpler times when he was a small boy," said Salim.

"Salim, things change. You should know better than the rest of us!" said Suzan.

"Why is that?" asked Salim.

"Ahmad how many Christians do you know that are married to a Muslim?" asked George.

"Falasteen and I know a few and we get together," said Ahmad.

"Yes, but how are you both treated in your families?" asked Sarah.

"Most accept us in their homes."

"That answer tells me a lot. That they are not all that happy with the inter-religious marriage. I understand that. My American family is finding it hard that I am marrying an Israeli. In part because I will not be in the States and safe from the political problems here, especially here in the West Bank. They remember the two Israeli Defense Force reservists who were lynched, mutilated, and dragged through the streets. They also can see, that when that episode is looked up on the web it gives more information about the Palestinians than the two soldiers. We are Christians and Moslems living together in the West Bank and since the Six Day War our peace is not the same," said Sarah.

"I understand what you are saying. The radicals in my family talk behind my back about Christians being hidden Jews behind a Cross. I have caught one of my uncles doing it with his friends. He said it was a joke. I told him I did not consider it a good joke," said Ahmad.

"What did he say?" asked Shiloh.

"He laughed and said he was sorry if he upset me. The others in the group I could feel it was true. I would leave this place if it was easier, but the Arab nations will not take Palestinian refugees and the Western world is turning against Muslim immigrants because of the rape and murders that are committed by Muslim immigrants in different countries. They are just like the Crusaders and see Christian or Moslem Palestinians as terrorists," said Ahmad.

"What about the Jews on the West Bank/" asked George

"The Jewish problem will take care of itself for the fact that the majority Jewish population on the West Bank is in decline. The lack of service from Israel, lack of employment opportunities, and low funds being divided from the six settlement divisions are part of the reasons for the decline. Maybe in time Jews, Christians, and Moslems will live in peace tighter." said Ahmad.

"Well it is September 2023 and the Middle East is making some progress at peace with the Saudi Crown Prince talking about the normalization with the State of Israel," said George.

"I do not want to burst your hope George but the men with my uncle were made-
up of Fatah, and Hamas, and there was one member from Hizballah. I do not think that guy was from the Gaza Strip for he looked like an Iranian and sounded Iranian. As I walked up I heard that the Iranian said the plan was almost complete and one of the other guys asked about the Christian here. That was when my uncle's joke came out. I feel like I have been watched ever since. Something big is being planned," said Ahmad.

"Well, we cannot do anything about today let us go and celebrate with our friends," said Samyah as they turned to go to a local café," said Falasteen as she walked into the small group.

CHAPTER TWENTY-THREE
Subversion

An investment in knowledge pays the best interest.
— Benjamin Franklin

We learn from failure, not from success.
— Bram Stoker

Learning is not attained by chance; it must be sought for with ardor and diligence.
— Abigail Adams

Education is what remains after one has forgotten what one has learned in school.
— Albert Einstein

2023 Lecture Hall

The lecture hall was packed with students most were on their phones and the rest were looking at their laptops or digital notebook. In the back of the room were Dan, Harriet, Naomi, and Jose. "I think this will be my best class this semester," said Harriet.

"Why is that?" asked Jose.

"A friend told me that Professor Andrei's lectures were presented with a real balance of the history," said Harriet.

"I also like the professor. I took another class from him and his lectures were the best," said Dan.

"Well, time will tell us if you are both right," said Jose as the professor walked into the room.

"Welcome to World History. I am Professor Andrei and in this section on Latin American, we will be discussing the American government's involvement in Guatemala, Nicaragua, and Cuba during the 1950s and 1960 with the actions being done under the idea of the Monroe Doctrine and the American paternalistic for the control of the Western Hemisphere. I have chosen these three countries as they were major targets of the CIA and operations during the Cold War to control the Red's infiltration into Central and South America.

"During the first for two weeks, we will cover Nicaragua from the Filibuster and Dollar Diplomacy to the intervention of 1906 with the military occupation of that country. This American expansionist has a long history in Nicaragua as far back as 1855 when the filibuster William Walker invaded the country and took control for a short while. Then during the Spanish-American war saw a more active role in the American expansion movement collecting territories in Latin America and the Pacific.

"By the Cold War, the American government was concerned and began an active position to control the spread of communism. The American government began active support for dictators like Anastasio Somoza Debayle in Nicaragua until he was driven from power by the Sandinistas.

"When Somoza left office the old Somoza military leaders formed a counter group called the Contras to fight the Sandinistas who were on the Left. The U.S. government began to fund the Contra who represented the Right. This funding was in direct violation of the Boland Amendment.

We will see that government lies, weapons, and drugs were used to support American foreign policy.

"When the U.S. Congress refused to support the Contra's, the then President coined the term 'Freedom Fighters' to win support. The funds were approved, and the fight continued.

"Next, we will move to Guatemala, and the United Fruit Company by 1950 was making $65 million from banana sales and other fruit. When the local government was acting against the American business community the CIA's used covert actions to help disrupt that nation's stability. The CIA plans for *Coup d'état* were a standard operation for power change in foreign nations to combat communism.

"The *Coup d'Etat* in 1954 allowed the CIA more operational control in the country and they set up training camps for anti-Castro soldiers for an invasion of our last country in this section. From there we will move to the numerous government plans to remove Fidel Castro from power in Cuba before and after the Bay of Pigs Invasion and the Cuban Missile Crisis."

He went on with more on what the class would cover and more details on the readings for the class. At the end of the class, he told them there would be a few extra curriculum sections on how protestors are formed and how they organize resistance to the powers. He told them they had the syllabus with the required books and films that are suggested for a more complete understanding of American foreign policy during the 20th Century in the western hemisphere. Everyone should have the first readings on the syllabus ready for the next meeting. "Thank you for your attention," said the professor as he walked away from the podium.

"I was told this was a great class to take and that Professor Andrei was the best instructor to get everyone involved in the class," said Harriet.

"What did you think Naomi?" asked Dan.

"I would rather hold my opinion until I have heard a few lectures," said Naomi.

"I, for one like what he has said so far. My family came from Nicaragua and fled from the Somoza government. I had uncles who fought beside Daniel Ortega. In fact, I was named after Ortega. Did you know he was the only communist leader to willing step down from power when he lost a popular election? I think this class will give an objective view of American foreign policy," said Dan.

INIQUITOUSNESS

"My family came from Cuba after Castro took power and Castro's brother Raul and that murderous thug Che Guevara killed three of my uncles at La Cabana. I will see how the Cuban revolution is presented before I say my opinion of the class," said Jose.

"I did not know your family came from Cuba," said Dan.

"It is something we do not talk about much. My family was not part of the elite in the first group of Cubans that came across to Florida. Once we reached the States we moved to northern California."

"If your family was not in the elite in Cuba why did your uncles die at La Cabana prison?" asked Harriet.

"They were army NCOs in the Cuban Army and that made them targets as anti-communist. As soon as the Castro's came to power the trials, if you call them that, were held and the executions started. Some say there may have been as many as a hundred thousand. I just know that Che seemed to enjoy the killing personally. La Cabana prison is where he was labeled the 'Butcher' and yet the liberals in the world still revere him as the perfect revolutionary and have his face printed on shirts," said Jose.

"Che was an educated man and wrote books on the revolution. Don't you think that you might be biased because of your family history," asked Dan.

"Dan, have you read anything that Che wrote?"

"To be honest, No!"

"What people tell you is always different from the actual subject. Hitler was a murderous thug who killed 11 million people in concentration and Death camps. He is the most hated individual in the last 200 years. Yet, Comrade Stalin was trained to become a priest and he was also a well-educated individual. During his reign of power Stalin was responsible for 20 million Russians dying of famine, in the Gulags, and in the numerous Purges that ended in execution. Yet, he is not viewed at the same level as Hitler. Both Hitler and Stalin killed targeted groups for the greater good. One is presented as an evil monster and the other as a misguided reformer," said Jose.

"I do not think you are right. They are both seen as evil!" said Harriet

"Really, Harriet? When people refer to real evil actions by an individual or a group it is Hitler or Nazi, not Stalin or communism. In fact, communism is still viewed as an acceptable political party despite its history of mass murder in whatever country it took power. No, Che is not what the popular image is of him," said Jose.

"Well, I think this will be a great class and I am looking forward to it,'" said Harriet.

"I have another class in 15 minutes. I'll see you tomorrow," said Jose.

"I have to get going also. I will meet you both at the pub at five," said Dan to Harriet and Naomi.

"Jose, why don't you stop by also?" said Naomi.

"Thanks, I will try to stop by."

THREE WEEKS LATER:

The parking lot was empty on a Sunday morning except for Professor Andrei and a dozen students from the Islamic club. The students carried various types of helmets from motorcycles to sports helmets and masks.

"Professor, should I get some trashcan lids?" asked Sandy.

"No, today we will focus on passive resistance suggested by men like Henry David Thoreau, Mahatma Gandhi, Martin Luther King Jr., and Cesar Chavez. Violence gets attention but draws, the attention away from the perpetrator of the violence. Passive resistance put to focus on the other side that will use force to resist or remove the protesters," said the Professor.

"Then why the helmets? It would be better to have heads cracked for the cameras," said Peggy.

"You are thinking of 1968 and the Democratic Convention. The violence of the police at that time was viewed by the public as horrible. Yet, that violence caused the Democrats to lose the election. Both sides in that struggle looked bad and the protesters created an image that they wanted chaos and not political and social change," said the Professor.

"So, why protest if it is a waste of time?" asked Peter.

"I did not say protests were a waste of time. When Thoreau wrote *Civil Disobedience,* he was telling people to break bad laws. By breaking the bad laws and arresting everyone that broke a bad law then who would be the jailer? When he was placed in jail for defining the law someone asked what he was doing in there. He responded by saying the question you should be asking is why are you out here!"

"I do not understand?" said Peter.

"A protest has one objective and that is to draw attention and make the oppressor look bad. One way to make the oppressors look bad is to have them drag individuals away from the group. So, if you all will lock arms you will see how difficult it is to remove one individual from the line. Then once an individual is drawn away from the group that individual should drop to the ground and become a lump like a baby. Do not resist and fight back the police dragging a person by force is a bad image. Also, for every person taken from the protest line it requires two to three of the oppressors," said the Professor.

"What about chanting at the police?" asked Sandy.

"All verbal conversation should be used to provoke negative actions from the oppressors. They have the responsibility to act without malice. It will not matter what is said or done for they must act with restraint of civil behavior and not overreact. Overreaction makes the news and headlines. So, everyone except Martin and Emanuel, I want the rest to join your arms at the elbows. Now, Martin will you both try to break the line."

The two boys went up to the smallest female, Sally, and tried to pull her away from the group. Their action caused a brief struggle with Sally kicking Martin in the groin. He immediately fell to the ground holding himself.

"Oh, My God, Martin I am so sorry," said Sally as she bent over to help as he rolled on the ground. "Marin I am so sorry, so sorry!"

After Martin recovered the Professor asked everyone, "What did we learn from this little exercise?"

"That Martin got knocked over by his girlfriend," said Peter to the laughter of the students.

Sally started to go after Peter with a kick. "Hold on for a minute you two. This is why passive resistance must be learned and practiced. Once it turns into a brawl it turns the focus back onto the demonstrators and not the oppressors. Once an image is created it is hard to reverse that image. I again refer to 1968. Many of us were pushing for change and the change we got was the Law and Order of Richard Nixon.

It has taken all this time to cause change for rights for all groups and to call out the colonizers and oppressors for their actions. Look at the political nature of America today. There is a democratic-socialist party, Green party, various Progressive parties, Libertarian Party, the Forward party, the Constitution party, and Antifa, plus the Democrat and Republican parties just to name a few," said the Professor.

"Professor the Antifa groups create violence and act like the old anarchist? It is an organization that does not like any form of government and yet it seems to have some form of governmental control," said Harriet.

"I know you all have questions, and many will be answered in the next class. Now, for everyone that is enough today. I hope you understand a little better how protesters must behave and act today. I will see everyone in class tomorrow," said the Professor as he went to his car and drove off.

Most of the group fell away and a few stayed to talk.

"So, Harriet we have now been to several classes and have moved from the three nations he introduced at the start of the semester. What do you think of Professor Andrei what is your opinion so far?" asked Jose.

"I think he is presenting a very balanced view of American foreign policy over the years that he has covered. The Monroe Doctrine is nothing more than an imperialistic weapon to control the poorer people of the world."

"Harriet, you cannot be serious that he is balanced. The Monroe Doctrine was used to keep the powerful European nations from dividing up the New World after Spanish power collapsed. The U.S. issued the document without a joint agreement with Great British. The new nation of America knew the British would follow the American policy to keep the other powerful European nations from carving out parts of the West," said Dan.

"The professor is still very balanced in the history," said Harriet.

"How can you say that? He is an anti-sematic and has slipped Zionism, colonialism, and imperialism in almost every lecture and he even suggested that the Rothchild's bankers were behind the funding dictators in Latin America," said Naomi.

"So, who are the Rothschilds?" asked Harriet.

"Oh! Brother!," said Dan.

"Don't you make fun of me Dan? I am not an economics or history major!" said Harriet.

"I am sorry, but the Rothchilds are known as one of the biggest banker families in the world. I just found it odd you did not know that. I am sorry," said Dan.

"Dan, the first rule of dating, is never to question your partner," said Jose.

"You should keep that in mind!" said Naomi.

"I still do not understand the antisemitism relationship?" said Harriet.

"The Rothschilds supported the first Zionist farming movement of Jews to Israel. The name is a way to remind the Jews of their homeland. Palestine was not the only location suggested at the time. The Jews that were spread in nations all over the world were separated from the groups in those nations. Religion is a common divide of groups even within the same religion look at the Christian faith. Protestant against Catholicism and within each of those there is a dispute on how to practice the faith. The Islam and Jewish faiths have the same problems of interpretation of the word.

"This country has a checkered past with civil rights. The African American group is not alone in being separated from the mainstream of society. The Jews have been in this country and built synagogues as early as 1654. New Port, Rhode Island has the oldest surviving synagogue in the United States. We, the Jews, have been here for a long time, and only in the last 60 years have we been allowed in some of the upper-class clubs. Antisemitism, racism, and anti-Catholic opinions pop up now and then. But recently the new wave of immigrants and many universities have begun to create a shift from tolerance to outright hate of Israel and any Jewish person," said Naomi.

"That is because of the Settlements that Israel has built on the land of Palestine! Professor Andrei explained in the last class meeting," said Harriet.

"Harriet, do you ever question what Professor Andrei is telling us?" asked Jose.

"Professor has two Doctorate degrees in Western Civilization and Western intellectual thought. Who am I to question Him?" asked Harriet.

"You are a student, and the job of every student is to ask questions for that is how we are expected to find excellence. The early Greeks used the word Arete for finding perfection or excellence. Socrates looked for Arete by asking questions. That is one of the many things the Greeks gave the modern world," said Jose.

"Are you telling me not to believe anything the professor tells us?" asked Harriet.

"Not at all, but you should question it outside the classroom to protect your grade. Harriet, how many times did the professor use the word oppressors in the last class?" asked Jose.

"I do not know. Several times I guess."

"Who was he referring to as the oppressors?" asked Jose.

"I did not really think about it, I guess at times the United States and the Israeli's foreign policy markers for allowing the settlements in Palestine."

"The professor presented true facts and left out important details. It is true the Israelis have built settlements on occupied land. He did not tell the reason for that from the Israeli side.

"That land has been occupied by Canaanites, Jews, Assyrians, Babylonians, Egyptians, Crusaders, and Ottoman Turks just to name a few and now the Palestinians claim it as their traditional homeland. Today their Arab neighbors have been willing to help kill the Jews and yet today they refuse to allow Palestinians in their countries as refugees.

"The professor has his agenda along with many professors in the American universities today. They are the products of the 1960s and what they call the New Left. That group is always willing to point out the faults in the presenting of the American history story by calling it imperialistic and the oppressors of the weak," said Jose.

"Well, they are right to point out those faults. Look at the history of slavery in this and the Japanese in this country. It is horrible and there should be amends made," said Harriet.

"True, history needs to be explained in complete context. Not with simple half facts that are stated as the complete truth," said Jose.

"The professor has presented a complete history of slavery. He gave both sides in the discussion!" said Harriet.

"Really! When, did the African slave trade start?" asked Dan.

"You all are ganging up on me! I do not want to talk about this anymore!" said Harriet.

"I am not doing that. I am trying to explain a fuller picture of the slave trade. The Arabs were in the trade some 600 years before the first Europeans. The Portuguese entered the slave market around 1444 on the west coast of Africa. The Europeans expanded the trade by arming West Coast African tribes with guns so those tribes could move into the interior of the continent to collect slaves for the European market.

'When they did this, it upset the political, economic, and social structures in the interior. It was the Africans who did the collecting and selling on the coast and on the East coast of Africa.

"The Arabs controlled the Eastern coast and had been doing it so long that the language of Swahili language developed. That trade is still a pattern in the Arab world today under different names. It is easy to point out the European and American slave trade and all of its horrible attributes. But that is not the whole story of slavery and the elite Western world is not the sole cause for the practice.

"That is all I will say and I am not trying to gang up on you. The professor has a point of view and he is pushing that point every class. I come from a country that saw communism take control and when my family left and came to the United States they found freedom with all its faults. The professor seems to be melancholy about the old Soviet Union," said Jose.

"If you are so smart, why are you taking the freshman class in history," asked Harriet.

"My counselor, who is no longer at this university, screwed up my records, and when it was all strengthened out I needed missing credits and this class provided those credits. Part of the problem was I transferred from an east coast university and that added to the problem, for their units did not always match this university's credits. Once I leave here I have been admitted to an Ivy League school to continue my doctorate in the Slave Trade," said Jose.

"Why did you choose the slave trade?" asked Dan.

"My family can trace our history back to Spain in the Extremadura area and were with the first conquistadors. Over all those years the family had mixed or married into native populations and slave populations. So, I find the issue important on an intellectual and personal level. I guess that is the simplest way to explain my interest," said Jose.

"I am getting hungry who wants to go and get something to eat and drink," asked Dan.

"Harriet and I will be happy to join the two of you," said Naomi.

"I am not sure Harriet wants to come with me right now," said Jose.

"Don't be silly Jose why would I give up the chance to make you feel bad? Besides you will need to apologize with more feelings," said Harriet as she smiled and everyone laughed.

CHAPTER TWENTY-FOUR
International Money

> Give all the power to the many, they will oppress the few.
> Give all the power to the few, they will oppress the many.
> — Alexander Hamilton

The Articles of Confederation joined the thirteen colonies into a confederation of independent states. Each state was allowed to make treaties, to print its own money and local bank were allowed to print notes for financial purposes. The economy had no unifying unit. Then Shays Rebellion began the call for reform. The meeting in Philadelphia tossed out the Articles and wrote the U.S. Constitution.

The first Secretary of Treasure Alexander Hamilton placed the new government on solid financial feet. First, he combined the national and state debts into one national debt. Then the plan called for the issuing of securities and bonds to pay off the debt and he pushed through the Congress a National Bank in an agreement with Thomas Jefferson. Hamilton argued the national debt would make America financially stronger.

His plan tax on whiskey set off a rebellion in western Pennsylvania.

2023 SEPTEMBER

The team had gathered in the office for an update on the progress that was going very slow but now seemed to be getting some breaks. Information had been collected for several years and was now connecting several different pieces together.

"Mary Jo, you have the floor bring us up to date," said the director.

"It has taken a while with a lot of help to put this thing into some kind of understanding. I am not sure we have a complete picture yet. This money trail goes back some 60 years. However, I will only focus on the most recent events of 2015.

"In 2015 the administration wanted a peace and nuclear deal with the Iranians and the Iranians wanted their money that we had tried up in foreign banks. The American banking laws were very specific on how transactions were to be done. That administration tried to sidestep its own financial system sanctions on Iran by allowing the Iranians to transfer funds from one bank to another and converting the funds into U.S. dollars and then into euros.

"All seemed to be working until the American bankers and their lawyers looked at American laws and said, no we cannot legally do this for they would be violating the banking laws and could be held responsible. This stopped the transfer of billions of dollars to the Iranian government.

"When the question was presented to the administration from Congress the administration denied the whole thing. Then there was the administration effort that dealt with an American deserter who was held as a hostage. In the end, Iran got the money, but I could not find out the process. A colleague in banking suggested that the funds were transferred in smaller amounts. He suggested Indian rupee be converted to dollars and then into euros. That was done by 2016."

"Excuse me, Mary Jo, you said 60 years. Why the 60-some years?" asked Nick.

"I was just about to get to that if I may continue,"

"Sorry, you are right. I should have waited for the full report. Once again I am sorry please continue," said Nick.

"Thank you, Agent Thomson!" Mary Joe said with a smile. "Now, this month this administration has agreed to release six billion in frozen

Iranian funds that were frozen by the last administration for American National interest according to a top administration official then. Once again hostages were involved.

"That money I am sure will or has found its way to various terrorist groups. I was able to trace some of the funds to banks that were involved in the stamp case that our agent Thomson and the consultant C.E. closed recently.

"Those radical individuals for the most part were poor money managers. That is not to say they were dumb for they did some pretty fancy trading with digital funds. It was with their personal funds that they made their mistakes.

"Now, I was able to trace funds to Blanco's organization from a front bank in Germany for the Iranians and payments made to a high official in the Communist Party in Beijing. The money trail ends in Beijing. Their real mistake was the American dollar. It is still the currency of finance with all other currencies used to convert from one to another and back into dollars or at times into euros. As far as I can tell those funds have not left their last location," said Mary Jo.

"I think I may have part of that answer. We picked up a coyote who was transporting illegals across the border two days ago. We were able to arrest the coyote but his passengers all escaped," said Casimir.

"Who are you?" asked Mary Jo

"My fault everyone this is Casimir Dubanowski an undercover agent of the Border Patrol. I had him added to the team yesterday. Please go on Casimir," said the director.

"Well, this poor guy just agreed to run these folks into the U.S. in a beat-up van. He is just 15 years old, and he was hoping to win a place in the cartel. After he was arrested, he was told he was being held as a terrorist."

"Wait a minute! What was the reason for the terrorist charges?" asked Nick.

"I am getting to that if I can continue? What is it with you Nick?" asked Mary Jo.

"Once again I am sorry. But in this case, if it is connected to the last case, then guys are without feelings and innocent lives mean nothing. I just cannot help but worry. Actually, I am scared of what may be going to happen," said Nick.

"I agree with Nick, these people are ruthless with other people's lives," said C.E.

"I think we all understand your concerns, so let us stay focused," said the director.

"I do not know what other case you are talking about, but I would say this one has me and my boss worried. So, when this kid was told the charges he said his boss was paid a bundle of money to get these guys into the country fast for one big special operation," said Casimir.

"Did he know what the operation was about?" asked Nick.

"No!"

"Then why all the attention on him?" asked C.E.

"Not on him, it was what they were carrying. Each of the eight guys and three women had with them these!" Casimir handed out the flyer calling for massive protests on an unknown topic one side flyer. The other side had instructions on how to obstruct the police.

"Something is being planned here in this country and we have no idea what it is and this is serious," said the director and turned back to Casimir.

"Then this morning, agents arrested a young female on this side of the border with a stack of these. She said she was told by a friend to hand them out on a college campus in the area," Casimir.

"Who was this friend?" asked Agent Barns.

"She said the girl was a friend of a friend and only knew her as Sally something. They only meet at a campus club for political action. When she asked about the flyer, her friend said everyone will know when to act," said Casimir.

"Alright, then what do we know about this club?" asked the director,

"It is one of several chapters on the universities that were started two years ago by a Russian dissident professor. Professor Andrei fled west as a young man and became a noted scholar on world history. His lectures are centered on the left of the political spectrum. His lectures are a bit odd and radical for someone who fled the Soviet system. He is crafty with his words," said agent Peterson.

"Would you care to explain?" asked C.E.

"I sat in his lecture when I was in university. The professor was presented as a Soviet dissident and then during his lectures, he would praise individuals in the Soviet system like the 'Bare Foot biologist' Trofin

Lysenko. If you do not know him he was a fraud and ruined Soviet agriculture for 20 years.

"At another time he remarked that Mao had saved the poor peasants of China by his good laws. Yet, he dismissed and ignored the millions of Chinese who died because of Mao's reform laws and following Lysenko's policies. Most of his lectures focus on the past bad deeds of American foreign and domestic policies. Most students left his classes with a negative opinion of America in their subconscious," said agent Peterson.

"The director and I met with Professor Andrei not long ago in a Chinese espionage case on that campus. In fact, we interrupted a lesson on riot control. Only to me, it seemed more like how to resist control," said C.E.

"That is classic Professor Andrei. Tell you one thing and do the opposite. His was the only class that I had with a minimum grade to pass. I had challenged him on Trofim's theory of evolution in a research paper. When I asked about the poor grade, I was told by the teacher's assistant that my paper did not meet the standards in the syllabus. I then went to the administration to challenge the grade and was told that I had no grounds for an appeal.

"I took my law diploma and started working for the FBI. At a reunion I met a fellow grad student of that same university and his story was that he was forced to transfer because of Professor Andrei. Anyways, I know the professor, and he is a jerk and I can see him behind these flyers!" said agent Peterson.

"To tell the truth our people are at a loss of what this is all about! Now, with these flyers even more if he is connected somehow. However, I think that C.E. and Nick have an update."

"Yes, we were able to get Mary Jo tied into the banking network of the old case and then we went to follow up on Diego's old organization that has been revised by this Leocadio Blanco. It seems that he is now into smuggling humans as much as drugs. My source in Panama said that Blanco is the number one smuggler of Arabs and Chinese into the States. The Arabs are paying top dollar, that is five to ten grand per person and the Chinese have a cut rate because of a deal with Asian drugs," said Nick.

"What about Asian drugs?" asked Peterson.

"That starting to make sense now, the Asian drug sellers control the

European market and Latin America controls the western hemisphere in heroin, and marijuana. The Chinese have been selling chemicals to the cartels to mix their own little pills of death. I've been hearing of a deal with the Chinese. They want to get more people into the country faster and are now using the open border as a way," said Casimir.

"O.K. we now have a connection between the Mexican drug guy, a connection to China," said the director.

CHAPTER TWENTY-FIVE
Funding Terrorism

The house built by the upright man is destroyed by the treacherous man.

— Sumerian Proverbs

In 1879 Iran revolutionaries took over the American Embassy and held Americans male hostages for 444 days. Every year after that the Iranian revolutionaries have funded and committed acts of terrorism around the world in the name of Islam. Funding Hezbollah, Hamas, al-Qaeda, al-Qassim Brigades, Isis and other groups in Iraq, Bahrain, Syria, Yemen, Palestine and others. For example:

In the year 2021 there were 26 international events of terror that were linked to Iran.

In the year 2022 there were 65 international events of terror that were linked to Iran.

This month of 2023 there were some 60 international events of terror linked to Iran.

2023 September 6

Israel

Rachel was sitting behind the desk reading reports from the night before when the door opened and Micah walked in without knocking and sat across from her. He looked like he had not slept in the last 72 hours. His clothes were covered with dirt.

"Micah you look like you have been busy! What is so important this early?"

"I am tired of sitting and waiting for the next rocket attack. I just returned from investigating the most recent tunnel."

"Why? That was discovered weeks ago."

"Right, and part of it was collapsed before we found it. Why do you think that was done?"

"Most likely poor construction techniques."

"You cannot be serious. We have found far too many that would compare to the construction methods of the Channel Tunnel from France to England. NO! Something is up and this tunnel was a decoy. I went through it again last night with a crew. After a little hard work and digging the walls of the tunnel did not extend beyond a few dozen meters from the collapse area. I know something is being planned. I just do not know what or when."

"I believe you. We had an agent in the West Bank send his daughter over to us last night with a message. That said an important Iranian meet with a member of the Hamas military group and were going over plans for some coming operation in Gaza. All he heard was the operation should derail the Saudi Crown Prince's peace plan. Plus, the Kurds have been telling the Americans about a senior Iranian military man and Mexican cartel contacts meetings with the Chinese businessman in Turkey about Gaza."

"What do you think? I am worried this might be big and we are in the dark!" said Micah.

"I have been sitting behind this desk for three and half years and during that time I have recorded nineteen different terrorist organizations that are on our border waiting to take us out. Each year hundreds of rockets have been fired into Israel from different directions. Do I think there could be a connection? I would be a fool if I did not think so! The problem is how do we piece each bit of information together to make a coherent picture?"

Lebanon

"Charbel the money has been sent from our contact in Iran. The bitcoins are ready to be used. You can see that the weapons dealer is paid for his shipment. Why has he insisted that the funds go through Bitcoin?" said Qateel.

"Bitcoin is the fastest and best way today to hide currency transactions from any of the Terrorist activities in the Finance market. Tracking Programs they use today have not caught up to the Cryptocurrency. Bitcoin is the preferred bank of illegal finance," replied Charbel.

"How is that possible?" asked Qateel.

"To put it in simple terms, it is that bitcoin is a Block Chain and that is a network of independent computers networked together. They are encrypted and are mathematically secure. To enter into the system one first installs what is called a wallet on a computer. This wallet controls the transactions with a code. If the owner of the wallet forgets the code the transaction is in limbo and unretrievable.

"Once a wallet is obtained, money is deposited into an online exchange that connects buyers and sellers, and the final step is to buy a bitcoin much like buying a share of stock. That is the simple explanation, but it is hard to follow the money," said Charbel.

"Then there is nothing to worry about on the money. How about the operation with the Hezbollah military units we have set in motion? asked Qateel.

"It is all set and will be closely controlled by hand-picked men," said Samir.

Iran

"The rockets to the Houthis in Yemen? Did they arrive?" asked Hadi.

"Yes, Erfan said they just arrived and two were used on an Indian ship as a test. The Americans were able to knock the rockets out before they hit the target. However, it is keeping their focus away from our other plans. The Western press is focused on the shipping lane to the Red Sea," said Hadi.

"The Saudis now appeared to be close to an agreement with the Jews. The journalist there has normalized criticisms for the Palestinians," said Erfan.

"This planned operation will knock the wind out of any cooperation between the Israelis and the Arab world. If everything goes as planned, this so-called peace plan is done. The Indians and Chinese are pushing the British and American influence out of the Middle East. The Chinese are pushing their economic plan for a Belt Road Initiative. It is also keeping them off balance. That is why we need to keep the door that appears to be open to western inspectors of our nuclear sites," said Hadi.

"Also, our last shipment of rockets entered Gaza last night. So, everything is in place," said Hadi.

"Excellent! Let's keep these Red Sea attacks limited until we need to increase them once the plan is in operation," said Erfan.

"One last thing we need to check and that is the U.N. workers," said Hadi.

"We have a number of them embedded with Hamas," said Cyrus.

"What will happen if the UN discovers their participation?"

"The UN is a joke. There are almost 50 nations on the U.N Human Rights Committee and Cuba and China are just two of the nations to oversee human rights! Those are the guardians of Human Rights. They hate the Israelis almost as much as the Palestinians," said Cyrus.

IRAQ

"These attacks on U.S. military bases have not been reported that much on western T.V., but the killing of Tiba al-Ali has caused a real blow to our image," said Rebaz.

"Who?" asked Haval.

"She was a woman living in Turkey with a man, and they made YouTube videos. Then she came home to see her family and her father went into her room one night and strangled her and condemned her to the family for her lifestyle of a whore. He confesses to the killing and many people saw it as an Honor killing. The whole thing caused a large protest here and around the world. The father was later sentenced to six months in jail," said Rebaz.

"Did that happen about the same time that the Swedish Embassy was set on fire by a radical? He claimed it was an insult to the *Quran* and was a desecration. Anyway, that was what the radical fire bugs told his captors."

"It might have been about the same time for I was in Sweden when it happened. It was big news there and it sparked more unrest with the Moslem immigrants. The Swedes suspended operation at their embassy if I remember right."

"Yes, and it shifts the world press to another issue and of the attacks on the U.S. military."

"Since 2020 Iran has helped us take the war to the Americans with some 150 drones, rockets, mortars, and a few close-range ballistic missiles attack on American bases in Syria and Iraq. The American administration and press ignore the attacks as just a nuance with a few injuries.

SAUDI ARABIA

"The Crown Prince is moving close to an Israeli agreement," said Abdullah.

"What about Hamas? Are they playing nice?" asked Saad.

"No! But only Iran and their proxies support Hamas. Those groups oppose us for now and will try to disrupt our efforts. However, we are gaining the moderate states' support for our peace position," said Abdullah.

"If we can do this, we stand a chance to become the Middle East leader. This could end the cold war we are playing with Iran. We need to remove the Iranian nuclear threat and that will be done with the United States and Israel. Those secret meetings we held with Israel back in 2015 set the stage for these talks," said Ibrahim.

"The Palestine situation has to be settled before and real peace can come!" said Ahmad.

"The work done by the last President's son-in-law went a long way with the Crown Prince," said Abdullah.

"Let us hope the radicals do not do something to set off a new war," said Saad.

"I was informed by an agent in Gaza that members of Hezbollah, Al-Qassane, Al-Nasser Salah al-Deen Brigades, and the Houthis were seen in Gaza in the last few months," said Saad.

"Do we know Why?"

"No, I have concerns and have people looking into it."

"As soon as I find out anything you will be informed."

2023 SEPTEMBER 20,

"We were lucky this week and were able to have two independent individuals who were able to make some connections between the dots. One was an Iranian woman named Nicole who was the victim of an attempted honor killing. It seems she was brought out of Iran by a CIA agent a few years ago. The agent said this Nicole was a valuable asset in Iran and that her life would be in danger if left behind. It was believed that her husband was arrested and eliminated with his father and brothers for various criminal crimes and for being traitors to the State of Iran the night she left.

However, it seems that her husband was not taken into custody at the time. It was our luck that this individual was Rashid Nicole's ex-husband whom she escaped from in Iran. His family was very powerful until Nika, now going by the name Nicole, escaped.

Information about the family's connections with the Russians came to light the night she escaped and the father and brothers were arrested and died in custody. Rashid escaped the roundup and was in Iraq at the time. He is still wanted in Iran for the rape and murder of a daughter of a high-ranking general in the Revolutionary Guard. Anyway, last week Rashid was in this country for a meeting with our Mexican friend when he saw his former wife Nicole at a shopping center and followed her home and was planning to kill her that night," said the director.

"I am guessing he did not make good on that plan," said C.E.

"You can say that these guys think they can do whatever they want with women. That the women will not fight back. He broke into her home and burst into her bedroom later that night yelling he was going to kill the rat whore that ruined his family and his name. Unfortunately for him, she had noticed him following her and was waiting and when he came into the room she shot him in the groin and he fell to the floor crying and was still crying when the police arrived. The funny thing was as they loaded him in the ambulance she walked up to him and said 'Rashid, never bring a knife to a gun fight'. The cops broke out laughing."

"How did this come to our attention?" asked Nick.

"Rashid wanted a deal and told the police he had important information for the FBI. He said he was afraid he would be sent back to Iran. He told the officers he had information on a drug cartel and a terrorist plot. That was what pulled us into the case. However, the bullet that entered the groin bounced off a bone and cut the femoral artery and he died in surgery before we could get someone there to question him," said the director.

"What about Nicole?" asked agent Wilson.

"She told us to contact agent Sarina. Our luck once more as she was in Washington and gave us all the information she had on the Rashid's family. They were involved in every piece of dirty activity inside and outside of Iran. We now have a direct connection between Iran and the Chinese with the Lecoadio cartel.

"The key for us right now is we focus on the second person in Leocadio's command change. A guy named Juan for he comes across the border twice each month. That is who Rashid was meeting. The police got that much out of Rashid before he went into surgery.

We will pick him up pick Juan up in a few days," said the director.

"What is the other break?" asked Mary Jo.

"I will let Agent Casimir explain."

"It is an often-told story on the Walking Trail…"

"Wait, what is the Walking Trail?" asked C.E.

"It is those individuals you see on T.V. walking across Mexico on the news. They start at a place called the Darien Gap in Panama. The immigrants fly into Brazil, Venezuela, and Columbia then journey on to Panama. There the cartels use it as an assembly location with various NGO's providing aid out of kindness and some shelter for the immigrants.

It is there that the cartel agents collect the money and make arrangements for payment in trade," said Casimir.

"What kind of trade?" asked Mary Jo.

"For most, it is labor in factories on farms up here that the cartels are involved. The newest area of this development is the illegal pot farms popping up in the western part of the country. The cartels are developing these farms in rural areas in states that have legalized pot.

They arrange the payment with the care of children that the cartel has stolen or purchased. The cartel pays individuals who agree to care for the kids on the trip and that care is part of the payment price that is cut off the cost of the trip. If the child is lost, the cost is added back onto the price of the trip in labor or other payment. The last method is forced on young females," said Casimir.

"You mean forced prostitution!" said Mary Jo.

"We try to stop it at the border, but fear of the cartel is too great and the cartels tell the women that we will sell them for life in the trade instead of the years promised. So, very few asked for help. This week was an exception a border agent was asking questions of the individuals when a woman walked up with two children who were five and six years old. She told the agent a story of betrayal. How she had to go and re-take the children from another couple before she approached the agent so she could see they would be safe.

"She told the agent her family lives in a small Columbian rural community. They had given her and her soon-to-be husband money for the trip to America. He then took the money and gave it to his uncle and made a deal with the cartel agent. That deal was to bring the two children along the trip and that care would cover the other half of the payment.

"Maria did not know about her family's money before they got into the Darien Gap. He told her what he had done with the money and that they had no choice but to continue the journey. She said she could not leave the children and continued with him. Then the night before the border crossing she heard her fiancé talking to a cartel guy. They were talking about the children and how her fiancé' was being paid a bonus for the children plus the release of his debt that was promised for her.

"She said he was selling her to the cartel. They planned to take her to a whorehouse after this cartel guy was tired of her. When her fiancé came back to her all smiles, she confronted him with what she had heard. He denied it at first. After a few minutes, he admitted it and said she was just a simple peasant female and that he was being paid well and there was nothing she could do about it now. That he was laughing."

"Wow! What a guy he must be," said C.E.

"I do not think he is too happy right now," said Casimir.

"Why?" asked Mary Jo.

"Maria, so mad she hit this fiancé', Hector, in the head with a rock and left him in a bush when the group moved to the border. He did survive the blow to the head. The cartel has him and he has real problems. If they bring him into this country we will take him into custody," said Casimir.

"How will you know him?" asked Mary Jo.

"Maria had a photo of him and told us what clothes he was wearing. It would seem that her family's money did not all go to his uncle if any. Hector would be one of the best-dressed immigrants to come across the border. She said she should have seen him for what he was before they left, but love is blinding at times.

"As soon as she was on this side she approached the border agent and told her story. As she was getting into the patrol vehicle she looked back across to border and she thought she saw Hector being tossed in a cartel vehicle. Did I tell you that Maria is a beautiful woman and the cartel is most likely very upset to lose such a prize? Hector will pay for his bad deeds."

"What is the break, that this incident gives us?" asked Nick.

"I am sorry! This story was so shocking to me that I forgot to tell you who the cartel guy was that Hector agreed to hand over Maria. It was Juan. She picked him out of a group of photos we showed her."

"O.K., and how is this a break?" asked C.E.

"There again I left out the meeting with Juan and Hector back at the Gap. It seems he tried to cover his real intentions and Hector told Maria of a meeting he had with Juan. That meeting was with an individual named Rashid. Hector told her that while he was meeting with Juan this guy came up to Juan and questioned if Juan and his boss would have everything by the end of September. That was when Juan told Hector to move along. He had told Maria that he was talking to Juan about the trip and was interrupted. She said she did not question him on that. Now, she sees that was when Hector was offering her to the cartel. When I showed her more photos she identified Rashid," said Casimir.

"Then we found in Rashid's clothes when we searched them a notebook in Farsi with one entry about a planned meeting in Nogales, Arizona with Juan on September 6th at a strip mall off North Grand Ave at noon. So we have the next few days to get surveillance set up so everything looks normal when Juan shows up," said the director.

CHAPTER TWENTY-SIX
October 7th 2023

Education is not preparation for life; education is life itself.

— John Dewey

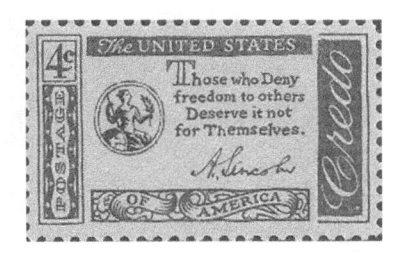

President Abraham Lincoln gave two speeches that addressed the nation in moving memorable words. First was the Gettysburg Address on November 4, 1863, just 272 words long. Next, was the Second Inaugural Address on March 4, 1865, just 701 words long and contained these words.

"...with malice toward none; with charity for all; with firmness in right, let us strive on to finish the work we are in..."

During the 1990's the United States Congress passed an immigration bill that was to fix the immigration system. The Congress and administration failed to follow up with border security section of the Bill. Then in 2001 President George W. Bush and President Vicente Fox of Mexico had an agreement on immigration reform that allowed then 8.5 million individuals in the country illegally a path to citizenship. That agreement collapsed on September 11, 2001.

2023 October 6th at 5:30 a.m. at Strip Mall

"All we can do now is wait for Juan to show up. I know you made some last-minute changes for who would be where on today's operation. May I ask why and who?" asked C.E.

"Nick is at the Morley Gate with Mary Jo and Peterson and Barns are at the DeConcini border walking crossing. The Casimir thinks Juan will walk across the border and be picked up on our side. But he could drive so Miller and Wilson are watching the vehicles. The reason for the switch was that Mary Jo and Nick could look like a couple and not draw attention to the surveillance. So Mary Jo switched with Peterson," said the director.

"Who's idea was to rent this storefront? It was a good idea, if Juan had the place watched or if there is a cartel operation in this strip mall," said C.E.

"We did a background on the owners and they all appeared to be normal small store owners or leaseholders doing average business. There is one that may be a concern the Mom-and-Pop store. We were lucky this place was in the perfect location to view the traffic in and out of the mall. Your idea of a phone/photoshop was great. We were able to set up cameras in the windows that look like display equipment and it covers the whole front," said the director.

"If Juan comes across like we think he will, he'll get here around noon. At peak time the crossing can take up to two hours. I hope this little operation works. I do not like the feeling I have of not knowing what is being planned by these guys," said C.E.

"I could not agree more but most of the time we are behind the bad guys. Remember you bought a stamp album and it became involved in an international crime organization," said the director.

9:30 a.m. at Strip Mall

"The guy that walked into the shop at the corner has just been identified as Ivan Pasternak a weapons guy with the Russian mob. I will have agent Tao do a quick deeper dive on the owner of the thar store," said the director.

"Who owns that Store?" asked C.E.

"It is a Mom-and-Pop store run by an elderly Chinese couple. The background on them came up with nothing suspicious. They came from Hong Kong in 2000. We will have to wait until Tao is done but for now, they are potential suspects!" said the director.

"This case just keeps getting stranger and bigger every day. I would sure like to know what is being planned!" said C.E.

"Look at who just walked into the same shop! I think that is another individual on our watch list. That guy's name is Zai and it is not a very common name today in China. The rumor is he is a go between the Chinese military and Korean leadership. Our source believes there is a Tong society connection. I better get this photo to Tao and have him run a background. This operation continues to get much bigger," said the director.

10:15 A.M. AT MORLEY GATE IN NOGALES

AsJuan was walking the short distance to the turnstiles at the international border in Nogales. He knew that Javier would be waiting with the car to drive him to see the three customers. He did not know why the Russian was at the meeting but the Iranians wanted him there. The Chinese guy is a thug with connections in the upper levels of Chinese leadership and he oversaw the shipments of chemicals. So, it was understood why he was at the meeting. Juan had been making this trip twice a month for several months now. He had always met with the Chinese thug and the older couple. Something was up!"

The crossing was easy for the Morley Avenue border gate crossing and it was the fastest way to cross the border. The one problem was it was only open from 10 a.m. to 6 p.m. and it was used mostly by day shoppers. As Juan left the U.S. Customs agent he was told to have a nice visit.

"Juan, Juan over here, I had to park far back in the parking lot. I knew your time was important and figured I better walk up here to meet you. The walking gate is busy today and I did not know how long it would take for you to clear the customs check," said Javier.

"Not a problem. We have more than enough time to get to the meeting."

10:26 A.M. AT STRIP MALL

The director answered his phone, "Yes!".

"Tao, here, director and I just ran a quick dive on the Chinese couple and this Zai individual. Their names came up along with him. I think that little shop is another secret Chinese police station. The couple and Zai had a link to the New York secret Chinese police station," said Tao.

"Stay on it and I want you to get a team of agents over here as soon as possible. Also, get the judge to sign a search warrant for this Mom-and-Pop shop. When we have them here a block away stand by until we are ready to act," said the director.

"I am on it!"

"What is happening?" asked C.E.

"This just got even bigger. It appears that quite a little Mom-and-Pop shop run by the old couple is also functioning as a secret police station for the People's Republic of China. I sure would like to know what is going on with this case!"

10:34 A.M.

"Director, we have another unknown individual entering the shop," said C.E.

"Get his photo to Tao. Any idea of who he is?" asked the director.

"No, but if I have to make a guess, I say he is Middle Eastern," said C.E

INSIDE THE MON-AND-POP STORE:

The shop door opened and a tall man entered the store and stopped. My name is Bahman. My partner Rashid and I were to have a meeting here at 11 a.m., but he is dead. So, I am here alone."

"What do you mean he is dead?" asked the older Chinese woman.

"We were at a shopping mall by the airport getting some things and Rashid saw a woman walking to the exit and said he would be right back. I was told he had a problem with women and to keep an eye on him. But he ran off before I could stop him."

"What do you mean a problem with women?" said the old woman.

"He likes to abuse them. We knew he was like that but he was very good at things we needed done. I was told to watch him and to keep him out of trouble. So, I was to follow him and watch what he was doing at all times. He got into our car and followed the woman. I got into a cab and followed behind. He followed the woman to her home and parked across the street. He was just sitting there in his car looking at the house. After a few minutes, I decided to go up and ask him what was he doing.

"I got out of my taxi to pay the driver and heard a noise behind me. I turned back around and saw that Rashid had jumped out of his car and rushed across the street. He broke into the front door of the house yelling something I could not understand. The next thing I heard was a gunshot and within minutes the police arrived. I think a neighbor called the police.

"The police then called for an ambulance that was there in minutes. I watched as Rashid was loaded into the ambulance and was taken to a hospital. I could not get close enough to hear what was being said other than what hospital he was being taken to. I went over to the car Rashid left across the street and the keys were still in the ignition. I got in and followed the ambulance to the hospital. There, I went inside and took a seat in the waiting room. The police were all over the place after about an hour then I heard a nurse say that the gunshot victim had died. So, here I am."

"Who was at the hospital?" asked the older Chinese man.

"I just said the place was crawling with police."

"Yes! But were there other officials present?" asked the older woman.

"Yes, there were some officers in suits that I took for local investigators."

"Could they have been FBI?" asked the Chinese man.

"I do not think so. They looked like local detectives. Most FBI have a similar look that these guys did not have."

10:57 A.M. IN A STRIP MALL PARKING LOT

The car pulled into the strip mall parking lot. "Javier, you can leave and I will call you when I need to be picked up. This meeting will take about two hours so go get some coffee," said Juan.

"Are you sure I can wait here?"

"No, if you are sitting in the car in the parking lot it will cause some suspicion and someone may call the police to investigate. It will be better if you are not sitting around," said Juan.

"All right I will not be far," he said as he drove off.

Javier stopped at the street waited to pull out of the lot and turned left. He stopped at a coffee shop and sat there thinking about Juan. Something was different.

In the Photo Shop

"Juan is getting out of that car. It looks like he has the driver leaving. Should we have Nick tail him?" asked C.E.

"Yes, No, wait let's have Nick get the local police to stop him and then have the U.S. Marshalls take him into custody at a safe house," said the director.

11:00 a.m. Two blocks away

Javier parked at a coffee shop and was getting out of his car when a police unit stopped behind his car and both officers got out, "Sir, please turn around and place your hands on the car roof."

"What is this about?" asked Javier.

Just then another car pulled in behind the police unit. A man and a woman climbed out, "Thank you officers. We will take him now and after my partner checks out the vehicle you can have the car towed to the yard. Thank you both for the quick response," said Nick as a second car with two U.S. Marshal pulled up.

"Our pleasure to assist the big guys," said the one officer.

"What is going on here? I have rights!" said Javier.

"That you do Javier Mendoza and you are being taken into protective custody for now," said Nick.

"Protective custody from what?"

"You will be told in due time, for now, you will go with these gentlemen in the car that is pulling up and two men got out. Nick turned to the passenger and said, "Marshal Adams take this gentleman to a safe house and both of you stay by his side and he is to have no contact with anybody period," said Nick.

After he was put into the car the driver asked, "Is there anything else we need to know."

"I think it would be best to keep him in cuffs. This guy is known as a want-strong-arm thug in a Mexican drug cartel. I would not turn our back on him," said Nick as he turned to Mary Jo, "We need to take up a position by the strip mall. Call the director and tell him Juan is in protective custody."

"I am on it. Just how bad is this Javier guy?"

"He is a small-time brutal killer trying to work his way up his organization! Tao ran a search on him and the Mexican police have him linked to four murders."

11:02 A.M. IN THE MOM-AND-POP STORE:

Juan walked into the small shop and looked around, "Where is Rashid?"

"He is dead!" said Bahman.

"What do you mean he is dead?" asked Juan.

"What is happening here?" asked the old Chinese woman.

"Nothing is happening here! Rashid is dead and that did not happen here, so there is no problem here!" said Juan standing over the old woman. Suddenly two more Chinese men stepped into the room from the storage area. The old woman became much younger and taller looking as she stood straight.

"You are very disrespectful and there is a problem here! You and your people had an unreliable person on your team in this fool Rashid. In the middle of an operation he runs off to get shot and we have no reason why he ran off or why he was shot. This companion of his has said Rashid was not trustworthy and had to be watched. That is a problem. This meeting is over now!" said, the not-so-old, Chinese woman.

"Who are you to give the orders here?" demanded Juan.

"I am the one with the power to make sure that my government is not compromised by some stupid action by you and your muddled eastern friends. If that is not enough for you my associates here will be glad to instruct you on your manners!" said the, not so old, woman.

11:08 A.M. IN PHOTO SHOP

"All units, we move in one minute. Nick you and Mary Jo will come in the front with C.E. and me. Barns you, Peterson, and Wilson cover the back. We do not know who is in there or if they are armed. So be ready for anything!" said the director.

The phone rang in the director's pocket, "Yes?"

"Sir, it is Tao, and that Middle Eastern guy is a top-level Hezbollah leader. I tracked him entering the country on a visa from Spain with another guy named Balian who is our guy going by the name Rashid that was killed this morning."

"Good to know, thanks Tao good work! It is a go time all units!"

IN THE STORE:

"You cannot do that there is too much a stake in this operation with all our countries!" demanded Juan.

"That is where you are wrong. I have orders not to jeopardize this office for any reason. Your operation is falling apart as of this morning with the killing of this fool Rashid. I do not know why and neither do you! So, right now leave this store or I will have my men here escort you out!" said the, now not so old, woman.

11:08:36 A.M.

Four people poured into the store with guns pointing at those in the store. "FBI, everyone stay where you are and do not move!" was yelled as they entered the building.

The back door swung open and an older Chinese male ran into more guns, "Stop, FBI, get on the ground NOW!"

"What is the purpose of this invasion of my small little store?" demanded, the not-so-old woman.

"All in due time miss," said the director as he handed her the search warrant.

"Search warrant under what cause?" demanded the woman.

"Read the warrant?" said the director.

"What! Is this terrorism?" said the not-so-old man as he walked back into the store.

"Oh, and one more thing on that list. This is an illegal establishment on United States Property acting as a police station for the People's Republic of China. So, we have more than enough to enter and search this establishment. Then we have the four Chinese nationals working in the same small storefront with a member of a Mexican cartel and a member of Hezbollah.

So, Miss Wang, you are being placed in the custody of the United States Federal Bureau of Investigation. Nick take her to the car," said the director.

7:39 P.M. AT FBI BUILDING

The room was filled with all the members of the team. The director stepped up to the board with photos of all the individuals. "We have a known agent from Hezbollah who was with a known terrorist from Hamas, four Chinese nationals acting as a secret police organization for the PRC, and a high-ranking member of a Mexican cartel. We have lots of pieces and they seem to fit together and yet what do have here?" asked the director.

"I do not know if this is connected but I have more information on the woman who shot Rashid," said Tao.

"Are we talking about this Nicole? Nika person?" asked the director,

"Yes, it seems that he was her husband in Iran and he beat her. When she left with the CIA agent she was told her husband and his father and brother were taken into custody and would not make it to trial. She said her husband Rashid was being arrested for the rape and murder of an important general in the Republican Army.

She was shocked to see him at the mall and became more worried when he followed her home. She waited for him to break into the house and the bedroom. He was yelling and rushed her when shot him. So, it was a chance that he saw her and left his partner and decided to go after her," said Tao.

"O.K. that answers one question. What about the Chinese?" asked the director.

"That looks like she goes back to Su Wu and attempts the removal of Mei at the lab fire and the top-secret bio-lab. During that part of the investigation, we learned that there were secret Chinese police stations set up in this country to intimidate Chinese dissidents. As for what part they play in this whole mess I cannot figure out!" said C.E.

"We do know that the Chinese are dumping their chemicals into Mexico so the cartels can manufacture enough fentanyl to kill millions of Americans. There is a rumor in Panama of a new cartel war starting over a net importer in the drug market. That link is to Iran and their surrogates. So could this be a wider war with Asian and Middle Eastern drug lords?" asked Mary Jo.

"That all fits together but I think this is a bigger operation. There are too many moving individuals in this puzzle. I do not think it is just this country that is part of the plan," said Nick.

"I agree with Nick," said C.E.

"O.K., how many think this is a bigger operation?" asked the director as all hands went up.

"The Chinese are out of our control. The administration has agreed to deport them tonight and all the questioning was ordered to stop," said the director.

"You're kidding!" said C.E.

"No! I am not and I hate the decision but this came almost as soon as we got them here. Once we asked for the search warrant the administration wheels went to work and the names of the six Chinese were on a list were to be sent back to China immediately. The administration does not want to upset the apple cart," said the director.

"You are telling us that these foreign agents were spying on American residents and citizens and our government is letting them walk!" said Tao.

"I am afraid so Tao," said the director.

"I escaped from China and my sister was in one of their re-education camps. I smuggle her story out of the camp and its barbaric brutality of beating and rumored organ transplants. I became an agent to expose the PRC. Now, I am sitting here being told to let these fatherless dogs go home!" said Tao.

"I know it is tough but if we did anything different we would become just like them. However, we did stop their illegal activity and broke up a spy ring. So I agree with you Tao but we did accomplish something," said Nick.

"It still sucks," said Tao.

"How about we get back on the subject in front of us!" said the director.

"Well, we still have Juan and Bahman. Why not let them stew tonight and run at them again tomorrow," said C.E.

"That sounds like a good plan. Everyone go home and get some rest we will continue at 9 a.m. in this room. Nick I would like you and C.E. to finish the paperwork before you two go. I also have some paperwork that has to go with the Chinese," said the director.

"Not a problem we are almost done. It will not take more than three-quarters of an hour," said Nick.

"Said, the man who cannot write his name and only proofreads my work," said C.E..

"I will admit you do have a nice way with words," said Nick

8:38 P.M.

The director burst into the room, "Nick and C.E. we have our answer to what was being planned. Hamas just attacked Israel with thousands of rockets and land troops," said the director.

"If that is true, why are these people here? Wait a minute! What were the flyers about?" asked C.E.

"Some kind of protest!" said Nick.

"Yes, they were but not some kind of protest," said C.E. as he looked for one of the flyers.

"These flyers that were being handed out on university campuses and other places were not about how to protest. Rather, they were disrupted as ways to block any attempts by the authorities who attempted to enforce the laws to stop protests. I think we need the team back here as fast," said Nick.

CHAPTER TWENTY-SEVEN

Massacre

To ignore evil is to become an accomplice to it.
— Martin Luther King Jr.

Between 66 C.E. and 136 C.E. the Romans and Jews fought three different wars. The Jews had been a majority population in that part of the Middle East at the time. Their final defeat by the Romans saw the destruction of the 2nd Temple and the scattering of the Jews throughout the Empire as a persecuted minority.

Later the Christian Church lay the blamed for the death of Christ on the Jews and vilified them. Then came the followers of Islam and expelled Jews from different locations. The Jews was allowed to stay and pay a tax.

By the 11th Century European countries and cities began expelling Jews or forced to live in certain locations. The Jew of Venice were subjected to being forced to live in an old foundry in the city on March 29, 1516. This was, in part, because of the influx of Jewish immigrants from Spain and the Spanish expulsion of the Jews in 1492.

The old foundry in Latin is Ghetto.

2023 October 7, Sneak Attack

The Wall that separated Gaza from Israel is made of several components with a 35-foot-high barrier with barbed wire, surveillance cameras, radar, sensors, and rotating remote-controlled machine guns every 500 feet. There is an underground reinforced concrete component to prevent Hamas from digging more tunnels into Israel. The wall covers 65 Kilometers (40 miles) between Gaza and Israel.

The Hama military arm of thugs breached the Israeli security wall in as many as 30 different locations. The cameras, radar, sensors barbed wire, and towers that were set 500 feet apart were all neutralized.

The attack included more than 1,500 militants who were to cause terror and chaos inside Israel. The attackers used quadcopter drones, paragliders, motor boats, motorcycles, bulldozers, pick-up in the assault on 20 communities, and a music festival. This brutal terrorist killed some 1,200 men, women, children and babies. Then took more than 250 hostages including babies. The thugs did confuse leaving 6,900 injured victims behind to pick up their lives.

The attack that morning started at 6:29 a.m. with 2,200 rockets launched into Israel that overwhelmed the Iron Dome defense system. The first wave of rockets was followed 20 minutes later with another 3,000 by the end of the day. This rocket attack was to cover the commercial quadcopter drones that would drop explosives into or in the observation towers along the wall separating Gaza from Israel. It was also to cover the fan-powered paragliders that flew terrorists into Israel to kill and rape.

6:29 Rockets were Launched into Israel

Running out of the tunnel the men rushed forward to create holes in the wall. Each man has his assignment. The leader began issuing commands.

An IDF soldier was lying on the ground with blood matting her hair.

"Samer get that bulldozer moving I want that wall breached NOW!" yelled Mostafa. Then turned to the man next to him and said, "Malik, as soon as the wall is breached get your motorbikes going."

"Do we head to the music festival or the kibbutz?"

"The paragliders will be at the festival. We need to cause as much panic and chaos as possible at the start. So, hit the kibbutz. The men in the vans and the pick-ups will be at both within minutes after you arrive. Remember we need hostages."

There appeared a gap in the wall and the bikes rushed through as the bulldozer backed up for another pass at the wall. The Bulldozer pushed forward once more and the hole was opened for the trucks.

"Samer, get off the dozer and get into the van." yelled Hasan "We are off to kill the Jewish dogs."

"Mostafa, what should I do with this Israeli soldier?" asked Hussein.

"It looks like you have done enough. She will be a hostage if she survives what you have already done," said Mostafa as he turned to another thug, "You take this Jewish trash to the hostage location we set up."

7:00 A.M. Supernova Music Festival

The festival was to have ended on the 6th but was extended an extra day. There were three stages and a camping ground for those who wanted to stay and enjoy the whole festival for one more day.

"Ava, why are you up"?

"There is a fireworks display going on, come look, Levi."

"What?"

"Levi, is there a paraglider demonstration scheduled this morning?" said Ava as Levi looked up.

"I do not think..." as he was cut off by a shower of bullets that fell from the sky.

"Run and get into the car!" he screamed to Ava as they started running.

"Stay low, once we get to the car get in the passenger side. I will drive."

"It is my car, Levi!"

"Do it, Ava! We do not have time to argue. I am the better driver and if you notice there are motorbikes headed this way with more gunmen."

"Why is everyone running to the terrorist?"

"Those riders are dressed like Israel Defense Force members. We need to go the other way and hope the paragliders have left an opening," as he started the car.

One of the motorbikes stopped and the man sitting behind the bike got off and held up his hand to stop a car with several young people. When it stopped he fired several rounds into the vehicle to scream. Other thugs came up and opened the driver's door yelling "Get out you filthy Jewish dogs!" Those that could get out were separated into men and women in lines. Four men and two women stood with their hands on their heads. One thug walked up behind the men and each one in the head as the women were dragged to a pick-up.

"Look at this pretty dog," said Abdel grabbed a wounded woman from the car and pulled her to the other terrorist around the car.

"Do not kill her. We need some for hostages. Put her into the back of the pick-up. There is more to do here. We need to show these occupiers that we are taking back our land." said their group leader. "Now, get to the job you were sent here to do!"

"You men go into the trees and search for these Jewish pigs that are hiding there. They ran like rabbits as we flew in. Remember we need hostages."

In the Trees

"Dad, it's me and terrorists have attacked here at the festival and they are killing everyone. Take care of the kids, Michael has been shot and I am running into the trees…" The call ended as Naomi ran and crawled into a small depression in the ground. She covered herself with brush and leaves and then lay still. She watched through the leaves as the men approached the trees and started to methodically hunt for people. She could hear screams and begging from those that were found.

As she lay there, she heard the raiders killing those they found and how they laughed as they dragged selected victims to waiting pick-up to take back to Gaza.

She stayed hidden and soon Naomi heard a different sound of gunfire. It was the IDF and volunteers who had arrived and were combating the terrorists. One member of the group was her father who had come as soon as her phone stopped.

7:00 A.M. AT A KIBBUTZ NEAR THE FESTIVAL

"Shiloh and Lilah come on hurry up if you want to get to Asher's birthday party. We need to get into the car and go, now!" said Eva standing beside the car.

The two girls came running out of the house and ran to the car. "STOP! Both of you run back into the house and get into the safe room NOW!" yelled Eva.

The girls stopped and looked at their mother. "Do, what I said now, hurry." Both children started to cry after being yelled at. The windshield of the car shattered with a spray of bullets. The crying turned into screams. Eva called the emergency call number.

As soon as the phone connected, "There are gunmen in my kibbutz with guns and they are shooting every…" the phone was dropped. Men rushed into the home and the crying and screaming stopped. The men moved to the next house yelling, "You unclean dogs we will step on you! We will wide you out!"

"Hold the door shut. This safe room is not going to stop these determined evil men. But if we can hold the door shut for a few minutes until help arrives." The grandfather looked at his wife who was holding her chest.

"Saul, I cannot help!" she said as he collapsed to the floor.

"Ava, Ava, …" he yelled as bullets tore through the door and his body. The men outside did not come into the room.

"Whoever is in there can stay. Burn the house and block the door so they cannot get out," said one of the men.

AT A MILITARY OUTPOST

The raiders went straight to the outpost without detection. A young female soldier looking out a barracks window saw the raiders approaching and yelled a warning. "Get up, we are under attack!" She was cut down by rapid fire.

"Everyone stay low and block the doors!" said one soldier who took command.

"Come out and no harm will come to you!" yelled one of the raiders as a grenade was tossed through a window.

"Everyone stay down and do not look out the windows. These men are not warriors they will not come in to fight!" said the woman who took command.

"How do you know that?" asked another female soldier.

"The guy that yelled for us to come out. They just want to kill without having to fight," she said as another grenade came into the room. "We just need to stay quiet and let them think we are all dead."

"Burn the building and let's move on," one of the raiders said as an Israeli fighter jet flew over the outpost. "Take cover"

After several Air Force jets flew several by-passes and strafed the raiders the terrorists loaded up what hostage they had captured and retreated to Gaza.

By the end of the day in Israel, most of the terrorists that were alive had retreated into Gaza leaving 1,200 dead including 30 children, 305 soldiers, and 58, police officers, and the taking of some 253 hostages. Many of the hostages were foreign nationals including a dozen Americans.

By mid-morning in Gaza a pick-up drove through the streets with the body of an Israeli woman in the bed laying on her back in only her underwear to the cheers of the local population yelling "Death to the Jews", and "From the River to the Sea" chants. News crews filmed the celebration and joy of these individuals in Gaza.

A dozen kibbutz had been attacked before the savages had been beaten back. A lone photograph of a woman in a black dress laying on her back on the ground at the music festival was the image that told the world of what had happened in Israel on October 7, 2024. These early images would fall to the sidelines for new images that told a different story.

The world of Terrorism had changed once more and was starting to use propaganda with the Big Lie. This attack by Hamas and the events after it would change the rules and methods of terrorism! The old pattern of suicide bombers that were directed by the leadership to blow up civilians at universities, coffee shops, restaurants, and buses was ending. Now, would begin isolated strikes with teams of terrorists to murder, rape, and mutilate bodies in the name of freedom. The civilian population would be used as protection from attacks and if they were killed or wounded so much the better for the propaganda. Hamza would become the victim and not the aggressor.

The atrocities committed this day would be lost in an orchestrated propaganda campaign by parties that wanted to bring about radical change to the world. Later, one of the last short videos that was played of the brutal attack showed five female Israeli soldiers being mishandled by the terrorist raiders. Images of Palestinians as victims of Israel's attacks against Hamas military targets.

NEW YORK 10:25 P.M.

The evening program was interrupted by a News Extra Flash. "We interrupt this program with a braking story in Israel! This is Chet Butler and the State of Israel has just suffered a massive rocket, air, land, and sea attack.

CHAPTER TWENTY-EIGHT

> The evil that is in the world almost always comes of ignorance, and good intentions may do as much harm as malevolence if they lack understanding.
> — Albert Camus

The United Nations eradicated Smallpox in the human population in 1980 in one of its only successful ventures. The Smallpox virus is stored and used for research in a number of research location. Those labs have done experiments for bioweapons and new vaccines that have not always complied with U.N. guidelines.

The U.N.t has failed to end wars, human rights violation of slavery, violence against women a children, antisemitism, corruption, appeasement and failure to cooperate.

2023 OCTOBER 8ᵀᴴ

"NEWS FLASH" There is a state of war between the State of Israel and Hamas in the Gaza Strip after the surprise attack yesterday. The reports out of Israel are horrifying with the killing and rape of civilians. We go to our reporter in Israel for the latest update. Eric are you there?" asked Chet.

"Yes, Chet I just left a briefing by the IDF and the situation is unfolding, and is unclear as to the extent of the disaster. I was told that Israel will not stop until Hamas is eliminated. I was shown video footage that was taken from one of the Palestinian invaders. The footage is shocking. The government here has begun to evacuate civilians from the northern border with Lebanon and increased activity on the West Bank territory.

There or rockets still being fired into Israel from Gaza and Hezbollah up in Lebanon has exchanged artillery and rocket fire with Israel. The situation here is still very unstable. Back to you Chet."

"You stay safe there Eric," said Chet....

"Nick would you switch channels and see what they are saying," said C.E. as a new picture emerged on the T.V. "...just interviewed two Palestinians and this is what they had to say about the attack on Israel." The image of two individuals with their faces covered with a black and white keffiyeh, " This attack conducted by us the Palestinian people as a legitimate and necessary action against the imperialistic occupying power of the Jewish colonialist!" yelled the man and the woman next to him screamed, "THE JEWS NEED TO BE TAUGHT A LESSON AND NOW THEY KNOW THE PALESTINIAN PEOPLE ARE WARRIORS!"

"As you can see this war is going to have many sides in the next few months. The Jews are in a state of shock and the Arab world is in a state of jubilation with massive street demonstrations for the Hamas attack yesterday. This is Sara Richardson reporting from Lebanon."

"Thank you, Sara, we will be right back…"

"Turn that off and let us come up with some kind of a plan," said the director.

"A plan for what? For all we know this thing may be tied to Leocadio and the Mexican cartels, the Chinese banks, and this Iranian Balian or

Rashid guy. The best we can do right now is keep a watch on all these things and see if we can start to make any connections," said C.E.

"There we have it director. I told you C.E. was good. He just put a plan together and did not even know he was giving us the plan," said Nick.

"I know you think that is a joke, Nick, but I think C.E. is right for now everyone watches and see if anything links all this together somehow," said the director.

October 13th

C.E. and Elaine were watching the evening news.

"NEWS FLASH" Israel has begun its bombard campaign in northern Gaza to wipe out the military and leadership of Hamas. They have warned the civilian population to move south that the military operation was about to start to remove Hamas's military capability.

The Israelis have established a blockade of Gaza that has included the shutting down of the electric power from Israel. That has reduced the electric power to Gaza by some 80%. The Operation is being called the Sword of Iron.

In response to the Israelis, the Hamas leadership has set up roadblocks to the south to keep the civilians in the north as shields for the Hamas fighters. The cost of civilian casualties so far has caused the NGOs here to react to the suffering of the civilian population in Gaza. When we come back from the break our correspondent in Israel has a report on the current military action where Hamas has accused Israel of attacking civilians near a school. The Israelis are investigating the claim.

"See what is on another channel," said C.E. as he brought two mugs of tea.

"You mean I can touch the control center?" said Elaine as she was changing the channel.

"Yes, that is if you want this tea."

"...the weather for the week will be in the low 60s and stay that way for a few days Burt," said Joan in front of a weather map.

"Thanks, Joan at least we will stay dry a little longer. Now, back to the world news.

Israel has started its massive assault against the civilians in the Gaza Strip. The Palestinian health agency has reported that an Israel bomb killed several civilians at a school," said Burt as the screen showed pictures of a bomb site with people being carried to cars with cries of pain and sorrow."

"I have seen and heard enough!" said Elaine as she turned off the TV.

"So, have I but I need to keep track of what is happening," said C.E.

"You can do that by watching an hour in the morning and one hour at night. Every channel just loops the information with a different set of newscasters for each program," said Elaine.

"You look like you have more to say?" said C.E.

"Yes, I do! You are right the news has become speculation and opinions by broadcasters and so-called experts that support one side or another. One station has lots of commentators telling you things that are facts when they are speculations that everyone on the panel agrees to it as fact. Then another station is selling books and special programs in between the news commentary they call news reports," said Elaine.

"True, but one has to view it all to filter out the real news," said C.E.

"Who has the time? When each station is giving its interpretation of the news instead of the facts," said Elaine

"You think we are being directed to a particular political position and we are. When I go into the office I watch the news from the Arab world and that is a completely different story with even more propaganda directed to the U.S. media," said C.E.

February 2024 Meeting with Professor Hellen

"Now that everyone is here let's get started. I have invited Professor Hellen to give us some background on the current intellectual thinking on university campuses. Recently, she gave a short history of terrorism to Nick and C.E. that helped in their investigation. I believe we need some clarity on the current intellectual climate on American campuses.

Since there seems to be a shift in the culture when on October 8, the day after the Hamas attack on Israel thirty-three Harvard groups met and signed a statement that held Israel entirely responsible for the violence of October 7, 2023.

"Professor it is a pleasure to meet you and thank you for taking the time to come in to give us this background on the situation in this county today," said the director as he introduced the team members to the professor.

"It is a pleasure to meet all of you and as the director said I know C.E. and Nick from a previous discussion we had on terrorism. But this topic for discussion today is far more complex and I will try to interrogate terrorist and antisemitism into a simple comprehensive format to explain the current protests that are in this country today," said the professor.

"Professor we are still trying to figure out what is happening with these demonstrations and protests around the world supporting the antisemitic terrorist. I think we all know what antisemitism is. So, maybe we could start with the protest against Israel?" said the director.

"No, disrespect director, but can you tell me what is antisemitism?" asked the professor.

"It is the disregard or hate of the Jewish people!" said the director.

"If that was the case, you would not need me to explain the current environment in the country. Antisemitism is not just the hate of the Jews. It is a political philosophy that is used to divide groups. The Jews just happened to be at the center of the political movement to remove the perceived opposition to society and culture.

"That all began in Germany in 1879 by Fredrick Wilhelm Adolph Marr who formed the Anti-Jewish League and created the term antisemitism. It was a method designed to remove a perceived competing group and cultural influence from the German nation.

"The method developed over time into four stages. The first, stage was to point the finger at a visible or hidden corruption. The second stage was to identify a scapegoat for individuals or a group to deflect or misdirect away from the real issues. The third stage was to use negative stereotypes to divide Left from Right, liberal from conservative, nationalist from internationalist. The fourth stage and most important was to build coalitions to increase power."

"What do you mean coalitions?" asked Nick.

"To join different groups of different goals for a common goal. For example, take Karl Marx and communism. Marx saw the Jews as an obstacle to communism. The Jew was a political problem and not a religious problem for Marx. He saw the religion of Judaism and its leaders as a group of hucksters to keep the Jews out of a more social world. The Jew needed to dissolve his anti-social religious practices in the name of progress and transition into the new citizen of communism and away from the colonial, Imperialist, racist world. Many of the early leaders in Marxism were Jewish and became non-Jews. Leon Trotsky is the most notable one.

"During the Twentieth Century, this antisemitism began to build a coalition with the Arab States and after 1945 it was formalized when the State of Israel was created. Closer relationships were built during the Israeli wars of 1967 and 1973. The Cold War between the West and the East played a part in this coalition building using the Palestinians.

"The Palestinians were now seen as victims of Israel's aggression even after PLO and other groups consistently conducted attacks terrorist on Israel. The United Nations became a coalition building block with the Arabs and the Soviet Union.

"On November 10, 1975, the United Nations passed resolution #3379 that was backed by the Soviet Union and the Arab Block that allowed the U.N. to use racism against the State of Israel. The Arab League then began to build coalitions with the Western universities with funds provided to Western universities to promote the Arab view of Western culture and they also lobbied Western politicians and business leaders with promises of oil."

"I do not understand their view of Western culture?" said Mary Jo.

"Like all history, if you teach it with only the facts that support your point of view it becomes haptoral facts. Take the Crusades the Europeans wanted to retake the Holy Land and Jerusalem back from the Muslims. This was after the Muslims had taken and occupied the Holy Land. There were a number of these the holly crusades fought over Jerusalem by the two warring factors of Christians and Muslims.

"At the time the Arab world was the most intellectual scholars reading Greek, Roman, as well as their and eastern scholars. During the Crusades, the Europeans were seen as uncultured barbarians killing all that they perceived to be Muslims. The facts are the Crusaders killed anyone, Muslims, Jews, and Christians, dressed in robes. The Arabs see the West as the invaders and colonizers of the Middle East," said the professor.

"But the Muslims also invaded Palestine to take Jerusalem?" said Mary Jo.

"There is the center of the problem! The Jews see that city as the site of the First and Second Temple, the Wailing Wall, today. The Christians value the site as the death and rising of Jesus. While the Muslims view the site as the place where Mohammad went to Heaven. All three religions are competing for what they perceive as theirs. Then you add the Twentieth Century deals with the Arabs, Jews, and the Western powers with failed promises.

: During this same period the War in Vietnam was beginning to expand and in 1968 the Free Speech movement hit American campuses. The consequence of this was the creation of ethnic studies departments; Black Studies, Hispanic Studies, Women Studies, and others. These were not to include outsiders in the general population but to show how they were never a part of the American experiment. They were promoted by individuals who told the young they were not included and the system was against them. The individuals who promoted this had all made it to the top with degrees or were in the process of getting degrees.

"The most damaging consequence, I feel, was the banishment of the ROTC programs on many university campuses. The military was then seen as the warriors of colonists and imperialists of the Western world or the modern world to the Muslim radicals. This image along with the alternate view of American history has had a negative on the national image with fewer and fewer individuals volunteering for military service."

"Wait, what do you mean by negative history?" asked Mary Jo.

"History books and classes that point out the negative side of history."

"I still do not understand?"

"Well, for example, the founding of the early settlements in the New World. Today it is presented as big bad Europeans coming and disrupting nature and peaceful loving native populations who protected the environment. The truth is that the native Americans were always being invaded or made war on other native Americans before 1492. Civilization rose and died before and during the Europeans arrived. Leave out native American history and you change the story from competing cultures to brutal conquest of native Americans, Spanish, and Mexicans.

"Jumping forward to the 2008 and the Presidential election when the then Democratic candidate repudiated his local churchman's attacks on the United States and the White race. However, that candidate did not repudiate the antisemitism. Instead went around the Arab world apologizing for American past actions in the Arab world.

"This country's civil rights political actions were more of a cosmetic fix at the top and left the bottom where they were or at times in worse shape with poor schools and economic opportunities. Then with the Globalist movement, the middle-class jobs of industry began to move overseas. The lower-class individuals did get handouts that helped to destroy the family over the next 50 years during and after the Great Society of the 1960s.

"The Feminist also played a part in this decline for they labeled men as misogynist and racist. This was followed by the *'Me Too'* movement that only wanted to defend women who were seen as worthy of defending. Those who claimed that a President attacked them were deemed as trailer trash or worse.

"This takes me to the Liberals of today. They asked, 'Who can we help?' at the same time they perceive those on the right as thugs, goons, and nonessentials. Today the Liberals do not confront any evil they try to negotiate with it," said the professor.

"Professor, I have one question. What do you mean by poor education?" asked C.E.

"The major universities began allowing minority students with low scores into the system. They are doing very little to nothing to prepare the students in K-12 education for the university workload. They just lowered the test scores required to enter. Some have even said the test scores are racist. The universities add a layer of cosmetics to the problem without fixing the problem. Many of these students who are admitted drop out over the workload before the second year. Sadly, many of these same students could make the grade give the right preparation. The universities then bragged about their enrollment of minorities and then let those individuals swim or sink."

"What should they have done?" asked Nick.

"Education begins in the early years and the universities and the business industry develop young athletes as young as thirteen, but do not do the same in academics. The American educational system develops the best athletics in the world and many Olympians from around the world train or go to American Universities. That training should start in the middle schools in the American educational system. Many middle school students do not read at what is considered grade level. Athletics has a proven record of developing the best.

"This could and should be replicated in the academic world without the loss of the individual. We train our athletes to weed out the best go to any secondary school and you will see non-suits who are left outside the class. The best go onto school teams or club teams. These teams go on to compete with other teams to build skills. The non-suits are placed in separate areas to sit or stand during the P.E. class.

"Then in the academic classroom world the grade of "A's" is the goal for parents, teachers, and students. When I was a high school teacher I never had anyone question me if I gave too many As. I was asked about too many Fs with the indication that I was not doing a good job of instruction.

"That was when I realized when they said raise the bar they were talking about Limbo bar, not High Jumping bar," said the professor as everyone laughed.

"Professor you are not given a very positive image!" said C.E.

"C.E. The nice thing about the American system of capitalism is we adjust to provide the maximum production. There will be a swing back the other way once it is discovered it is not working," said the professor.

"Are we not there now?" asked Mary Jo.

"I do not think so. I think by May or April things will get more radical like the summer of 2020. Then the coalitions will join together behind the Palestinians. The Summer of Love as it was called did not result in many criminal prosecutions. The environmentalists, Antifa, Black Lives Matter, and others will join the *'River to the Sea'* protest not understanding what they are demanding," said the professor.

"I do not understand why would they join together?" said Mary Jo.

"By this summer they will all see the corruption they were decorated with and perceive that is stage one. Israel is the scapegoat in stage two. Those with them are positive and those against are negative stereotypes in stage three. The fourth stage is to bring all these parties together in one coalition to bring down the existing power structure. Antisemitism is just the focus of the power attack. I think that pretty much covers the topic in this brief lesson," said the professor.

"Thank you for coming in to go over the topic with us. You were right I did not understand the real definition of antisemitism," said the director.

"I hope I was able to give everyone a little better understanding of the current society with some historical background. C.E. I will see you and Elaine later at home," said the professor.

"I will walk you out of the building," said C.E.

"C.E. and everyone I think we can call it a day. I will see everyone back here in the morning," said the director.

CHAPTER TWENTY-NINE

A child without education is like a bird without wings.
— Tibetan Proverb

The study of history is more than just the facts of past historical positive and negative or passive or aggressive actions. German expansion in the Second World War was stopped by Winston Churchill and the British people who stood alone for months holding the German war machine at bay until the Soviet Union was forced to trade sides and the United States entered the war.

Just one nation stood alone on the European continent to resist German demands to identify Jews with a Yellow Star of David. King Christian of Denmark as told by a legend wore a Yellow Star one morning and by that afternoon the people of Denmark were wearing the Yellow Star. The truth is that did not happen but it is symbolic for Denmark did save most of their Jews in Denmark.

Today Israel stands alone against Iran and their terrorist supporters. The goal of Iran and those following their leaders is the total elimination of the Jewish State of Israel. Israel has agreed to many truces and peace agreements that have failed to settle the demands of the radicals of the Arab world.

April 17th Office Meeting

The team was assembled in the office for a meeting while the nightly news was on a split screen covering the protest on university campuses. The liberal stations focused on Palestinians being attacked and killed and the occupation of Gaza by Israel. The conservative stations focused on the hostages and the Palestinians using civilians as shields to protect their military elements. The director walked over and turned off the set.

"Now that we are all present for the weekly briefing Tao has put together a small summary of what we are beginning to think is what is at play. So, the floor is all yours, Tao," said the director.

"This is a report on one of the liberal T.V. channels as he brought up the video. *'NEWS FLASH tonight the war in Palestine has added more suffering for Palestinian civilians. The Israeli forces have again admitted the strike that was to take out two high-level Hamas leaders who were located behind a first aid station.*

Hamas claims a high number of wounded and dead from the air strike. The clip ended.

This is a different channel on the same incident, *'Israel has reported that the attack on the two high-level Hamas leaders was near the aid station but the explosion that killed and wounded the civilians was at a parking lot a good distance away from the bomb target. The IDF information person showed these photos of the bomb site and the parking lot you can see that there is a good distance between the two sites. The IDF officer said they believe that the parking lot explosion was caused by a Hamas rocket that failed,'* as you can see the story is told with a different focus and is part of a propaganda program. All the information from Gaza is from Hamas. So is it to be believed?" asked Tao.

"We all know that the news coverage is biased, so is there a point to your position?" asked Nick.

"I believe that there has been a part of this media bias on Israel ever since October 7th. I think that there has been a propaganda element to the overall strategy from the beginning. Professor Hellen made me start to think more globally after her brief lecture," said Tao.

"What do you mean a propaganda element?" asked Mary Jo.

"Once the Israel Army entered Gaza, the cry of Israeli aggression increased threefold or more. The focus was on what Israel has done and not on what Hamas did. The hostages are being exchanged at a very favorable rate for Hamas and the Arab world in the exchange. Those in Israel who have loved ones held by Hamas already are demanding the government stop the war and get the hostages back. There is in Tel Aviv a public square where people gather on Saturday nights making demands.

"Israel is a divided nation with liberal views and ultranationalist views. Those views will be used by the international press to influence public views. Antisemitism is still widespread in the world and Israel is seen as part of the Western developed world that will only re-enforce antiwesternism views in the Third World. These images will help share alternate views on America. For example, American T.V. will show protest individuals beaten and kicked as victims on the ground in America. The violent acts committed by Hamas terrorists in Israel on October 7th are no longer shown. They just show burned-out cars and homes, but very few if any of the brutality acts committed that day on the victims," said Tao.

"Who would want to see them?" asked Mary Jo.

"That is a good point and the answer is nobody wants to see the real horror committed by our fellow men. When I escaped from China I carried a description by my sister of life in the re-education camp that she was forced into for the simple crime of speaking against the party line. The report told of the horrors that were being committed inside the camp.

"The beating and killing were described in detail. These were accepted as facts. What could not be accepted was the mining of organs from individuals for replacement parts for top elites who needed new organs. That was just too much for people to believe and the CCP was capable of doing. The CCP denied that it was happening in the camps and that was accepted without any verification.

"This denying of the facts is the same thing that is happening with the state of Israel and the October 7th attack. The *Al-Qassam* news agency has reported with their video evidence that Hamas only targeted the border fence and military targets. That any civilian casualties were caused by the Israeli response in their state of confession and there was confession in

INIQUITOUSNESS

Israel's military response with exaggerated reports. They are accusing Israel of what they have and are doing." said Tao.

"So, just what are you saying, Tao?" asked Nick.

"That the war on terrorism is no longer a war of suicide attacks and hijackings but is now spread to a war of words and denials. Some people still do not believe that a man walked on the Moon and there are still those that deny that the Holocaust happened. In both cases, they argue that it is all done by Hollywood. The novelist Albert Camus once said, *'The evil that is in the world almost always comes of ignorance, and good intentions may do as much harm as malevolence if they lack understanding.'* and I think he was right," said Tao.

"If I understand your point it is that propaganda is now part of the terrorist war not just on Israel but also, on the West," said the director.

"Yes, remember the professor said the situation would most likely get worse before it would get better. University students are today camping on campuses demanding the university divest from anything tied to Israel. I think the universities will negotiate with the students and fail to control the situation," said Tao.

"I hate to be the wet blanket here," said agent Peterson. "But, we have a case that is far from settled and we are off on campus unrest."

"That is my point, Greg! I think they are the same!" said Tao.

"O.K. now you have lost me completely,"

"This whole thing started with a small Chinese spy ring on a university campus back in 2020. That then turned into a bio-lab and illegal Chinese police station scandal. The bio-lab had a connection to the cartels in Mexico that led us to the human smuggling and drug trade that has exploded since 2020. Every time we turn over a new rock a new problem pops up. This last year we have tied Arab banks and Chinese banks to human and drug traffic at the border to launder money. Then we discovered the pamphlets that were to be passed out on campuses. The question is what do we do?" asked Tao.

"I have the same question," said C.E.

"Look, I know you are all wanting to do more. The problem is we cannot make concrete connections to all the participants. Plus, the resistance from the top. I have been blocked by one or more higher-ups with almost every request for action. The administration is unwilling to challenge the regime in Iran and still insists that the border is secure. Then just this morning I was told to stop our investigation into the Chinese bank and that it was in conflict with another investigation," said the director.

"Was there a reason given?" asked Nick.

"Yes, they said there is a parallel investigation going on that is investigating underground Chinese criminal banks and the cartels with drugs and money laundering."

"That is also our case!" said Nick.

"True, but it seems our case is small potatoes in the finance world. The way it was explained to me was Chinese government will only allow $50,000 to leave the country per year. Therefore, influential individuals in China use Chinese criminal syndicates as an alternative method of moving funds to launder money into the West mainly the United States. The cartels use this to import and distribute cocaine, Methamphetamines, and Fentanyl into the United States. I had to turn over all our documents to this other investigating team," said the director.

"You mean our investigation into Iran banking has also been taking over. It seems that our European allies have done some work to stop violations of U.S. banking sanctions. This February two banks in London evaded sanctions by saying the banks they dealt with were not on the United States list and the amounts were small," said C.E.

"Yes, then a German bank was caught laundering funds for front companies for the Islamic Revolutionary Guard Corps. They claimed the funds were for 'Humanitarian Goods'. The Europeans allow Iranian banks to operate in the open in Europe and provide funds for Hezbollah, Houthis, and Hamas to name a few terrorist groups.

"On top of this, the flood of illegals pouring across the border is a problem that is a political party football. That each side is kicking around for political advantage. The next election may or may not create a change.

"I have also, been told of a rumor is circulating that this unit will be discontinued by the end of next week. Plus, C.E. the rumor is also that you will no longer be used as a consultant for the bureau. The power above wants you out. I have it on a good source that this is a fact. I am sorry," said the director.

"How can this happen? There is a real threat to this nation and the leadership is ignoring the evidence!" said Nick and Mary Jo together.

"Listen we all know that the government conflicts with opposing groups trying to take power or stay in power. I just hope the state of the ship can right itself soon so for now we have to carry on and do your job the best we can," said the director.

"We have spent three years trying to build a good case with government obstruction at every turn. I will be glad to be out of this mess. I will have my withdrawal letter on your desk before I leave," said C.E.

"C.E. this is only a rumor do not overreact and jump ship too soon," said Nick.

"I agree with Nick!" said the director.

"No, I have been thinking about doing this for some time. My private investigation practice has suffered and Elaine and I need more time together. So, this happens to push my decision ahead," said C.E.

"C.E. I have been proud to work with you," said the director, and everyone there agreed. "If things change, I hope you will rethink about coming back!"

The next week the unit was disbanded and everyone was sent back to their old department and workload. The director was sent to an office in the Midwest and Nick stayed in the local office.

"Is Nick coming by this evening? asked Elaine.

"He called a said he would be a little late that he was in the valley this afternoon," said C.E.

"It has been a while since you stopped with the FBI. How are you feeling?" asked Elaine.

"That is a good question for I have not had many thoughts about it since I walked out of the building. I will miss the people I was working beside I will say that. But I will not miss the bureaucratic shuffling that goes on with every project. Yet, I feel guilty for just walking away. Thomas Jefferson said that *'Evil triumphs when good men do nothing.'* I wonder if I could have done more," said C.E.

"You are a good man C.E. and should not feel any quilt."

"I could have spoken up rather than just walk away,"

"What would that have gotten you?"

"You know that during the Holocaust the German *SS* are told to be the source of the killings. There were Police Battalions and common soldiers that were made up of ordinary citizens who conducted a large part of the killings. In many of the villages where the killings took place, many of the villagers came out to witness the killing and celebrate. Those stories were hidden for years until researchers uncovered the stories.

Dictators always find supporters to hold on to power. Evil lives on hate. In Rwanda during the Hutus and Tutsi genocide in 1990 priests, clergymen and nuns took part in the killings the hate was so great."

"O.K. that is enough of this talk the world is in conflict and you and I will have a nice evening with Nick and forget about these problems for tonight," said Elaine.

"One last thing I have to say is that someone said, *"One can always find ordinary people to carry out evil actions in the name of the general good!*

Printed in the USA
CPSIA information can be obtained
at www.ICGtesting.com
LVHW092137161124
796607LV00007B/495